MESSY BUSINESS

MESSY BUSINESS

LUCIA NARDO

Published by Clean Sweep Press
www.cleansweeppress.com

A catalogue record for this
book is available from the
National Library of Australia

ISBNs
ISBN: 978-0-6454341-0-1 (print)
ISBN: 978-0-6454341-1-8 (epub)

Cover and text design by Chris Nardo

For my father, Salvatore Romita
Thank you for your daily example of
living an extraordinary, creative life.

CHAPTER ONE

For someone who believed image was everything, this couldn't have looked worse. Me, slumped in the front seat of my car in the predawn stillness, watching a building. Inside, there was a party for two going on. I didn't have an invitation, but I was dressed for the occasion, decked out in black from top-to-toe. Not Little-Black-Dress elegant, more Grungy-Drug-Dealer inelegant – if the definition of 'drug dealer' included a woman on the wrong side of thirty, with bad hair, a worse attitude, and no knowledge of illicit substances.

The Admiral's Retreat was as I remembered. Seeing it again recalled days when life was simpler, especially mine. The building faced the beach where waves whooshed back and forward on the shoreline, their tips glistening in the moon's waning light. A bluestone wall separated the sand from the footpath. Rohan and I had strolled that path in the past, holding hands, promising each other we'd be together forever.

Lights dotted the verandah of the mid-nineteenth century cottage.
Beyond a wrought iron gate, the path to the entrance was lined with standard roses. A former private home reincarnated as a boutique Bed and Breakfast, The Admiral's Retreat was an ideal cover for a multitude of sins. My only interest was one specific transgression being committed within its walls.

I checked my watch. 4.15am. Two hours had passed since I'd parked, choosing a spot behind a leafy tree that segmented the nature strip and kept me inconspicuous. I needn't have worried; people see only what they want to see.

Until today, I'd been blind, too.

My nether regions were numb and I shifted constantly to wake them. This was what came of working all day and running a surveillance mission in the early hours of the morning. Your bum goes to sleep, although your brain never stops.

I poured coffee from a thermos into a plastic cup and took a sip.

The hot liquid scalded my tongue and I jumped. Coffee spilled between my thighs. I sat glumly in the puddle and rubbed my gritty eyes, then lowered the window to let in cool air. I had a mission to complete. A mission that had started around twenty-four hours earlier when Draga had waddled through the rear door, carrying her canvas tote and a bulging bag of groceries.

The pinnacle of housekeepers, Draga was old enough to be my mother. With more energy than a six-year-old on a sugar rush, she could kill a germ at forty paces. She'd arrived to do her daily clean-vacuum-bleach-cook routine early enough to make breakfast for me, served with a side order of unsavoury news.

'Good morning, Missus Jac.'

As I switched on the coffee machine, Draga put down her load, then bumped me aside with her hip. The kitchen was her territory and she asserted it at every opportunity. 'I fix coffee, then I make the strangled eggs for you.'

Draga's English wasn't great. She didn't know her 'you' from her 'your', disregarded plurals, confused pronouns, and considered correct tense optional. Every day, I had to pick through her convoluted sentences. Still, she was a sunny presence in the house and, although I would never tell her, I missed her on the weekends. Our offbeat conversations had become part of my life.

Soon she was clashing utensils like a discordant one-woman band, muttering in Croatian. My Croatian was negligible, but I'd learned enough to know there was something on her mind. It didn't stop her dishing up the goodies. In the short time it took to pack my work bag, she'd set out a plate piled high with fluffy scrambled eggs and two slices of perfectly toasted sourdough bread.

Hiring Draga had turned out to be one of my better recruitment choices. As the owner of All Class Recruitment – a name I chose to reflect the ethical and reliable service my company provided – I took pride in picking the best person for the job.

While I scoffed breakfast, she unloaded the dishwasher. 'Mister Ruin be home tonight?' she asked, stacking plates into the cupboard with a little more force than usual.

'That's what he said when I spoke with him yesterday.'

Knowing I treated coffee as a nutrient, Draga poured me another large mugful and a demitasse for herself. Her face creased in consternation. 'You husband be gone many nights.'

'Why are you so worried?'

'Why you not be worry? That man go more meeting than Prime Minister.'

'Stop fussing.' True, the number of overnight meetings Rohan attended had increased, and he was preoccupied when at home. He stuck to his study, mobile phone glued to his ear and paperwork scattered across the desk. But Rohan's work ethic had been one of his most attractive traits. 'He's running a large firm, Draga. I understand why he's away so often.'

'You think this good thing?' She slipped on her glasses and blinked rapidly. Her eyes magnified through the lenses, giving her the appearance of an owl.

One with grey curls and an abundance of off-centre wisdom.

A fork-load of eggs stopped midway to my mouth. 'What?'

'I think long time if I should say. I think da, no, da, no. Up, down like toilet seat.'

'What?' A clump of egg tumbled off my fork and splattered onto the bench.

Draga pounced to wipe it away and expelled a resigned

sigh. 'Bah! I show you.'

She fetched a laundry basket. From a jumble of clothes, she retrieved a pair of tiny men's briefs. She held them in front of her and stretched the waistband. 'Mr Ruin buy like this. All new. So small, I not know how he cover his business.'

Granted, jockettes weren't Rohan's typical choice. His taste was more conventional. Cotton boxers. Usually grey. Usually boring.

'So?' I paused, trying to recall the last time I'd seen Rohan in his underwear.

Draga's eyes narrowed. Her shoulders sagged, affirming her disappointment with my lack of insight. 'You smart lady, but not today. Man buy new underpants for one reason.'

'If you're implying Rohan is up to something, you're wrong. Why would he be? I'm a good wife and a good stepmother to his son. I keep the household running. We're happy.'

Draga crossed herself and looked to the heavens. 'Forgive me to say this, Missus Jac. Three thing.' She raised four fingers and began a countdown. 'One, you not go nowhere with Mr Ruin for long time. Two, you not like the boy much. Three, I the one who make everything in this house to run good.' She glanced at her uncounted pinkie finger and abruptly brought her hand down.

Bad maths aside, I hated it when she was right, although it was a little unfair to bring 'the boy' – my teen stepson, Anthony – into the equation. Rohan and I hardly saw him. Still, I wasn't ready to concede anything.

'Rohan loves me,' I said, but my conviction had developed a hairline crack.

'You not count the chicken if is burning in oven,' Draga said.

'What the hell does that mean?' I threw her a challenging look. 'Anyway, how is this any of your business, Draga?'

'I with you long time, Missus Jac. You always my business.'

For the last four-plus years, Draga had had the full run of our domestic world. She'd washed my husband's – and my – underwear for a substantial portion of our marriage. A certain level of intimate knowledge had to be assumed. This had to be just another of Draga's crazy notions. But she wasn't cruel and would never say anything to hurt me.

Okay, so Rohan had bought new underwear. And he was absent more often and for longer than usual. His mobile chirped every few minutes, although he tended to end calls and pocket it whenever I came into the room. None of it proved he was having an affair.

I took a swig of coffee, my lipstick leaving a cutthroat red slash on the cup rim as a small cloud of doubt gathered.

Draga reached into her apron pocket, extracting a business card. Her eyes grew dark as she offered it with stubby fingers. 'I not want to give you this, but I must. I find in Mr Ruin pocket when I wash shirt.'

I snatched it and ran my finger over the raised lettering, embossed on silky paper stock and bearing an address printed in gold – The Admiral's Retreat. It was once our favourite getaway. Memories of lazy Sunday morning beach walks with Rohan flooded back. My hand trembled as I flipped over the card to see a message written in an unfamiliar script.

Darling, I've booked the night of Wednesday 15th for our anniversary celebration.

The signature was a large cursive 'J' followed by a string of kisses.

Anniversary. I stared at the word.

'Fifteen is today,' Draga said.

'I don't need a calendar,' I said. My mouth had gone dry.

Her gaze softened. 'Missus Jac, you be kind to me when I look for work. I look many years, but no one want give me job. But you do. You help me much. I like look after you. I not like you be hurt but is better you know before is too late.'

It was already too late. My life was a cliché based on the notion that all cheating husbands invest in new underwear.

Draga set her mouth like a hyphen and fetched a broom. It was her cleaning weapon of choice and she had a collection of them. Her favourite was a blue, bristled one with a dark, wooden handle. She clung to it when she had a problem to solve, claiming she could think better while holding it. Her knuckles tensed around the handle as she waited for me to speak.

'I hate it when you're right,' I said.

'Sometime, me, too.' Draga wrapped a thick arm around my shoulder and pressed her head against mine.

There was no going back. I should know the problem with any contract is the fine print. A marriage contract was no different and I hadn't read all the terms and conditions before I'd signed on the emotional dotted line. The 'out' clause had been revealed by those few words written by my husband's lover. A lover he'd been with long enough to celebrate an anniversary. The hurt went all the way to my bones.

I had to see it for myself, which is why I now had my gaze glued to the front door of The Admiral's Retreat, waiting on the painful proof.

I leaned against the headrest, closed my eyes, and drifted. A dog barked from behind a nearby fence. I sat up, disoriented, and checked the time. Only three minutes had passed. I sighed. This was torture. I wished Rohan would hurry up and come out.

On cue, the front door opened, and light flooded out onto the verandah. I bolted upright, raising the opera glasses I'd included in my surveillance kit. I hadn't used them since Rohan and I saw La Bohème years ago. Now the lorgnettes confirmed my life had more drama than Puccini could ever have composed.

Rohan was silhouetted by the light. Twelve years older than

me, he was tall, with a strong jawline and salt-and-pepper hair at his temples that branded him 'distinguished'. He stepped out in his dark business suit, clutching his briefcase and a small overnight bag. A woman followed him out.

I peered through the lenses, assessing her features, prepared for what I'd imagined his lover to be – tall, blonde, and youthful. She was the opposite – short, redheaded, and old. Okay, she wasn't quite pension-worthy, but I guessed older than me by a good fifteen years. That made her older than Rohan.

He hugged her. She raised her face and they kissed. He helped her shrug on a jacket, button it, then kissed her again. It looked so effortless, so normal. So damned ... practised.

I bit my lip and tasted blood.

A cab drew up at the entrance. Rohan held the woman for another long squeeze before he slipped into the front passenger seat. The cab's interior light illuminated his smile as he waved goodbye. Exhaust streamed into the cool air as the cab accelerated away and turned at the end of the street.

The woman began to walk towards my car.

I ducked, hitting my head on the steering wheel. Ouch. I counted. One, two, three, and reached ten before daring to peek over the dashboard to see her pulling away in a white Toyota Corolla parked a few spots ahead of me. Had I known it was hers, I would have keyed the damn thing. As an investigator, I was clueless.

For once, I was unsure of what to do. Confrontation wasn't in my nature, which was why I was hiding in the car, parked behind a tree. A self-respecting woman would have marched up to Rohan and kicked him in his new jockettes. Not me. My first reaction was denial, followed by rationalisation. I could be misinterpreting what I'd seen. It could have been a business meeting, a passing phase, an hallucination. I slapped my forehead. They've had an anniversary, idiot. Worse, Rohan had taken her to a place special to us. She wasn't only stealing my husband – she was stealing my memories.

I needed to know a whole lot more before I decided what to do: who she was, how they met, and what she could offer Rohan that I couldn't. What was Rohan planning to do? Was my marriage over? First, I'd find out where Rohan's lover lived. I started the engine and, with my cap pulled low, I followed the Toyota.

On the open road, I surrendered to tears, remembering how in love I'd been in those early days. After years of too many first-but-last dates, I'd met 'the one'. We had business in common. He was charming, handsome, and filled my days with flowers, nice restaurants, and surprise gifts. Two months later, he slipped a ring with a diamond the diameter of a five-cent coin on my finger. A circle of diamonds in a wedding band followed a month later. It happened so fast, I was giddy.

That was only five years ago, but now it seemed a lifetime.

I trailed the Toyota along the meandering beach road, through the suburbs. My grip on the steering wheel was so tight, the stones in my wedding ring cut into my finger. Its solitaire partner was now worth little more than the five-cent coin it resembled.

The woman's car slowed. In the distance, a garage door went up on a white, rendered house with a sea view balcony across the upper level. I pulled over, near enough to see the car swing into the garage and disappear behind the descending door. The street stilled again.

Watching my rival's home, my internal critic's voice was louder than usual, chanting how unlovable I was. The bump on my forehead pulsed. A long time passed, then a priority one message from my bladder urged me to restart the engine. I hung a U-turn and sped home. I wanted my bed and my doona. I wanted to hide from Rohan's betrayal and everything else I couldn't control, including my spinelessness.

Everything Draga had noticed about our relationship

was correct. I shouldn't be angry with her, but I cursed her for making me face it. It was easier than acknowledging my stupidity and humiliation. I should be angry with myself for being so gullible when it came to Rohan's behaviour. I'd refused to see him drawing away. Now he'd found someone else. I could forgive a lot, but never that. I knew the answer to the most important question – my marriage was over.

I'd divorce him. I was young enough to take my share and start over – if I got my share. Marriage is supposed to be grand, but divorce could be several hundred grand. Even a civilised settlement could take years to reach. Given Rohan's capacity for deviousness, that might be difficult. He ran an investment business, that's why I'd agreed to let him handle our joint finances in the first place. Like an idiot, I'd trusted him. A deep chill ran through me. He could have our assets tied up in complex schemes, which even a slick Cheat'em & Fastbuck-style law firm wouldn't be able to unravel.

Why make it easy for him and her then, whoever she was? I should be as sneaky and calculating as Rohan. Okay, I'd need to consult an instruction manual on the subject, but I could learn. I wasn't stupid, just blind.

My tears dried. A fire ignited in my belly and grew. I slowed to a steady speed, and I sat up tall. The road ahead opened out and so did my thinking. I cruised homeward as the summer sunrise inked a blood-red line along the horizon, underscoring what I knew beyond certainty – Rohan Anthony Burne, my 'devoted' husband, was a lying, cheating dog. I wasn't going to let him take anything more from me. Not my assets nor what was left of my self-respect.

The streetlights went out. It was a new day. With it came a new solution to my problem.

I was going to kill the mongrel.

CHAPTER TWO

I braked my car to a stop in the garage just after 7am. Rohan's BMW wasn't there.

Usually, he drove to meetings, but he'd left The Admiral's Retreat in a cab. Given his nocturnal activities, he could have hidden the Beemer anywhere. I considered calling his offices – Burne and Campbell Investment Consultants – to find out about his movements for the day, but I'd look an idiot not knowing my husband's whereabouts.

Surveillance kit in hand, I went out through the garage side door to the patio with its cushioned, cane day beds arranged under a shade sail that spanned half the yard. The swimming pool sparkled in the morning sun. Another thing we didn't need and rarely used, given there was a beach opposite our front door. Rohan had installed the pool the year we were married, with notions of doing morning laps.

'Have to work on this to keep up with the trophy wife,' he'd said, patting his belly.

Calling me a 'trophy wife' should have been a clue. That phrase could never be a compliment. If I was any sort of 'trophy' to Rohan, it's the sort kept in pride of place for a while then pushed to the back of the shelf. It had taken five years, a cranky housekeeper, and a business card, to realise I was coated in dust.

The back door was unlocked. It scraped as I slid it open and stepped into the cool living area facing the kitchen. I dropped my kit and dashed to the powder room where a long sit allowed me scheming time and a healthy list of punishing possibilities to consider before I did the cheater in. I could put peroxide in his mouthwash, superglue his eyes shut while he was sleeping, or set his pubic hair alight.

'Missus Jac, is you?' Draga's gravelly voice boomed from the kitchen.

Damn. She was early.

She had my surveillance bag hooked on one finger. Her other hand rested on her hip and a cleaning cloth was draped over her shoulder. Steely blue eyes drilled into me over the rims of her glasses, which balanced lopsidedly on the tip of her nose. She scanned my drug dealer garb. 'I see what you have in bag. Where you be?'

'Dobro jutro, Draga.'

She ignored the morning greeting in my best Croatian.

'You not do right thing.' She wiped down the bag with the cloth. 'I put this where you not find any more.' She stomped out of the room and continued to reprove me at a distance. 'Not waste time with looking, looking, looking. What good do?'

Soon she was back, the evidence of my misdeed gone.

'You must learn osveta.' She contemplated the ceiling as if the English word she was looking for was written there. 'How you say? Da! Revenge. That make Mr Ruin think about things he do then he change for sure.'

I already had my revenge in mind. 'Mind your own business, Draga.'

'You my business.' She waggled her finger and flicked the cleaning rag. 'Bah! I go fix the bed you not sleep in.'

Draga's bossiness didn't bother me. I took it as an expression of her well-meaning nature and the fact she liked things to run perfectly. We shared that value. But now my life wasn't running quite perfectly, and it was logical Draga would double her efforts to protect me. I hated feeling so exposed and vulnerable.

In the shower, I rubbed hard with a loofah sponge as though enough scrubbing could shed the years I'd wasted with

Rohan. The fact he had a lover was hard enough. But someone older? I wished the hot water could wash away my humiliation.

When I stepped out, my skin was patchy red. Great. It added to my overall plain features. Mine wasn't a face to grace a fashion magazine. My nose was too big, my mouth too wide, and I had one slightly crooked tooth, which made me shy about smiling. My eyes were green, and today the whites were bloodshot.

Then there was my hair, which I was constantly at war with. I battled to get it to sit, but it was pointless. In the end, I pulled it into a chignon, pinning it with clips and slides. They stuck out all over like an experimental art installation.

I applied concealer to cover the dark circles under my eyes, adding a thick coat to my forehead where the bump was now beginning to bruise. Blusher gave me a healthier glow and a slash of lipstick heightened my pout. I was good at acting confident, but today I was fraught with nerves and uncertainty. Whatever direction my life was about to take, it would never be the same.

Draga passed the open bedroom door, pushing the vacuum cleaner ahead of her as if the fate of the global environment depended on sucking up every speck of dust. She stopped the machine to impart a vital piece of information. 'You not look good,' she said before she continued her dirt-eradicating mission.

I slammed the door shut and dressed in a charcoal linen suit with a crisp, white shirt underneath, stud earrings and corporate black heels. I cast a critical eye over my image. The outfit should have made me the consummate businesswoman, but Draga was right. I didn't look good and, in the recruitment business, it was all about making the right impression. Image is everything.

The vacuum cleaner whined to a stop and Draga flung open the door. 'I no like when you cry, Missus Jac.' Her tone grew gentle. 'You cry too much.'

'I'm not crying.' I marched downstairs.

'You stay home. You must sleep,' she said, standing on the landing with her hands on her hips.

Despite what Rohan had done, there wasn't time to wallow. I had a business to run and staff to think of.

'I can't, Draga. I know you worry about me, and I appreciate it. I'm sure if my mum was alive, she'd be doing the same.'

Draga's hard look softened.

'But I have to deal with this my way. And I do have to get to work. I'll see you tonight.'

'Okay, Missus Jac. Have the nice day.'

Not likely. In the last twenty-four hours, I'd learned about the vagaries of marital fine print and about how long I could hold my bladder. I'd learned I was a naïve fool. Since then, my emotions had tumbled like wet rags in a washing machine, dampening my pride. I needed to salvage what was left.

In the car, I plugged my phone into the car's speaker system and punched up my music app. I selected Blondie's 'One Way or Another'. Debbie Harry belted out my new anthem, warning some man she would get him, one way or another.

Yep, Rohan. I was right there with Ms Harry.

With the track on repeat, I sang all the way to the Westgate Bridge. Peak hour traffic snaked ahead to the crest, car brake lights glowing intermittently. Low, dark clouds reached down into the city skyline, threatening to turn the day wet and humid. Rain splattered the windscreen as the summer storm set in. The wipers came on and thudded like a metronome across the glass. Although the air conditioner was running, I tingled with heat. In the drama of discovering Rohan's betrayal, I'd lost sight of the biggest problem confronting my business – it might go bust at any minute. When the economy had nose-dived, thanks to shoddy banking practices on a global scale, All Class had taken a hit. It had recovered somewhat, and since then, the business had some good years. In others, I'd barely managed to pay the bills. This year was one of the bad ones.

I clung to one hope – a tender to provide recruitment services to a group of affiliated financial institutions. If All Class was successful, it would be three years' worth of guaranteed work. It would save my staff's jobs. The tender deadline was looming and I couldn't afford to let my personal life distract me.

I turned my plans for Rohan down to a simmer.

Finding the right employees for clients and the right employers for candidates gave me satisfaction. It took energy and commitment, both of which I lacked today. I wasn't ready for anything more demanding than a few callbacks and a little reading time in my office, but there were urgent decisions to make.

A gap opened, and I inched forward and nudged my way to the off-ramp. I accelerated and followed the road to Port Melbourne and my company's offices. 'All Class Recruitment' was emblazoned on the building in bold red letters. In the rear carpark, I swung into my allocated spot.

The receptionist, Paulette Antonelli, had parked her Hyundai two bays away. It needed a wash. I should send her an email reminding her that image is everything.

Except for last night's coffee stain on the seat, my modest VW Golf was still as shiny as it had been on the car showroom floor. I took it to the local car wash every week. For Rohan, car cleaning was a Sunday ritual. I called it The Church of the Holy Chamois. Worship began after breakfast. He would spend hours on his pride and joy, a black BMW 5 series. A beautiful car, but now I suspected Rohan's cleaning was less about pride and more about removing any evidence of his indiscretions. A kind of washing of his cheating soul.

Before I got rid of him, I should seek payback via that damn car. I could let down his tyres, tip sugar into the fuel tank, put a dead fish under the seat. My shortlist took on new momentum.

Draga's voice, reminding me I was 'smart lady, but not today', echoed in my head. Her notion of revenge and mine varied. Ruining his car wouldn't be in her repertoire.

The wind fussed with my hair, making me more irritated. My work bag dragged my arm down under the weight of many documents.

The company's offices were a modest section of a shared building. Large windows spilled natural light onto the latte chairs in the reception area. They were faux leather, but I didn't care; they looked the part. Inexpensive abstract artwork painted in reds put a shot of hot chilli into the décor, giving the office a sophisticated look.

Paulette sat at the reception desk in her usual black business suit; today's shirt was emerald green. Big silver hoops dangled from her ears. Her hair pulled high into a sleek, jet black ponytail, she was the perfect company face.

'Morning, Jacqueline,' she chirped and flashed whitened teeth. Her makeup was glamour-shot ready and the scent of Coco Mademoiselle wafted around her. 'Good thing you're here.' She lowered her voice. 'Sandi's not coming in. She's got a virus.' She said virus while making air quotation marks with her fingers.

Paulette had a long history of unexpressed tension towards Sandi Watson. Sandi never noticed. She was the sort of person who could never imagine anyone thinking a single unpleasant thing about her. So far, it hadn't caused a problem and it suited me. Both were good at their jobs and I didn't want anything bringing their animosity to the surface.

As head of the Permanent Placement Division, Sandi was great with clients. Smart and reliable in a 'keep the client happy' kind of way, she'd been the ideal hamster on my organisational wheel until some months ago when her attendance and interest in the job waned. I let it ride as a temporary glitch. Everyone had rough patches, as I'd discovered in my own life.

'Sandi forgot to log off last night, so I can get onto her PC and print her client list for today if you want it,' Paulette said.

'Great, bring it in.' I headed into my small office.

The 'in' and 'out' trays were aligned on my desk. Books occupied their shelves in height order. Everything was in place, except for the crimson roses in the vase on my desk. Their heads were bowed in death nods with some fallen petals scattered around the vase base. Clients often sent bouquets in gratitude, but I felt most appreciated when an account was paid on time.

I buzzed Paulette over the intercom. 'Please throw out the roses in my office as soon as you can.'

She appeared a few minutes later, ticking off the items she carried. 'Thought you might like a coffee.' She set down a mug with the All Class logo on it. 'Here's Sandi's client list and today's vacancy postings. And I'll take this.' She whisked up the vase and hurried out, hips moving like a pendulum.

One red petal remained on the desk. I picked it up and crushed it between my fingers. It left a blood-like stain and Rohan jumped to the top of my thoughts. I was such an idiot to keep believing his excuses for being away so often. I imagined him with that woman, then brushed it aside. I needed to deal with my business's demands and focus on collating the material for the Financial Services Sector tender.

The staff and the company expenses were always my number one priority when it came to doling out money. Nobody knew I topped up those expenses from my savings, thanks to a small inheritance from Dad. The rest of his estate had gone to my stepmother, a woman who had even less time for me than he'd had.

I spread the printouts, picked up the mug and took a mouthful. I needed a massive caffeine boost to work through Sandi's schedule. Surely, she didn't work this hard.

There was a long list of client calls to follow up, and a midmorning meeting with Globe General Bank, a potential client we'd been courting. There was also a lunch appointment. I didn't recognise her companion's name or the venue address.

I sipped more coffee, flipping over the pages. There was one after-hours appointment listed. This address I knew – the offices of Keene Recruiting. I leaned closer to the printout. It didn't make the situation look any better, especially when I read the name of the person she was meeting. Jason Keene. Why was Sandi meeting my most hated rival?

I slammed the mug onto the desk so hard it toppled. Coffee puddled onto the paper, before cascading over the desk's edge. I grabbed tissues and pressed them into the carpet to sop up the spill, cursing the man. Every time Jason Keene was around, things went downhill.

It hadn't started that way. The first time I'd spotted him was at a conference. Wearing Armani, he was the sort of man women wanted to follow home. In our networking session, he'd introduced himself. He held the right qualifications and had a bit of experience under his calfskin belt. 'I hope to head an executive search firm one day,' he said, flashing a toothpaste commercial smile and oozing enthusiasm. He was smooth and dropped so many names I almost needed to borrow Draga's broom. Yet there was something about him.

We chatted during the breaks, and before the conference ended, he offered me his business card. We shook hands, and then he disappeared into the crowd.

A few phone calls to people in the industry revealed a lot about Jason Keene. His Information Technology experience and recruitment expertise were what All Class had needed at the time. He also knew what I knew about this field – no matter which way it was spun, it's a sales game dressed up as a service industry. One great big numbers game and Mr Keene could count high.

I recruited him and soon Jason was handing out All Class Recruitment business cards. I put him in the Contracting Division where he grew our client base with tech talk and charisma. He was great with clients, charming and clever. At least it appeared that way, but he was the worst recruitment decision I ever made.

He didn't deliver the numbers he'd promised. Worse, he couldn't keep his mouth shut, or his fly. A candidate's complaint brought it to my attention and we narrowly avoided a lawsuit. He was the only employee I'd ever terminated. The last time I saw Jason Keene, he said I'd regret what I'd done, but I only regretted I'd employed him for those six months. I learned from the experience and decided that All Class would be classier and put service ahead of sales.

I'd kept track of him and the small firm he'd started. Now he was on the fringe of my business again and I was suspicious. Still, Sandi had always been cool towards him when he'd worked here, and I couldn't imagine them staying in touch.

The intercom light flashed. 'What's up, Paulette?'

'Sandi rang back. She's updated her calendar and asked if I needed her password to print it. I said yes.'

'You didn't tell her she'd left her PC on?'

'Nope.'

I imagined Paulette's glossed lips forming a satisfied pout. I bet she wasn't telling Sandi anything she didn't have to. She wasn't so dumb after all.

She sashayed in a few minutes later, a glint in her eye as she gave me the documents.

'Here you go. Ohmygod, your coffee.' Paulette's tone was all 'breaking news'.

She didn't know that in today's grand scheme of problems, splattered coffee meant zilch compared to a senior member of my staff meeting with my nemesis, plus my husband having an affair. Possibly in that order of disaster.

'I'll get that cleaned up.' Paulette's tone segued to 'police rescue' and she left with fitting urgency.

'Thanks, Paulette.' I scanned the new schedule.

Keene Recruiting and Jason Keene's names were gone.

One thing was sure, Sandi had no idea I knew about her clandestine appointment. If I confronted her, she might become extra careful and I'd never find out what was going on between them. I'd have to keep a close eye on my little hamster as well as my rat of a husband.

I might have to go into rodent extermination.

CHAPTER THREE

My mobile rang as I entered a trendy eatery at the west end of Collins Street.

Draga barked down the line, 'Missus Jac, boy mother ring house
two time.'

Ant's mother was Trish Burne-Spencer, Rohan's first wife. To me, she was 'Triple-T': teeth, tits, and a tart. Her teeth were veneered, her breasts enlarged, and her face was pulled so tightly with cosmetic procedures, it looked like she was permanently in a wind tunnel. Triple-T had married and discarded another husband after Rohan. She'd kept both their names and any assets they hadn't secured.

Draga's voice showed no sign of her earlier frustration. 'She not happy. I tell her she must call on you mobility phone. Okay?'

'No. I'll call her when ...'

There was a click as Draga disconnected.

Whatever Triple-T wanted, I didn't want to deal with her today, or any other day. Our conversations at the best of times were perfunctory, limited to issues of Ant's sporadic visits to his father, and occasionally being the message-bearer when Triple-T was looking for more child support. I switched off my 'mobility' phone.

In the café, pendulum lights lit the beech tables. The staff were hipsters. I sat at a table and waited for Maddison Parker from Globe General Bank, Sandi's main appointment for today – if I discounted Jason Keene. I brooded for fifteen long minutes until a young woman entered and scanned the room.

I stood and signalled her. 'Maddison?'

She hesitated then came towards me.

'Jacqueline Burne, All Class Recruitment.' I offered her my hand.

Maddison's handshake was so light, I wondered if her muscles had atrophied.

'I was expecting Sandi Watson.'

'I'm sorry, she couldn't make it today.'

Maddison sighed and slid into a chair. 'It's so nice to get out of the office.'

'I'm sure you appreciate the break.' I forced a smile until my cheeks hurt.

She handed me her business card – Maddison Parker, Manager Human Investment.

Someone, somewhere, was paid to create these stupid titles. According to her card, the office she'd escaped was on the thirty-fifth floor of the bank's headquarters, which overlooked the river. Yep, life was tough in Maddison Land.

I gave her my card. Maddison dropped it into her handbag. She'd probably file it under F for Forget.

'Congratulations on your recent promotion, Maddison.' I'd read about it in Sandi's notes and sometimes I had to suck up to clients. They liked to feel important and it was my job to nurture that belief. I didn't have to like them, but I did respect their power to sign off contracts, no matter how pretentious their job title.

'Thank you.' The skin between her expertly shaped eyebrows crinkled. 'It was tough. I've worked for the company for three years, but I should have been promoted ages ago. I can't understand why it took them so long.'

I suspected it was because Maddison was an idiot. If someone came up with a perfume called 'Entitlement', Maddison would be dabbing it on her wrists.

A waiter hovered. 'Ready to order?' He eyed Maddison as if

she was a serve of his favourite ice cream.

Maddison tossed her brunette locks. 'Skinny soy latte and absolutely nothing sprinkled on the top.' She emphasised 'nothing' with a sharp hand swipe. Long lashes almost brushed her cheek when she looked down. I wondered if she employed them tactically in office politics.

The waiter's mood evaporated, and he gave an almost imperceptible head shake as he swivelled to me. 'For you, ma'am?'

I ordered a double-shot black coffee. I wanted a Jack Daniels, neat. Pity it was only eleven in the morning or I'd be tempted.

Maddison's eyes fired daggers into the waiter's departing figure. 'Men are jerks.'

And Rohan was the King of Jerks. He'd promised me the world, but instead had taken everything. My mind flew back to The Admiral's Retreat.

'Jacqueline?' Maddison's lashes blinked double time.

'Sorry. I'm a bit thrown today with Sandi being ill.' I delivered the line with a bucket load of sincerity.

Rattling on in corporate jargon, Maddison handed over a brief.

I perused it, puzzled by one element. There were six vacant positions, not four as in Sandi's background notes. This was better than I'd expected. I did a quick mental calculation. At the designated fee of between twelve and twenty per cent of the gross salary package, All Class would be looking at a decent boost to the coffers. This could keep us above the line for the next few months while we waited for the tender outcome. For that kind of money, Maddison Parker could call herself whatever she liked.

'I see you've increased the number of positions from four to six since your conversation with Sandi.'

Maddison's cheeks flushed, and she snatched back the

documents. She pulled two position descriptions from the staple. 'These two don't belong here. We need a shortlist by month's end. Absolutely no extension.'

Perhaps she believed Globe General Bank's annual profit depended on her deadline.

'I don't anticipate it'll be a problem.' I was happy to be sidetracked from my concerns with Rohan by the prospect of money coming into the business. My staff's jobs would be safe for a while longer. That notion and more caffeine saw me through Maddison's next 'me, me, me' story.

Our meeting ended outside the café with her limp handshake and some small talk.

Maddison tottered off on skyscraper heels. She was the sort of airhead who'd be a good candidate for Rohan's fling. I imagined her in her office, shuffling papers at her desk, doing a bit of online shopping, yet never coming to terms with the fact she had no idea how to find decent staff. Lucky for her, she'd found a good recruitment company.

In the underground carpark, I counted down the levels as I rode the grimy elevator to the bowels of the building. I was buoyed by the business opportunity, but something about the two extra positions niggled.

At the pay station, I inserted my ticket.

A patrolling security guard strolled by. 'G'day.' He smiled at me in the way men hadn't for a long time. I was tempted to look around in case Maddison was standing behind me. There was a wedding ring on his finger.

I whizzed up the parking levels with dizzy speed. The boom gate rose, and I powered out the exit.

It was only late morning and my inventory already included a cheating husband, a nagging housekeeper, a suspect employee, a conceited client and a flirty, married, carpark attendant.

A stack of messages was waiting for me at the office. My mobile phone showed two missed calls. One from Triple-T, one from Rohan. Neither had left messages. It made it easier to ignore them.

I focused my limited energy on the assignment for Globe General Bank. It'd be good to show a touch of zeal and get the shortlist in before the due date. That should impress Maddison Parker down to her French-tipped fingernails. The sooner I filled the positions, the quicker the fees would come in. I read all the position descriptions, made notes, and then wrote queries for the database, hoping it would spit out a long list of suitable candidates. Failing that, I'd draft an advertisement to post online.

After an hour, my eyes stung, and my neck was stiff, but I kept going. Nothing would stop me putting in my best effort.

Not even getting rid of my cheating husband.

I pulled into the garage, next to the BMW. My shoulders tensed at the thought of facing Rohan, but until I worked out exactly what to do, I wasn't ready to let him know I'd caught him out.

Draga had the kitchen secured like a piece of sacred ground. A floral apron around her ample waist, she chopped vegetables with a quick hand. It was scary how fast the knife blade moved.

'You come late, Missus Jac.'

Exhaustion gripped me, and I could hardly move. All day, I'd mused over my problems and fought off sleep, but my tension eased on hearing her voice. I'd grown used to her presence since the one-week trial we agreed on. It had morphed into Monday to Friday attendance, a flourishing potted herb supply in my back garden, and meals calculated to feed MCG Grand Finals crowds. Draga's cooking was worth the few extra kilos around my hips.

'It's been a long, hard day.' I threw my bag and jacket onto a chair.

Draga hurried to put them away.

'I can do it, Draga. I don't expect you to pick up after me.'
I almost added 'as Rohan does', but today's list of complaints
against him was long enough. 'And I'm sorry I was so grumpy
with you this morning.'

I waited for her to continue remonstrating about my spy
mission, but she didn't.

'Is okay, Missus Jac. You much tired and I think now
somebody give you more trouble, da?' she asked over her
shoulder as she went to the kitchen. Her head disappeared
into the fridge. She emerged juggling fresh tomatoes and a cos
lettuce.

'Big trouble.' I kicked off my shoes, flopped onto the sofa,
and wiggled my toes into the rug's deep pile. I should go and
find Rohan, but my gut clenched at having to see him. I stayed
put. 'Can you put the coffee gadget on please, Draga?'

'Coffee fix nothing tonight. You need strong drink.'

'Thank you.' My head had been thumping since this
morning; I hoped it wouldn't develop into a migraine. I'd been
getting them frequently. I should have thought twice about
drinking on an empty stomach, but I took the cab-sav she
handed me. 'Hvala.'

Draga produced a small plate of sliced cheeses, Ligurian
olives, and water crackers.

'You eat little bit. I cook something special for the dinner.'

Within a few minutes, the scent of oregano and garlic
wafted from the kitchen.

I nibbled on a piece of pecorino picante. 'Where's Rohan?'

Draga stirred the simmering pan. 'Mr Ruin not home.'

'But his car's in the garage.'

Even though I'd ignored his phone calls today, I'd expected
the lying sod to put in an appearance and make a show of being
a good husband.

'He say he have the meeting late, but I not believe he go
work. He think I stupid because I not speak the English good.

He more stupid than me.' She shook her head and her curls flounced in emphasis.

'Go on.'

'He say he call taxi-car, but I look from window and see he not go in taxi-car.' She waved the wooden spoon in the direction of the street.

My neck prickled. 'What did he go in?'

Draga's face scrunched with annoyance. 'White car take Mr Ruin.'

I put down the glass on the coffee table with a clunk. 'Did you see the driver?'

'Was lady. She have the big sunglass and hair like fire.'

The same woman I'd seen him with at The Admiral's Retreat. How could he be so brazen? I picked up the glass and gulped the remainder of the wine. 'What time did he leave?'

'He come home five clock. He go in shower. He stay long time. I tell him when he come downstair, Mr Ruin, you use much water.'

'Draga!'

'He go half past six,' she finished in a hurry.

'Thank you.' I handed her the empty glass.

'You think this woman write the letter to Mr Ruin?'

'It wasn't a whole letter. It was only a few words.'

'Tsk. Was important word. Mr Ruin not treat you like the husband must do.'

'He must be having a midlife crisis.'

'Then he have the crisis for one year.' Draga's tone sharpened. 'He think he is young rooster. Make me angry, Missus Jac.'

'I can handle him.'

'Then why you face like the ripe tomato?'

I left and went to the bathroom and drew a bath. I poured in frangipani-scented foaming gel. The scent wove its way to my brain and began to soothe me. I blew bubbles through a fingertip circle. One formed perfectly and floated upward. It did a fragile dance, bounced off the tiles and popped. I wished it was Rohan's head.

'Who is she?' I asked. 'Do you think I can't find out? I have one word for you, mongrel: Google. I'll find out everything I can about her.' Once I'd worked out her name.

'Missus Jac, who you talk to?' Draga rapped on the bathroom door.

'Myself.'

'Not make me to worry more.'

'Mind your own business.'

'You my business.'

I bristled at the memory of Rohan and his lover's goodbye and how much they looked like they belonged together.

I blew more bubbles. Each carried off an item on my list of 'do rights'. I was faithful and supportive. The popping bubbles answered: you married in haste, you replaced your absent father, and you have no self-respect.

Draga was right – my relationships weren't in good shape. I avoided Rohan and I didn't like Ant. I was in the home stretch to forty with little to show. The twelve-year age difference wasn't the only gap in my marriage. There was a bigger, emptier space dividing us – no children.

I'd assumed having a family would be on the agenda when we married. Then, one night, as Rohan had hung up from a terse phone call with Triple-T, he'd said, 'Good thing I won't have to deal with any more kids.'

'What about our kids?'

'We'll see. Anthony's more than anyone can handle at the moment.' He kissed my forehead as if I was a petulant child.

It should have been another clue to the contract's fine print.

Over the years, we had a few conversations about a family, enough to create a little hope, but never a commitment. Then, eight months ago, when the lines on the home testing kit confirmed my surprise pregnancy, I didn't know how to tell Rohan. I held in my joy while I made the rounds of early medical appointments and strategised ways to announce it. I'd hoped he would change his mind when presented with the news. I never had the chance to find out.

Six weeks after the doctor's confirmation, I woke with cramping and bleeding. I went alone to my local doctor who examined me, said something about complications, and called an ambulance. The ride seemed to take forever. At the hospital, there was a flurry of activity to have me admitted. In the operating theatre, the temperature was low, as was my desire to live.

'Miscarriages happen for many reasons. Sometimes there's no obvious reason. Sometimes it's chromosomal. We could organise further tests, but they might not show up anything definitive. The good news is you conceived once, so you probably can again.' The specialist left me in the care of a nurse who had kind eyes and a gentle manner.

'Can I contact someone for you, Mrs Burne?' she asked.

'My husband's interstate on business. I don't want to worry him.' I said, too embarrassed to tell her I hadn't told Rohan about the pregnancy. The only other person I could call was Draga, but in the announcement hierarchy, my husband should hear the news about my pregnancy before the housekeeper. Now, there was nothing to announce, and all my strategising was in vain.

I'd watched the rain dribble down the window. The peak hour traffic crawled along the streets in the fading light. Long snakes of red and amber lights flickered. Pedestrians hurried with winter coats tightly wrapped around them and their heads bowed against the bitter wind.

My baby had slipped away, unformed, and unnamed, leaving me hollow. I sobbed until my eyes felt as if metal filings were in them. I vowed never to tell Rohan. The irony didn't escape me. It was the last time Rohan and I had had sex, and I'd fallen pregnant.

What were the odds?

On discharge, I'd gone straight to the office. When Rohan returned from his interstate trip, he said I looked pale but didn't ask if anything was wrong.

I should have left him then, but I hadn't had the energy to leave the house, let alone leave the marriage.

In the six months since the miscarriage, I'd put all my grief neatly aside and pretended everything was fine. Instead of admitting it was the turning point in our relationship, I'd lied to myself, living in denial so long I knew its postcode. Now, I took solace in knowing I had a plan to extricate myself from the relationship. Not an exact plan; more like a plan to make a plan.

I sank under the bubbles. When I came up, my breasts wore foam like a strapless gown. The small breasts I'd hated as a teenager had retained a degree of pertness because there wasn't a lot of flesh to head south. There was a strange advantage in that. By my age, my boobs could be touching my toes. Women I knew complained birth took a toll on their bodies. Big deal. I would trade my circumstances for sagging breasts or even a fashionable C-section. I could live with stretch marks. All a small price to pay for motherhood.

'Missus Jac, dinner ready.' Draga's voice boomed through the door.

I stood, and the bubble bath crackled as it dissolved to nothing. 'Coming.'

'I not want food be cold,' she called back.

'I'll be two minutes.'

'Hurry.'

When it concerned food, everything was urgent to Draga.

I dried myself with a towel as soft as cotton wool and slipped into a crocheted cotton dressing-gown handmade by Draga. I discarded the used towel, just as I'd discarded any ideas about saving my marriage. My relationship with Rohan was over. I could never forgive infidelity. Even God herself would understand why I couldn't let him get away with it. All I needed was to orchestrate my exit strategy – more accurately, his exit strategy. The only real part of my life that mattered now was my business. It was my biggest asset. And there was the interfering, but well-meaning Draga. She counted as an asset of sorts.

The house had the scent of an upmarket restaurant as I went downstairs. It hit me. My best relationship was with a late sixties-something Croatian housekeeper who was about to feed and fuss over me. This might be the closest I'd ever get to domestic bliss. I tried to mentally balanced happiness and sadness at the thought. In the end I gave up.

After dinner, I read through paperwork while Draga tidied around me, hovering attentively.

'Missus Jac, what you learn today is not easy thing.'

'No, it's not, Draga, but I'll work it out.' I doodled it'll work out in the page margin. Who was I kidding?

'When you lose the husband is bad. But when you lose the trust, you never get back. You trust no one after. Mr Ruin make me be much angry. He should think how important is be good husband.'

Draga wiped the bench making vigorous circles as if she imagined polishing sense into Rohan's thick skull. 'He should think how important is be good father, too.'

He was neither. A lump formed in my throat.

'He think I not see. I have the big eyes. I see everything.' She spread her arms in a circle.

I buried my head in the paperwork. I sensed Draga move towards me, and I held up my palm. 'Stop. I'm okay.'

'You not okay, Missus Jac. You suffer much this year.' Her voice dropped. 'I know why you go to the hospital for four days.'

Damn. I thought I'd covered my tracks. 'How?'

'I smartie,' she said, tapping a finger to her temple. 'Mr Ruin be gone one week. You call me to say you go for the business, but was all of the sudden. I not believe you. Then, I find blood on sheet when I wash. When you come home, you much sad and not want to speak. I put two with the two.' She crossed one index finger over the other.

I fiddled with my wedding ring. 'I didn't tell anyone. Not even Rohan.'

'This break you heart.' Draga sat opposite, her squat legs crossed at the knee. 'What doctor say?'

'It happens. Sometimes they don't know why. I had an infection, too.' I paused, remembering the pain. 'He suggested I have further tests, but warned they might not give me any answers.'

'You do these tests?'

'I didn't bother.'

'Why you not do? Maybe they help you.'

'Lots of people don't have kids, Draga, and they do fine.' But I didn't count myself as one of those doing fine. I didn't have the requisites for motherhood: a supportive partner, a reliable reproductive system, and the most basic one – a sex life.

'If they choose no children is okay, but you not choose, Missus Jac.' Draga kept probing, wearing me down with tender understanding. In one day, she'd already uncovered most of my secrets. There was no way I wanted to add to my humiliation by telling her Rohan didn't want a child with me, regardless of the test outcomes.

I'd learned not to look in the windows of baby goods stores. I changed channels on the television when ads with babies came on. I recalled the card for counselling services the hospital had given me. Where had I put it?

'It wasn't meant to be. Anyway, why are we talking about this, Draga?'

'Because you sad all the time. I know what is be sad like you be. When you lose the husband and the child. Feel like nothing left. Is weight to carry you whole life.' She lifted the apron hem to dab her eyes.

'Are you talking about your family, Draga?' Although she'd mentioned in the job interview that she'd come to Australia after the Bosnian war, she'd never elaborated. I wanted to slap myself. How could I not have realised?

'Did something happen to them during the war?' I asked.

'Many people suffer in war,' Draga said. 'You not worry for me. I find place to put the love.' She squeezed my arm. 'You need somebody look after you. I do this. You always be my business. I see you tomorrow.'

As the sound of Draga's car engine faded, her words echoed in my head.

A place to put the love.

In bed, I stared at the ceiling until I fell into a dreamless sleep, waking when Rohan came in.

His clothes rustled as he undressed. The clock glowed 2am and I wasn't up for flimsy explanations or a screaming match. I'd already decided I was going to get rid of the jerk and didn't plan to give him any hints or reasons to get out of the way. I wanted him right in the firing line for when the time was right.

Rohan pulled up the covers and rolled over. Within seconds, he was snoring.

When I woke, light had already flooded the room. Rohan's side was empty and cold. Only rumpled sheets and a crushed pillow remained.

He'd vanished, leaving indentations on the bed made by the ghost he'd become.

CHAPTER FOUR

Traffic was light, and I arrived at the office before anyone else. I fired up the coffee machine and poured a strong cup, fortifying myself to read a stack of query reports regarding All Class's recent performance. The bottom line was unhealthy with figures that teetered at the edge of a financial cliff.

I reviewed everything that generated business. I understood the market. I approached clients without being so aggressive that I ran the risk of having an intervention order issued against me. The business had excellent processes and procedures. The website was up to date and social media was relevant. Staff had as many professional development opportunities as I could afford. Still, times were tough.

I thumbed through a heap of overdue accounts; utilities sat at the top, followed by the offsite data backup services. I had two months of payroll, max. If things didn't pick up soon, I'd be out of business. Perspiration bathed my neck, although it was nothing to do with the hot morning sun radiating through the window.

I gathered the documents into a red folder, shoved them into the top drawer, and then headed to the cool of the tiled bathroom. I wadded a wet paper towel and dabbed it around my neck. The business will bounce back. Rohan will be out of my life. I will find a way through this.

I'd never accepted anyone's help. Not even from my late father whose style was to buy solutions rather than make himself available. My independence had been attractive to Rohan. He'd doted on me, and I'd basked in his attention. He'd seemed perfect. I should have consulted Recruiting 101.

The door swung open and Sandi Watson swanned in on designer heels. She gave me a slow up and down. 'You okay, Jacqueline? You look ... out of sorts.'

There wasn't a shred of concern in her voice.

On any given day, Sandi looked like she'd stepped out of the latest edition of Vogue. This morning was no exception. She stood before the mirror, turning one way and the other, inspecting the silhouette of her well-cut suit. She adjusted an expensive silver pendant.

A surge of self-consciousness flowed through me as I turned from my reflection and made a show of smoothing down my skirt.

'I'm surprised to see you. Paulette said you were sick.' She didn't look like she was recovering from any sort of virus.

'I'm much better,' Sandi said. She flashed the fake smile she'd perfected over the past six months. She leaned into the mirror and fine-tuned strands of shiny ash-blonde hair with manicured fingers. Her 'do' sat perfectly in place.

My waves were rampant. I tucked loose strands behind my ears.

'We're meeting this afternoon on the tender. You're available?' I asked, my back to her while I wiped my sweaty hands on a paper towel. I sensed Sandi's judgment boring into the back of my head.

'Wouldn't miss it.' She added more gloss to her lips and twirled, allowing herself a last satisfied once-over before she left.

Damn. I should have mentioned I was working on Globe General Bank's assignment and asked what she knew about the extra two positions Maddison Parker had pulled from the brief. I decided not to chase her. I had a niggling feeling something else was going on, and I didn't want to show my hand.

I re-examined my face, imagining my problems were written in its noticeable lines. I'd always believed I could decide what happened and when. Who to like, dislike, or trust. The last six months had shattered the illusion. Changes had crept stealthily into my personal and professional lives.

Back in my office, I didn't want to deal with anyone. I checked a few phone messages but set them aside. The trivia on my desk became the focus of my attention. I hated dirt and disorder, so I tidied up the top drawer, organised the paperclips, pulled out fluffy clumps of dust, lined up pens, and stacked Post-it notes in a neat pile. The red folder demand attention. The bills bulged from its edges, taunting my poor management and performance. Any other time I would have asked Rohan for advice.

I stayed in my office dealing with all the small things that didn't matter to my future life while hiding from all the big things that did. It took every ounce of my energy to concentrate. I put together an agenda, ran reports, and printed out copies for the meeting.

By the time I headed to the meeting room, my head ached. I adjusted the blinds to stop the sun's glare piercing my eyes, then laid out copies of the documents around the conference table.

Will Grenfell and Claire Sandhurst were the first to arrive, chorusing, 'Afternoon, Jac.'

They were the sort of employees I was proud to have at All Class. I never needed to chase them for anything.

Will was a solid family man whose face lit up when he spoke of his wife and two kids. Pictures of them covered his desk. From all accounts, his wife's primary occupation was shopping.

Claire was the company's Swiss watch – dependable and methodical. Detail-minded to the point of obsession, even her tiny permanent frown was precisely drawn. Rumour was she did a lot of charity work. Something to do with lost cats or dogs. Maybe it was native fauna. I knew little else of Claire's life. I couldn't remember the last time I had a social conversation with her.

'Where are Andrew and Sandi?' Will asked, checking his watch.

Just then, the door opened, and Andrew de Witt hurried in. 'Sorry I'm late, Chief,' he said. 'I had to sort out a technical problem.' He acknowledged Will and Claire with a nod. He sat down and began reading.

At thirty, Andrew looked much younger. He was a gem I'd found during a recruitment assignment for an information technology company. He'd made the shortlist although he didn't get across the line with the client. His youthful features belied his toughness, which I discovered when, unlike most candidates, he didn't brush off the rejection when he didn't get the job. When I'd told him, there was a brief silence on the other end before he let me have it. His rant involved a lot of swearing – some words with which I was unfamiliar – and it lasted about three minutes. Job hunting for months had pushed Andrew to boiling point around the time he landed on my hotplate. When he'd calmed down, I offered him a job as All Class's IT and Administration Manager. I knew a good one when I saw one, or I used to know. My radar for good quality was a tad off these days.

'We might give Sandi another minute,' I said.

Claire peeped up. 'She left the building about ten minutes ago.'

'Left?' I dialled Sandi's extension. It diverted to Paulette.

'Sorry, Jac, she didn't say where she was going but she was in a hurry. Hang on a tic. I'll ring her mobile.'

I waited while she dialled from another line.

'It went straight to voicemail.'

'Thanks, Paulette. When she returns, remind her she should be in this meeting.'

I smiled at the others. 'We should get started. You're all aware that the closing date for the Financial Services Sector tender is looming. If we're successful, there'll be plenty of work for All Class Recruitment for the next three years.'

'Things are okay at present, aren't they, Jac?' Will asked. His brow furrowed, probably estimating the next payment due on his wife's Visa card.

'Of course.' If no one examined the books too closely. The financial pressure was like holding up a mountain – a mountain of debt. I couldn't let any of them know.

'If we win the tender, will we have to take on extra staff?' Claire asked.

'Possibly. There'd be a lot of interviews to be done.'

'Do we need to do all those interviews?' Will asked. 'If we use the right filters, the database will do most of the work. I don't see why we couldn't run the whole project the same way.'

'True, but I want to look our clients in the eye and say the consultants working on their requirements have met with every single candidate we think is qualified,' I said.

'Always admired your ethics, Jac,' he said.

If he knew my dark heart, he'd change his mind.

'We could bring in extra people for data input,' Claire said.

'Yes, I'd expect we'd have to employ casual staff for a few weeks.' I turned to Andrew who was engrossed in the documents. 'Any thoughts?'

'Huh? No, not really.' He scratched his head and glanced away.

The meeting ran for two hours, and still Sandi was a no-show. Just as we wrapped, Paulette poked her head around the door. 'Sandi just came back.'

I jumped up. 'Thanks, all. Please email me your divisional information as soon as possible.'

Andrew hovered. He ran his tongue over his lips. 'Chief, got a minute? It's important.'

'Sorry, Andrew. I have to see Sandi.' I pushed past him and down the corridor.

I marched to Sandi's office. Without knocking, I flung the

door wide and stormed in, catching the tail end of the lilting laughter Sandi sent down the phone line.

Her eyes slid to me then she said into the receiver, 'I'll have to call you back.' She cradled the phone. 'Jac, what can I do for you?' She blinked, looking as innocent as a death row inmate.

'You missed the tender meeting. Where were you?'

She shrugged. 'Something came up.'

I wanted to bury the sharp stiletto into her skull. 'What was more important than the tender meeting?'

Sandi returned to her monitor. 'Globe General Bank.'

'I took care of the GGB assignment when I met with Maddison Parker.'

Sandi blinked, and her cold stare turned the summer day into the dead of winter.

'Maddison had some further concerns. She wanted immediate action, and she wanted me there in person.' A tiny smile played on her lips.

I attempted to keep my voice firm and even. 'Sandi, I'm the CEO of this company. I expect to be informed of any changes impacting current assignments.'

'Of course.' Sandi's voice dripped with artificial sweetness. 'But you didn't want to lose a potential big client, did you?'

'No, but ...'

'Didn't think so.' She sighed as if she was talking to a trainee.

'What was Maddison Parker concerned about?'

Sandi checked her watch and stood. 'I'm sorry, Jac, but I have a candidate waiting.'

I gaped after her as my brain scrambled for something to say, something to assert my haemorrhaging authority. All I came up with was a feeble, 'Hey.' My voice dissipated in the empty office.

For the second time that day, the painted cow had left me without a comeback.

CHAPTER FIVE

I arrived home, my head muddled with problems and relieved to find Rohan wasn't there. Good. I needed time to plan. Plan the tender, plan to save my business, plan to get rid of Rohan. No wonder my head was ready to explode.

'You look very bad, Missus Jac. You go lie on bed,' Draga insisted. 'I stay longer. I make juha for you. Is good for the sore head.'

I napped for an hour and woke to the scents of her culinary skills.

Draga served the juha in an oversized bowl. Over the years, her vegetable and chicken soup had helped heal any part of my body that hurt. I sipped it while I fired the remote control at the television, catching snippets of police procedurals, and some doco on forensics investigation on the Crime Channel. I discovered victims are frequently murdered by someone they know. I'd have to be extra careful. As the wife who'd uncovered her husband's affair, I'd be at the top of the suspect list. There were other obstacles: pesky DNA testing, Luminol, and hazmat-suited crime scene specialists.

I fantasised making it look like an accident or suicide; natural causes would be a stretch. I shelved each idea, as one-episode TV justice dispatched the perpetrators who quickly found themselves behind barred metal doors with impossible-to-escape locks.

Draga came in to remove the empty bowl. She paused, observing my frenzied channel surfing. 'Missus Jac, why you watch this television program? Too much people die. Bah!' She flicked her hand and returned to the kitchen.

'You're the one who said osveta,' I called after her.

'Kill somebody is not good revenge. The good revenge make person feel the guilt all the time. Make they life hard like they make you life. You too nice kill somebody. You not can spray the Mortein when come the spider.'

I ignored her comment, pausing on a rerun of a police procedural episode in which the scenario was spookily familiar. The dead guy was having an affair. Now his body was sprawled in the stairwell of an apartment block. The scene was gruesome, with deep cuts, rivers of blood, and lifeless, open eyes. While I saluted the artistry of special effects, I made a mental note, resolving to make my murder the non-messy variety. I hated untidiness.

The weepy widow appeared on screen looking like she wouldn't survive another minute without her departed love. She was in for more bad luck because the lead character, a detective genius, caught the case. He had the widow rattled, his head cocked to one side, firing questions, closing in. The detective got in the wife's face. He was turning red; she was turning white. The suspect sweated. Any minute the trap would spring. She listed her husband's misdeeds, justifying her crime. Her list was point-for-point like mine. I noted the stupid mistakes predicting her downfall, culminating with a PC trail of visited websites, all on poisons. I mentally crossed poisons off my list. They were too forensic-friendly.

Draga returned with a tall glass of iced tea. She'd added a slice of lemon and ice cubes into which she'd frozen sprigs of mint.

All this loving care had almost fixed my sore head. I sipped the tea with one hand and continued surfing with the other.

Draga, arms folded across her chest, watched the screen jump from one channel to the next. 'You hurt you finger press so much. How you can understand when everything go fast?'

'Shh.' I leaned towards the screen where handcuffs clicked

into place. They always got their man or woman. The same fundamental problem confronted all murderers. The tricky bit wasn't the doing, it was the getting away with. My stomach churned at the sight of so much blood. Even if I could get away with it, I was starting to think my constitution couldn't stand up to committing a murder.

Draga said, 'Oofah!' then waddled to the kitchen, humming.

'How can you be so cheerful all the time?' I asked as the credits rolled.

'Because I choose.'

'You what?'

'Choose. I choose be happy.' As she cleaned, the cacophony of clanging pots and pans increased. Draga yelled over the din. 'I like peace. You should choose same. Then maybe you do something good for youself.'

'Mind your own business.'

'You my ...' Draga began, but the ringing house phone cut her off. 'Ullo.' she barked into the handset. 'Srce.'

I pricked up my ears. Dear heart? I muted the television.

'Mr Ruin not home.' A pause. 'Da, she here.' She covered the mouthpiece and said in a stage whisper, 'Missus Jac, you must speak.'

'Who is it?' I mouthed.

She offered me the phone, concern caught in every brow crease. 'Is boy. Is little Anthony. He be much upset.'

I sighed. What trouble was the Angry Ant in this time?

I spent two hours at the police station, where a hulking great copper gave Ant a stern talking to about shoplifting before letting him go. We'd only been home fifteen minutes and already I was tempted to move him up next to Rohan on my hit list.

Ant opened and closed the fridge door three times without taking out anything. He slammed the door shut, sending a blast of cold air across the bench.

'What are you looking for, Ant?' I asked with unmasked irritation.

'Nuthin.'

'I could make you something to eat,' I offered, which was code for 'Draga can make you something to eat'.

Ant shook his head.

'Would you like to ring your father?'

His hand tensed on the fridge handle. 'Nah.'

'What about your mum? Does she know you've come to Melbourne?' It might be why Triple-T had called.

'No!' he snapped. 'Don't call her.'

Draga said he got his ever-present grumpiness from me. She must think it was via step-DNA. Fact was, I didn't see him often enough to teach him anything.

There'd been a time when I'd hoped Ant's curls and big eyes might make me swell with step-maternal pride; back when I believed he'd be the older brother to the children Rohan and I would have. I'd wanted to be the type of stepmother he'd describe to his mates as 'cool'. They'd shake their heads in disbelief and say, 'You're lucky, dude.'

That's how I'd imagined our relationship would be, but my imagination was overactive. In reality, our contact with Ant was intermittent. Melbourne was where he came when he needed money, or when Triple-T wanted him out of her over-bleached hair. As he grew, I was convinced nature was winning the war over nurture, and he was growing into his father: self-absorbed, sneaky, and expecting someone else to clean up after him.

In fairness, nurture had done little for the kid. His relationship with both his parents was erratic and fragmented. Rohan complained Triple-T had treated Ant as currency in the divorce. When she moved to Sydney, she dragged the then six-year-old along for the ride. She'd hit the social circuit while he spent his time in the company of an assortment of nannies. That was the story Rohan told me in the early days when he was harnessing my sympathy and goodwill. The truth was Rohan hadn't fought for more time with Ant.

When I came onto the scene, we'd tried a little harder. Still, the number of Ant's visits had barely reached double digits. Now seventeen, he hadn't returned to secondary school this year and lived on government benefits. Impressive for a lad with a private school education and a loaded dad. At least he must be good at filling out welfare forms.

Step-maternal pride had a short shelf life in this household, especially tonight. Why should I have to deal with this problem child while Rohan was ... who knows where?

'Are you staying for a while, Ant?' I asked, not sure I wanted to know.

'If I can. I ... um ... just want to stay with Dad for a while.'

I was tempted to ask why, but he stretched and dragged back his long hair revealing an angry dark welt running down his neck. I opened my mouth to say something just as Draga came in carrying a laundry basket.

'Little Ant, you have the dirty washing?'

Ant dropped his hair and developed a sudden interest in his feet. 'Nuh.'

Draga gave him a prison guard stare. 'Why you tell the lie? Bag in you room smell. You be smell, too.'

He reeked of sweat and stale cigarettes. The hems of his jeans dragged on the ground, and a faded t-shirt hung on his bony frame. His arms were thin, and his wrist bones prominent. What had happened to this kid?

Draga shoved the laundry basket at him, 'You bring dirty clothes, or I burn all you porny books.'

Ant blushed. He took the basket and disappeared.

Draga winked. 'I not know for sure, but I think all boys

have the porny books somewhere.' She crossed herself. 'Ja ne razumijem. I not understand these things.'

I wasn't paying attention. Instead, I thought about the bruise on Ant's neck and his fragility. I had no idea what my authority or responsibility was in these circumstances, but I knew the kid was in some sort of trouble.

Curse Rohan for never being around when he should be.

Draga lowered her voice, one eye on the door in case Ant came back to defend his porny book collection. 'You think little Ant go prison?'

'I doubt it.'

'But he try steal.'

'He was cautioned, so I don't think they'll bring charges.'

'They catch him quick.'

'I don't understand how he figured he'd get away with it. There's CCTV everywhere these days.' He should watch more crime shows.

Draga wiped the kitchen benches. 'Maybe he want,' she said.

'You think he wanted to be caught?'

'Not be caught. Be notice. No one notice this boy.'

Ant reappeared with the laundry basket in which there was a meagre collection of dark-toned clothes. A sock with a huge hole in the heel poked through the plastic slats.

'You leave on top of wash machine. I fix after.' Draga flashed him a grandma-style smile.

'It's okay.' Ant took the basket into the laundry, and soon the washing machine buttons beeped in an odd musical sequence until he decided on a cycle. Water gushed into the tub. He came to the door. 'I'm going to crash.' His hand shook as he brushed curls off his face. The look in his eyes was too old for someone so young.

'I already fix bed in you room,' Draga said.

Ant's room had stayed the same since Triple-T had left

Rohan, taking the child with her. The Bob the Builder lamp and bed cover were suited to a six-year-old, not a teenager. There hadn't been any point in redecorating it for the infrequent visits Ant made in the ensuing years, so we'd kept the door shut and ignored the reminders of him behind it.

'Tomorrow things be better.' Draga bearhugged him, crushing his thin frame into hers. 'You good boy, little Ant.'

Ant pulled back, his face red.

'Draga's right, Ant,' I said. 'Tomorrow things will be better.'

Who was I kidding? Whatever had brought him to Melbourne couldn't be good.

Ant shoved his hands deep in his pockets and hunched his shoulders, not looking at me. 'Um ... sorry about the hassle with the cops, Jac. Thanks for letting me stay.' He rubbed his neck.

'I wish you'd tell me what's wrong, Ant.'

'It's all good.' He left, taking his secrets with him.

Draga folded thick arms across her chest. 'See? He need be notice. He father house should be he home too, Missus Jac.'

True. Rohan didn't want him, Triple-T used him as a bargaining chip, and I was ambivalent at best. Bottom line – no one gave a toss.

Better than anyone, I should understand. My father had been an executive who lived on planes, and in other cities, more than at home. He took to the skies even more after Mum developed cancer. He remarried within a year of her death and accepted a job in Perth. At nine years old, I was left at a Melbourne boarding school, discarded and alone. My pillow was tearstained every night. I'd never acknowledged the same in Ant. Poor kid was in the same boat as I'd been, and the boat was sinking.

'Boy need the love and the guidance to grow to good man. Sometime children not have chance for this.' Sadness clouded Draga's eyes. She paused, then straightened. 'I go home now.'

Draga cared about Ant more than any other adult in his

life. A lump formed in my throat and I wore my shame like a well-cut coat.

Before bed, I made several calls to Rohan, reaching his message bank each time. I left increasingly terse messages. When I fell asleep, I was plagued by a dream in which I was in my office interviewing Rohan for a job, but he wouldn't answer any questions.

It was 7am when I woke and checked my phone. He hadn't replied. There was no way he'd been at meetings so late. He must be with her.

I dragged myself downstairs and made coffee, planning a day at the office. There would be no one there on a Saturday, giving me peace to work on the tender. With all the computers at my disposal, I might also be able to find out something else about Jason Keene in Sandi's online diary.

I was on my second cup of coffee when Rohan telephoned.

'Where have you been? I've been worried sick,' I barked, although my reasons for worrying were more about my own welfare.

'I was out with clients. Had a few too many drinks, so I stayed at the RACV Club.'

Yeah, right. I told him about Ant.

'Jacqueline, I don't have time for this,' he said.

It was a bad sign when he called me Jacqueline instead of Jac.

'What do you expect me to do, Rohan? You're the one who needs to talk to Ant.'

I pressed fingers to my forehead and shut my eyes while Rohan prattled on.

'I've got an important meeting about to start,' he said.

'What meeting? It's the weekend.'

'It has to be today,' he said. 'We have an interstate delegation here. They have a packed schedule next week, so we've had to fit them in. And they want me to be there. You wouldn't understand.'

'What's that supposed to mean?'

'You don't understand the importance of my business. It's more complex than that tiny company you run.'

'Excuse me ...' My voice pitched up an octave, but he cut me off.

'How many times do I have to tell you? I. Don't. Have. Time.'

I imagined the vein pulsing at his temple. 'Then find the time. Your son's in trouble with the police.'

'It's not like he's been charged,' he thundered down the line, then snorted. 'You call yourself a CEO and you can't handle a tiny problem like this.'

'He's your son, not mine. You can damn well ring Trish and tell her he's here. This shouldn't be my problem.'

We argued round and round like a Ferris wheel minus the fun until I pressed the end button and threw the handset at the wall. It rebounded with a clunk, followed by a plaintive tingle, and skidded across the floorboards. I followed its path until it stopped.

Against Ant's bare feet.

He stood in the doorway, a white singlet making his skin look even paler. Ragged jeans skimmed his hips. His eyes, full of shock and hurt, were fixed on me. I might as well have shot a bullet between them.

My cheeks burned. 'Ant. I ...'

He picked up the handset and held it out. 'I've heard worse. Doesn't bother me.'

The corners of his mouth quivered.

'I didn't mean it the way it sounded.' It sounded like the bottom of the excuse barrel that it was.

'Don't expect him to call you,' Ant said, fixing me with a look, which I couldn't interpret at first. Anger? Hate?

God help me. The kid pitied me.

He took out a hand-rolled cigarette and a plastic lighter. There was a long tear in the seat of his jeans. He went out the screen door and let it slide shut with a bang. The bright daylight swallowed him up until I could just make out his skinny shape at the edge of the pool, legs dangling in the water, the jeans legs wet. He lit the cigarette, shielding the flame. He took a drag and tilted his head to blow out smoke.

In the street, early traffic picked up with the day's promised warmth and the beach's call. Amped-up cars, people's voices, and quarrelling seagulls floated from the world outside. Yet Ant, who should be part of the fun world of youth, stayed by the poolside and continued to suck on the cigarette. He ground the butt into the tiles and slumped into a question mark, staring into the water. He looked as if he was made of tissue paper, all crumpled and fragile. I'd torn him further with my words.

My chest started to burn. Much as I was furious with Rohan and that cow, Triple-T, I was no better. Other people hurt, too. Not only me. Ant's problems weren't all his own making. He was the ball in an emotional pinball machine, pinging between one apathetic adult and the next. I didn't like the person I'd become. I wanted to kill my husband, and I was killing my stepson with indifference. Although I couldn't help thinking Rohan deserved his fate, Ant didn't.

The side gate clanged open and Draga appeared.

'Ullo, little Ant,' she boomed. She rattled on and I caught 'sleep', 'eat', and 'hot'.

Ant's side of the conversation was mainly grunting.

Draga barrelled through the door, 'Good morning, Missus Jac.' She cracked a wide grin; our household's officer-in-charge of cheerfulness. A French breadstick protruded out of her overloaded tote, along with wrapped parcels I recognised as being from the local deli.

'Why are you here on a Saturday, Draga?'

'I come because boy here. He need food. You need much

company.'

'You're kind Draga, but you don't need to be here all the time, you have your own life. You must have lots to do.'

'What you think I do Saturday?'

'Um …' I was reminded how little I knew about Draga's life.

'I always free the Saturday. Is good for me be here,' Draga said, although her happy expression clouded a little. She went into the kitchen and unloaded the tote's contents onto the bench. 'Why you have the angry face, Missus Jac?'

'I argued with Rohan. He's not coming home until tomorrow. And before you say anything, I don't want to talk about it. I'm more worried about Ant. He overheard something I said about him to Rohan. It sounded like I didn't care about him. He's pretty upset.'

'Tsk, tsk, tsk.' Draga shook her head. 'I make breakfast for you and boy. Food make everything be better. Then we sit together and talk like family.'

'Like a family?' Good luck with that.

Draga sighed. 'We must do for boy. This not just the house, this home.'

'Not much of a distinction,' I said.

'Be big difference, Missus Jac. House be outside, home be inside.'

CHAPTER SIX

Heat crept into the house and Saturday developed into a scorcher.

Not as hot as my temper, brought on by poor sleep, a cheating husband, and a fair dollop of newly acquired guilt about my stepson.

We spent breakfast in stilted 'family conversation', with Draga taking the lead and me feeling sheepish. Afterwards, Ant went outside.

I attempted to help Draga clean up. It shamed me when I realised how little I knew about where things belonged in my own kitchen. All I did was rotate dishes from one location to the next.

'You not helping as much as you think you do, Missus Jac,' Draga said. 'You go. I fix here. Then we go the Kmuck and buy things for boy. He have sock with much hole and the broken underpants.'

I checked the time; almost 10am and I was nowhere near getting to the office. 'I can't go to Kmart. I need to go to work.'

'This more important. He clothes look like rag. Only good for rubbish.'

'I don't think Ant would be happy about us buying his underwear. He's seventeen, remember? If you're worried, I'll give him money and he can buy them himself.'

'Why you think crazy? Boy not know how buy these things. He not know we can see his dupe through the holes.' Draga pushed her behind out and pointed to it in case I didn't know where to locate that part of the human anatomy.

I opened my mouth, but she put her hands together in

prayer and waggled them.

'Missus Jac, mother do these thing for children. You not his mother, but somebody must care for boy. He live here little bit now. You be one who see problem. You be one who must fix. Understand?'

Live here for a little bit?

Her heart was in the right place even if mine wasn't. When seen through her eyes, Ant wasn't the problem child I thought.

I sighed. There was no way I was getting to the office today. 'Okay, you win. But he'll be angry.'

'I not worry for that.'

'You're a tough woman, Draga.' I picked up my handbag and keys.

'Not because I tough. Is because I will say to him was you idea.'

When we arrived at 'Kmuck', Draga discarded several hand baskets before selecting the one she preferred and barrelling towards the menswear section, me following. She sorted through the hangers of men's underwear, examining each as if she expected to find Ant's initials monogrammed on one of them.

I'd never bought underwear for anyone except myself. Never for Rohan. I wasn't sure if replenishing a husband's underwear supply was a wifely responsibility because I wasn't a traditional wife, so how would I know? Running a household was a prickly issue for me. I'd managed the basics, but before Draga exploded onto my domestic scene, dishes had semipermanent residence in the sink, the vacuum cleaner rarely came out from the cupboard, and the washing machine's array of buttons perplexed me. The closest I came to cooking was transferring takeaway food from a container to a plate. I could make tea, coffee, and a basic sandwich.

On nearby hangers, I caught sight of the same style jockettes Draga had used as mundane evidence of Rohan's sins.

I couldn't imagine him coming to 'Kmuck' for them. He could have asked his lover to buy them. Maybe she'd bought them without prompting. I wondered if I could stuff them down Rohan's throat and let him choke on them. I made a note to myself to keep the option on my 'possible methods of murder' list. My face flushed, and I fanned the stifling air. 'It's so hot in here.'

Perspiration coated Draga's brow, but she ignored it. She picked up a pair of boxer shorts and held them across her abdomen. 'What you think?' She twisted her body left and right in a model's pose.

'He won't like the Mickey Mouse print.'

'You be sure? He has like this already.'

'Shows how old they must be.' I selected grey cotton boxers with white banding and handed them to her. 'Can't go wrong with these.'

I peeked over Draga's shoulder to the store entrance facing the food court. The centre was crowded with weekend activity. Shoppers wrangled bags and harassed parents chased children. It was a sea of moving colours and people. Among them, someone I knew.

Sandi Watson.

Even on a weekend, her makeup and hair were perfect. She wore a cropped jacket over skin-tight jeans and bright red heeled boots. She fawned over her main accessory – a man on her arm. I couldn't see his face, yet his stance was familiar. They sat, he with his back to me while Sandi faced straight into the store, all the while keeping a proprietary hand on her companion.

I grabbed Draga and pulled her down behind the rack.

'Ai! What you do?' Draga asked.

I put my finger up to my lips. 'Shh.'

'You want shh in here?' Draga raised her voice in competition with the store's cacophony of announcements and music. 'What is matter with you?'

'It's Sandi Watson. She's in the café across the way. I don't want her to see me.'

'She be the one work in you office? One like the Missus Trish?'

I returned a blank look. 'What do you mean?'

Draga cupped her hands in front of her breasts, holding two invisible basketballs.

'The woman who is like the pie.'

'Tart.'

'Da.' Draga crossed herself.

'Heaven won't help her, Draga.'

'Is not for her. Is for you. You need the prayer. You got plenty trouble.'

I peeked over the rack.

Sandi fiddled with her phone, occasionally flicking back her hair, leaning to whisper into the man's ear. He turned. Jason Keene. They kissed.

'What you see?' Draga asked from somewhere around my knees.

I ducked down. 'She's with the man I fired. Kissing him!' I swore.

'Bah! Bad words, Missus Jac.' Draga admonished. She raised her head over the rack like a fluffy grey periscope to sneak a look.

I yanked her arm and pulled her down; she tumbled forward, her gold cross swinging on its chain.

'What is wrong? You be crazy.' Draga waved the underwear in her hand.

'Why wouldn't I be crazy? My husband is having an affair and those two are up to something. I'm sure of it,' I said.

'And what you can fix when you be hiding? Bah!'

'I don't know. It's not easy being the boss. Sometimes I don't know what to do. And look at me.' Of all days, I picked today to forget image is everything. My track pants were on the verge of falling into the saggy category and my unkempt hair was bundled under a headband. I sagged onto the floor. 'I'll be wearing velour next.'

Draga knelt beside me. 'You much stupid for smart person. You have the business for many year. You have the nice car, the nice house, and the nice family.' Her gaze travelled over me. 'Okay, today you not dress nice.'

'Nice family? My husband cheats on me. I've got a thieving stepson who's in … in … broken underpants.' My voice notched up several octaves. 'I need help.'

'Can I help you?' A staff member peered over the rack, his hair sculpted into some sort of skyscraper. From the corner of my eye, I caught a little girl staring at us from behind her mother's legs. The mother pulled her close and scurried away.

Draga wobbled her way to standing then brushed herself down. She flashed the sales assistant a smile. 'We come here for the underpants, but my friend drop something on floor. Is all right, we can find. You go.' She shooed him away.

The assistant left, casting looks back at us.

Draga scratched her head. 'How he make the hair to stand up? Neznam!'

I rose and peered into the food court where the sea of movement and colour still ebbed, but Sandi and Jason were gone.

'You must not worry, Missus Jac. You find way fix everything.'

Draga was right. I'd worked since my late teens, then found the courage to start All Class Recruitment and to keep it going. Yet, despite my achievements, my confidence had never been high. This was a bad time to lose the little that remained.

I trailed Draga along the aisles while I tried mentally to answer the questions lining up like dominoes. I kept looking towards the doors in case Sandi and Jason reappeared.

In the toiletries section, Draga opened several bottles of shower gel and smelled each one. She sprayed deodorant options into the air, sniffing them and added the selected ones to the basket, which was brimming with jocks, socks, and t-shirts. She threw in a pack of disposable razors and some shaving foam.

'Is Ant shaving already?' I asked.

'Even if he have little bit hair for the shave, is good he know we think he already man.'

True, the kid could do with someone having confidence in him. 'I guess.'

'What more boy need?' Draga asked.

'Nothing. No, wait. He needs a lamp and a bedspread.'

'Now you be think right, Missus Jac.'

We selected a metal bedside lamp, sheets, and a doona cover in a blue and grey-accented geometric print.

At the register, Draga attempted to haggle with the shop assistant for a discount. I gave the girl an understanding nod as I handed over my credit card. She wished us a nice day as we left, but I suspected she knew we weren't having one.

On the drive home, Draga said, 'Missus Jac, I worry for you. You unhappy and when you see woman from you work, you be unhappy more. If you have problem, you must fix. Like we fix boy underpants.'

'Life's more complicated than underwear, Draga.'

'You think I not know? I understand better than you think.'

I let her prattle on. What a way to spend my Saturday morning. I should be at the office, working on saving my business. Better still, in a gym getting my bum into shape, or drinking lattes with friends. The fact was, I was short on friends and when I wasn't at work, I spent most of my free time with a woman who was decades older, and who had an opinion on every aspect of my life. Before I knew it, I was crying. The road ahead became a blur.

'Stop car, Missus Jac,' Draga said, planting her hands against the dashboard.

I pulled over and cut the engine. Draga didn't speak while I blubbered and used up all the tissues she found in the glove box. I honked into them. They lined up on the dashboard like bad decorations in a wedding limousine.

'You feel better?' Draga asked as I snuffled.

'Not really.' I checked my face in the rear-view mirror. Puffy eyes and the tip of my nose like a maraschino cherry.

Draga touched my arm. 'Missus Jac. You like daughter. I not like you be sad all time. I old. I know much things, but I not can speak good English. But you must listen and understand what I say.' She tucked a straggly lock of hair back under my headband. 'You must change your life. No one can do this for you. I help, but help not same as do youself. Only you can fix.'

Draga had all the qualities I didn't possess – kindness, unselfishness, a lack of self-pity. I started to cry again. This time, her arm went around me, and I leaned into her, slobbering tears onto her chest. I smelled lavender soap and mild perspiration. Her gold cross pressed into my cheek.

Draga murmured in Croatian as she rubbed my back. After some time, she said, 'You make me to worry.'

'I'm sorry. None of this is your problem, Draga.'

'Is my problem when you my business.'

We stayed until I calmed. My eyes felt heavy and I wanted to sleep; a lengthy, magical sleep during which all my problems would disappear and when I woke, I'd start again. But there would be no magic. As Draga said, I was the only one who could fix my life. If I wanted things to be different, I needed to do things differently.

'Am I really like a daughter?' My question came in a small voice.

My head rose and fell with Draga's chest as she sighed. 'Da.

Like bad one.'

We arrived home to find Ant lying on the outdoor lounge, riveted to his phone. He'd seemed so fragile this morning, but I relaxed a little when he waved at us.

'I take things to boy room.' Draga chugged up the stairs with the overladen shopping bags.

The house phone rang, I answered with a distracted, 'Hello.'

'Jacqueline, it's Trish.'

Damn. Triple-T had nailed me. I thumped my forehead and sighed, loud enough for her to hear, but I didn't care. 'How are you, Trish?'

'Fine as ever. You?' Trish's singsong voice grated down the line. She couldn't be as happy as she made out. All the boozing and partying would catch up with her soon. I was surprised she didn't have a permanent hangover.

'Things are good.' I said, knowing how pleased she'd be if she knew the unhappy state of my marriage.

'I can't reach Rohan on his mobile. Is he home?'

'Rohan's away at meetings.'

'Ever the workhorse.' She laughed. 'I was wondering if Anthony is there.'

She could have asked me in the first place, but that was typical of Triple-T.

'He is.' I didn't mention the theft, the police, and the fact the kid looked like he'd been starving for months. 'Didn't he tell you he was coming?'

'He's an adult. He doesn't need to tell his mother all his movements.' There was a slight edge to her tone. 'I've left messages on his mobile, but he's not returning my calls. Like father, like son, I guess.'

'I'll get him to come to the phone.'

'Don't bother. Just tell him to call his friend.'

'Which friend?'

'No idea of his name. Obviously, someone Anthony's upset.

He's leaving angry messages for him on my answering machine. I've arrived home from a few weeks in Noosa. The stress is undoing all my zen.'

I imagined her frowning, if her Botox-filled face allowed.

'What kind of angry messages?'

'Oh, you know.'

'No, Trish, I don't know.' The mark on Ant's neck flashed to mind.

'Kids mucking around, I expect. I suppose it's one of those things between boys.'

I wanted to remind her she'd considered him an adult a few seconds ago.

'He's saying silly things; leaving stupid threats.'

The hairs on my arm pricked up. 'What sort of threats?'

'Oh, I can't remember the exact wording. I don't think he means them. Anyway, I wiped the machine. I don't have time for all this.'

Cold cow. And she got to be a mother. 'What would you like me to do, Trish?'

'Tell him to contact his mate and sort it out.'

Then she was gone, leaving the dial tone reverberating in my ear. I hung up the phone, my gut tight. Something was off in Ant's life, and it was more than having a self-absorbed mother. I wasn't great at parenthood, but I should try to find out what that 'something' was.

I went outside and found Ant snoring on the banana lounge; his hand rested on his chest clutching his phone. Curls fell around his neck and, although I was tempted to lift them to check his injury, I didn't want to risk waking him.

Draga appeared at the door. 'You go office, Missus Jac?' Her voiced boomed.

I put a finger to my lips and pointed to Ant. I joined her inside. 'It's too late to go to the office. I'll work on the tender redraft here.'

Draga set about the kitchen with her favourite household product – bleach. The house smelled like a hospital after one of Draga's cleaning jags. She was excellent at controlling contaminants. I should take a lesson and apply it to Sandi, Jason, Triple-T, and the big one, Rohan.

With a draft of the tender spread across the study desk, I shut the door against Draga's cheerful humming and the scent of germ-annihilating chemicals. I checked the document, section by section, making editing notes, and picking up typos I'd missed onscreen.

Although I was confident in All Class's technical capabilities, I scribbled comments in the margins, noting where I could make my words more precise. The financial information presented showed we were solvent. What it didn't show on paper was the amount of capital I'd injected. Dad wouldn't have been happy about me using the money he'd left me in this way. I didn't mind because it made the company look better on paper and if I could save the staff's jobs, it was worth it. Next, I checked the staff CVs to be included. Sandi's name was first on the list. I flashed back to her and Jason. I remembered his 'you'll regret it' speech when I'd fired him. He could be using Sandi to get to me. But how? Even if she was oblivious to his manipulation, I couldn't trust her. Women in love can make crazy decisions. Who knew better than I did?

It would be nice to get rid of her, but I couldn't without a reason or due process. For summary dismissal, I'd have needed a list of reasons outlined in her employment contract at the time she'd signed. But my staff's employment contracts were straightforward and didn't include such details. Lesson learned. I added rewrite future employments contract templates to my 'to do' list.

Draga and Ant weren't in the house when I emerged from the study around 6pm.

I had a shower, letting the warm water ease my neck

muscles and wash away the heat of the day. I dressed in light workout gear and headed downstairs. The only workout I planned for this evening consisted of pouring a white wine and curling onto the sofa. I didn't want to think about Rohan, but I couldn't help it. Every idea I had to get rid of him came with a 'Yes, but'. At least I didn't have to face him until tomorrow night. Figuring out what was happening in Ant's life was a more pressing problem. I'd have to talk with him, even if it was awkward. I'd go in as 'peer-not-parent' or should it be 'parent-not-peer'?

On the tail end of my second wine, Draga and Ant returned. Amid their chatter, shopping bags rustled, and the fridge door opened and closed.

Ant came in chomping on a thick hunk of bread. In his other hand, a plate of crackers and cheese. 'Draga said to give you this, and to say dinner won't be long.'

He had colour in his cheeks. Draga's food must be helping.

'Ant, I'm so sorry for what I said this morning.'

'Forget it.' He focused on the ground and put the last piece of bread in his mouth.

'No need to let me off lightly. It was hurtful, and I was wrong.'

He was about to leave when I remembered Triple-T. 'Your mum rang.'

Ant folded his arms. 'What did she want?'

'Something about phone messages she's been getting at home. Threats, she said. She thinks it's your friends mucking around. Does that make sense to you?'

The veins in Ant's neck stood out.

'Ant? What's going on?'

'Nuthin'. My mates are losers.'

I opened my mouth, but he scurried out past Draga who came in clutching her broom.

'Missus Jac, you be finish work?'

'For today. Draga, I think Ant's in trouble.'

She banged the broom head onto the floor. 'What trouble?'

'I'm not sure.' I told her about Triple-T's call, but held back about the mark on Ant's neck. She'd be onto it with all the subtlety of a tank. Ant would clam up and I'd never learn anything. 'Triple-T doesn't know anything about his friends, or care about his life.'

'Is sad for boy. With mother like she be, is not surprise he have trouble. She not pay attention when she should. She not know how lucky she be. Family important.' Draga stared into the distance. 'You must look after. When you lose, can be forever.'

After she left, a cloud of sadness lingered in the room.

I went upstairs. The door to Ant's room was ajar. The t-shirts, socks, and the underwear that were the subject of Draga and my debate at 'Kmuck' were on the bed. Ant picked up the boxer shorts, one at a time. He folded each one with care and built a neat pile. When he picked up the ones with the Mickey Mouse print, I waited for his look of horror, but he held them up and smiled. The first time he'd done so since he'd arrived.

He saw me and blushed. 'Thanks for these, Jac. Draga said you bought them for me.'

'I can't take all the credit. I said you'd be upset, but she insisted you wouldn't.'

'They're cool in an old school way,' he said, looking about ten years old. 'Reminds me of stuff I had as a kid. I like the lamp and bedspread. It was nice of you guys.'

'Our pleasure.' I paused. 'Ant, is everything else okay? You've been a bit on edge since you arrived. I know sometimes it's hard to talk about things, but I'm worried.'

The light in his eyes vanished. 'All good.' He opened a drawer and began to put his new clothes inside.

I didn't press him further. I'd already put a dent in his rare good mood.

Draga called from downstairs. 'Food get cold. Hurry. Not make me to wait.'

Ant scampered ahead of me. As he did, I caught a whiff of the spray deodorant Draga had chosen.

I followed him downstairs, musing on the fact Micky Mouse could still make kids – and adults – smile.

Well played, Draga.

CHAPTER SEVEN

The back door slid open with a scrape and Rohan's curt greeting followed. 'Morning, Draga.'

Damn. He wasn't due home until tonight. My shoulders tensed. I stayed in the lounge room where I was editing a mountain of documents.

'Ullo, Mr Ruin,' Draga said.

'Why are you here on a Sunday?' he asked.

'I come extra days because boy here.'

Rohan grunted. His briefcase and overnight bag thudded to the floor in sequence. His habit was to drop anything he carried near the kitchen bench, leaving Draga to carry the 'work suitcase' to the study, and the bag to the bedroom.

The fridge door opened and the glub-glub of wine tumbled into a glass. Not even noon and he was drinking.

I steeled myself to stay focused on my document review. I needed to find better ways to expand on All Class's capabilities, a process that necessitated lots of thinking, as well as self-admonition about how bad I was at this today.

Rohan entered and set the wine bottle and a glass on the coffee table with a loud clunk. The deep cushion squelched loudly as he sank into the chair opposite me.

'You're home early. How were your meetings?' I glanced at him, conscious of the icy drip in my voice. His eyelids were hooded and the silver hair at his temples had gathered like cotton balls.

'Same old. I gather you worked all weekend.' He raised his glass in a toast to the documents. 'It's becoming a habit.'

'You know what they say – no rest for the wicked.'

'Have you been wicked?' he asked. His voice stirred memories of intimate times. Long conversations in bed; whispered promises. All shattered.

Mongrel. I added other things I could do to him to my list – delete the contacts from his phone, slash his suits, key his Beemer. Better still, all three.

I met his gaze. 'No, I haven't. What about you?'

Rohan put his head down. An expanding hairless circle on the crown took me by surprise; another small change that had crept in without me noticing. Once, we hadn't been able to stop looking at one another. I didn't want to feel nostalgic. I wanted to stay angry. I reminded myself this was as monk-like as he would ever be.

He placed his wine glass on the side table and locked his fingers together. The kind of position that warned I was about to hear something I didn't want to.

Rohan sighed and rested his chin on his fist. 'We have to talk, Jacqueline.'

My full name again.

'If this is about Ant ...'

'It's not.'

Any second, he would say he wanted out of the marriage, his lover was 'the one' and he was leaving for a new life. Rohan would be out of my life. I should be dancing in the street. Still, I pressed my lips together to stop myself from screaming.

'Geoff Campbell wants to buy my share of the business.'

I sat upright. 'Buy you out? Why?' I waited for him to answer while he stared upwards.

'We haven't agreed on business strategy for a long time. Geoff wants to expand and I'm not sure I have the energy to deal with anything so ambitious.' Rohan loosened his tie, tugging hard. 'I want to sell, but ...'

'You want to sell? Yesterday you were telling me how important you are to the business.'

He slid the tie out from under his collar. 'I am, but I'm sick of thinking about other people's futures; their investments, their finances, their retirement funds. I'm just tired.'

He wouldn't be so tired if he wasn't running around with another woman. Crow's feet bunched around his eyes. Eyes that once looked at me with love were now as cold as slate.

'So, what are you unsure about?' I asked.

'It's a slog selling an investment company. We'd have to do due diligence, examine all the books. There'd be audits. There's so much paperwork. It's an expensive and complicated process.' Rohan's eyes darted around the room, landing on pieces of furniture; probably checking inventory.

What were the implications of the business sale in my 'bump him off' scenario?

'I'm confused. You're sick of working, but you don't want to sell. Which is it? You can't have the best of both worlds, Rohan.' But he had a lover and a life with me. Two worlds in which he seemed to have the best. 'For someone obsessed with present and future security, you sound uncertain.'

'I know. I know.' He massaged his temples.

'What else is bothering you?' I asked.

Rohan picked up the wine bottle, filled my water glass and topped up his. 'Well, there is something.'

I stiffened. Someone else, he meant. Suddenly, I needed wine. I downed the glass in one long swallow. I stood and paced the floor like a patrolling security guard.

'Jacqueline, please sit down.'

'I'd rather stand.'

Rohan sat forward and did the handclasp thing again. He sighed, opened his mouth, and then jolted as Ant's voice filtered into the room.

'Hey, Dad.' Ant was at the door, rocking back and forth on his heels.

'Anthony.' Rohan stood. 'I forgot you were here.'

Ant scratched his neck and turned away.

How does a child feel when a parent 'forgets' he's around? I knew very well.

'I've told Ant he can stay as long as he wants, Rohan.' I hadn't, and the conviction in my voice as I lied surprised me. 'He's long overdue to have some time with us. Ant agreed, didn't you?'

Ant shuffled, slight confusion furrowing his brow. 'Um ... yeah.'

'Sounds like you two have settled the matter already,' Rohan said in his formal business tone. 'Well, I'm going to unpack, then wash the car. We'll finish our discussion later, Jacqueline.' He walked out, glass in hand, and patted Ant on the shoulder without making eye contact. 'Good to see you, Ant.'

When Rohan was out of earshot, Ant said, 'Thanks, Jac.'

What had I done?

All I knew was, it was the right thing.

Draga prepared a lunch large enough to cater a wedding reception.

She never understood moderation when it came to food. Each year, the grocery bill grew steeper and our waists a little wider. Still, I wouldn't give up Draga for anything. She brought chaotic sanity to the household, and copious good recipes. And she was caring in a 'drive-me-crazy' way. The house wasn't the same when she wasn't there.

Rohan, Ant and I ate lunch outside, shaded by a large market umbrella. Draga, who refused to sit with us, scurried in and out with plates of cold meats, antipasto, crusty bread, and green salads.

The afternoon sun bounced off the deck and a small breeze brushed my face. The pool sparkled as though diamonds were scattered across the water. The scene could be from a G-rated happy family movie. In our case, one with a bad script in which no one came out happy.

In any other circumstances, I'd be enjoying life. I picked at a little salad and fended off Draga's dirty looks at my refusal to participate in the family feast.

Rohan tucked into the huge pile of food on his plate. Attendance at the Church of the Holy Chamois must have given him an appetite.

'How's school, Ant?' Rohan sounded stilted like he was reading badly prepared lines for an audition.

Ant sighed. 'I don't go to school, Dad.'

How did the idiot not remember Ant left school at the end of last year?

'Really?' Rohan kept his eyes on the mobile phone, picking it up every time the message tone sounded. 'Are you keeping busy?'

'Kinda.' Ant bit into a large chunk of bread laden with ham.

Rohan didn't ask what 'kinda' meant. Instead, he checked his phone.

'Rohan, can you stop playing with the phone at the table?' I clamped fists either side of my head.

'I'm expecting an important message.' On cue, the phone chirped, and he grabbed it. He frowned as he read the text, then went back to eating.

'Everything okay?' I asked.

'Yeah ... um ... organised a meeting after the conference I'm going to.'

I took a good stab at who he'd be conferring with – the fire-hair lady. I should shove the phone down his throat.

Draga appeared with a fruit platter.

Ant dived into the pineapple pieces. Whatever problems he had, his appetite was making a comeback.

'Sit with us, Draga. Have something to eat,' I said.

'No, thank you, Missus Jac. I not like eat much. I watch figure.' She patted her spare tyre then turned to Rohan. 'Mr Ruin, I put work suitcase in study, but I not see you little computer.'

Rohan's flicked skyward as if the answer was on the inside of his eyelids. 'My laptop? Oh ... I left it at the office.'

'Didn't you come straight from the conference?' I waited to see if he'd slip up and reveal something incriminating to add to my accumulating list of grievances.

Rohan shifted. 'Er ... I called into the office on the way home. I had papers to drop off, and there were a couple of things I needed to check.' He topped up his wine glass.

If I owned a gun, I'd pop him one between those lying eyes. Not that I had any idea of where to get a gun, or how to use one.

I changed the subject. 'Ant, do you have your learner's permit?'

Ant sat up. 'Yeah. Why?'

'It might be a good chance to have some driving lessons while you're staying here.'

'Not in the BMW,' Rohan said, looking as though his throat was about to be slit.

Ant's expression hardened, and his jaw muscle worked. 'I didn't expect to.'

'We should book some lessons with a driving school first,' Rohan backpedalled.

'No need. I'm happy to give Ant lessons in my car. We could go this afternoon.'

The look I sent Rohan was more smug than necessary.

Ant sat up. 'Yeah? Haven't you got work to do?'

'It'll keep.' It couldn't, but I didn't want to stay around Rohan, and the more time I spent with Ant, the better the chance of finding out what was happening in his life. There was still the mysterious mark on his neck, and the nervous tension hovering around him like a toxic cloud.

Rohan shuffled in his seat. 'Jacqueline, I wanted to finish our discussion after lunch. I'm leaving early tomorrow.'

'If it's so important, we shouldn't discuss things in a rush. My work's full-on and I don't have the energy for anything else.' Except getting rid of him. 'Let me get the work done then we'll have plenty of time to talk.'

I got up and walked away before Rohan could argue. Let him live with uncertainty for a change.

An hour later, I drove down the freeway with the sunroof open. Ant leaned back against the headrest, eyes closed, and his arms folded. If I didn't know better, I'd think he was smiling. He wore a pair of shorts, highlighting spindly legs that stretched down to his sneakers. A few more weeks with Draga would fatten him up.

'Have you had any driving lessons yet, Ant?'

'Mum tried a couple of times, but she cracked it when I made mistakes.'

No surprise coming from Triple-T.

'I'll take you onto a back road near some of the freight terminals in Port Melbourne. They're wide and there's not much traffic around to bother us on a weekend.' It was also a short detour to the office.

I dropped a gear and overtook a slow-moving Toyota then slipped back into the lane, narrowly avoiding the back bumper of a car ahead.

Good thing Ant didn't notice.

'Bit risky, wasn't it?' he asked.

'How did you see that? Anyway, I knew what I was doing. Do you mind if we call into the office?'

Ant shrugged. I took it as an okay.

I checked my speed, took the freeway exit at Todd Road, and wound through to the prime real estate of Beacon Cove, then up Bay Street. When we arrived at the office, I slid into my parking spot. 'I'll only be a minute.'

Ant had already opened the door and climbed out. 'Can I come?' He bit his lip, like a small child waiting for permission.

How had I never stopped to see how vulnerable he was?
'Sure thing.'

Without the air conditioning running, the office was overheated. The air was oppressive, and the quietness foreign.

Ant wandered around the offices while I fired up my PC. I printed off copies of what I needed, and for surety, emailed the documents to home. I also transferred them to a USB.

Ant lingered at my office door. 'Is this all yours, Jac?'

'Sort of. We rent the office space and lease the equipment. The only thing that's really mine is the goodwill.'

'What's that?'

'It means the reputation of the business. It's worth something because the clients use us and trust us.'

'You can't see that by looking around,' he said.

'No, you can't.'

'What was your first job?' he asked.

'My first job was in an office, running errands and photocopying. Mundane stuff. I wasn't much older than you.'

'Were you scared?'

'Of what?'

'Of screwing up.'

'I was. I was sure any minute they'd realise I didn't have a clue. I cringe when I remember all the mistakes I made, but I kept turning up and paying attention. Eventually, I did something right because I was promoted a few times and ended up in Human Resources. It's where I learned about hiring and firing.'

'Is that when you started your business?'

'Not then. Three years later, I moved to a bigger firm where my manager suggested I enrol in some part-time studies, which I did. The job gave me a lot of interviewing practice. Then, I decided to start my own recruitment service. I saved a little money, I created a business plan and a marketing strategy. And here I am.'

I gazed around with pride, then I remembered that something in my business was off. I placed the documents into the folder and slipped the USB into my bag.

Ant drew lines on the carpet with his foot. 'I'll never get a job.'

'What makes you say that?'

He shoved his hands into his pocket. 'I wouldn't know how to do anything. Sometimes I wish Dad talked to me more about stuff like business and handling money. I guess I'm just too stupid.'

No wonder the world of work appeared incomprehensible. Who'd ever bothered to teach him anything or encourage him? As Draga said no one notice this boy.

'You're not stupid, Ant. Work's like anything. It takes practice to learn what you need to know. You'll be fine.' I wasn't sure it was true, but the kid had to have some hope.

Ant gave me a tiny smile. It looked like it'd taken all his energy.

I locked the doors and we headed to the car.

Summer had drawn people into the streets. Café tables spilled onto the footpaths, the scent of coffee, spiced food and the murmur of the crowds filled the air.

'This is way better than being in Sydney,' Ant said.

'Don't you miss your friends?'

'Not really.'

'I suppose you can stay in touch with them over social media.'

'I deactivated my accounts.'

'Why?'

Ant shrugged. 'Just did.'

It would be a slow process getting him to disclose anything. What reason did he have to trust me? All I could offer him were small demonstrations of my faith in him, like letting him drive my car.

'Next stop, driving lesson.' I glanced across at Ant, but he was staring out of the passenger window.

I turned into Cook Road and passed the terminals, looking for a spot where it would be safe for Ant to have his lesson without too much traffic around. I pulled over on a deserted section where the road widened and stretched a long way ahead, flanked by warehouses.

'This is perfect. Except the views aren't fantastic,' I said. 'I'll put the L-plates on.'

Ant stared ahead, his expression blank.

I guessed his mind was focussed on whatever he was running from.

Something he couldn't escape, even on an endless road.

CHAPTER EIGHT

Monday morning and the office hummed with activity.

Paulette was a broken record on the reception phone. 'Welcome to All Class Recruitment. This is Paulette, how can I help you?' There was a smile in her voice. 'I'm sorry; she's not available. May I put you through to her voicemail?'

'What's going on?' I was feeling chipper this morning, given Ant hadn't pranged my car, and I'd avoided Rohan who'd left as early as he'd promised.

Paulette moved the headset microphone away from her mouth. 'There's a bunch of people ringing for Sandi this morning. She'll probably be on the phone all day once she gets in.' She picked up another call and her cheerful voice returned. 'Welcome to All Class Recruitment. This is Paulette, how may I help you?'

Had I misjudged Sandi? Still, my instincts said something wasn't right. But even if you're paranoid it doesn't mean they're not out to get you. I had to remain logical. I'd see what I could find in Sandi's records, but if I found something amiss, I wasn't looking forward to the sick feeling that would come with proof.

The tender documents were perched on the corner of my desk, begging for attention. I kept a guilty eye on them and called Andrew, who picked up within two rings.

'Andrew, can you run the performance figures of each consultant for the last six months?'

'Ten minutes, Chief.'

In seven, he knocked and cracked open the office door.

I waved him in. Andrew's 'thing' was ties with movie characters printed on them. An image of the Three Stooges watched from a shiny blue background. As a model for corporate attire, Andrew made a great database whiz.

He handed over a printout. 'Checking up on the workers?'

'None of your business,' I said, feigning a casual tone.

He laughed.

I scanned down the numbers. Claire Sandhurst's Temporary Division was a little below target, but temporary work often went up and down. Will Grenfell's Contracting Division and his two staff were above target. Sandi's low Permanent Placement Division figures made me catch my breath. I squinted at the numbers, trying to read between the lines.

'Some results aren't good, are they?' Andrew asked.

No point letting on how nervous the figures made me. 'Hmm. Things are tough for most businesses these days. It's been one economic downturn after another.'

'At least we're making the payroll,' Andrew said. He bit his lip. He ran the payroll and knew I took a minimum wage for myself. Some weeks I took nothing.

'I have a few opportunities up my sleeve. We have a chance at the tender. Three years of supplying staff to a conglomerate of businesses are nothing to sneeze at.'

'The deadline's next week,' he said.

As if I needed reminding. 'I'm on it. Oh, what was so important on Friday?'

'Friday?' Andrew pondered for a few seconds. 'Oh, yeah. I ran some database reports, but they didn't work. I think it was a glitch. It's okay today.'

'Good.' I didn't need another thing dumped in the 'too hard' basket, especially not anything to do with the database where we kept all clients' and candidates' details for current or future job searches. Every assignment that came in, we matched candidates against the criteria. Often people who applied for roles years ago came onto the job market again. The database saved us additional advertising and provided a pattern of candidate qualifications and experiences. It was the blood supply of the business and was backed up offsite every day.

'Are you sure., Andrew?'

'Absolutely, Chief.'

'I'm glad it's sorted. Can I have a printout of Sandi's outcomes by client for the past twelve months, please?' It would indicate what was happening with her client group before and since Jason Keene had left All Class.

When Andrew returned, he dropped the document onto my desk without comment and bolted from the room before I picked it up.

I checked all the assignments on which Sandi had worked. Two were coded 'AFI', meaning Assignment Filled Internally. Six had the code 'CWA', meaning Client Withdrew Assignment. It was an unusually high number because, while it did happen on rare occasions, clients didn't engage a recruitment firm unless they were sure they needed to recruit for a role. Sandi hadn't noted on the memo line the reasons why the clients had withdrawn.

Like most recruitment companies, All Class operated on contingency. Unless we made a placement, we didn't get our fee. Not ideal, but competition was tough, and we followed what most other recruitment companies did. On the occasions when we lost an assignment because the client withdrew it, or because the client appointed someone to the role from within the existing staff, we couldn't recoup the money spent on our background work, including advertising, time spent on candidates' enquiries, interviewing, and all reports. That was the risk we carried.

I calculated the revenue lost on Sandi's withdrawn assignments over the period in question and flinched at the amount: just over fifty thousand dollars. What had happened to those placements? If I asked Sandi directly, it would raise a red flag. I had enough of those flying already. I cursed myself for only asking for summary documents in the last twelve months. I should have been on top of this.

I buzzed Andrew. 'Can you come back?' I hadn't cradled the handset before he scurried into my office and closed the door, playing with his tie.

'Can you get past email passwords?'

He frowned. 'If I have to. Why?'

'I need to get into Sandi's email account.'

Andrew shifted from one foot to another. 'What about the privacy policy?'

'What about your details on a Centrelink dole application?' I grinned. I couldn't imagine ever firing Andrew.

He made a face and held up his hands. 'You're the chief.' He came around to my side and took over my PC. His fingers flew over the keys. He waited, biting his thumbnail, while the system churned, preparing to surrender Sandi's secrets. 'There you go.' He rotated the keyboard and monitor around to face me.

'Thanks, Andrew. You were never here.'

'Where?' He pulled the door behind him as if there was a bomb in the room.

Sandi's Inbox was the usual fare. There were a stack from clients – all standard, all bland. I sorted the Inbox by sender and searched for anything unusual. I stared at the screen, willing Sandi's Inbox to reveal something to help me figure out what was going on.

I searched for 'Keene Recruiting' and found nothing. My next search was for 'Jason'. The screen data jumbled and came up empty. I sorted by topic and finger-drummed an accompaniment while the processing icon whirred. Whatever Sandi was up to, I could almost smell it. My nose was an inch from the screen as the messages rearranged into reverse alpha order.

The intercom beeped. 'Jacqueline, your husband's on hold. Line four.'

Rohan always rang via the switchboard. I suspected it made him feel important.

My finger dragged down the list. Nothing stood out.

Paulette repeated the message.

'Tell him I'll call him later,' I said. I could only deal with one cheat at a time. I set the phone to 'Do Not Disturb'. For good measure, I muted my mobile.

I was getting nowhere with my investigation. About to give up, I checked the last few emails and noticed a subject header, 'Bank Account Details'. The sender, 'jk_hunk'. I highlighted the message and hit enter.

Thx for sending thru a/c details. Funds by the end of the quarter. Love the arrangements. JK.

JK could only be Jason Keene. The date was six months ago, about the time Sandi's numbers started to drop. What account details was he referring to, and what arrangements?

I flipped to the Sent folder and searched for the word 'account'. Hundreds of emails still bypassed the filter. Of course – client accounts. Next, I used 'bank' as a search term for all mailboxes. Three emails popped up. One promised millions of dollars paid into a bank account if the recipient sent twenty thousand dollars to some lawyer in Nigeria with Esq after his name. Andrew really should upgrade the spam filter. The next email was from a friend referring to someone she'd bumped into at the bank. Blah, blah, blah, who cares? Third time lucky they say. The last email told me what I wanted to know.

JK, got a shortlist for the Marketing Exec. S

I read it again and the words blurred. But was this evidence? Sandi could simply be telling Jason she'd done that part of her job. His email might be promising to pay back the money he owed her. Neither scenario was likely. There must be something more damning.

I pulled up the Marketing Executive position at Best Breaks Travel on the database. It was one of the assignments

Sandi had coded as Client Withdrew Assignment but with no explanation. I could call the client to ask except that would look like I didn't know my own business.

I ran a report on the applicants for the role. The results indicated interviews were conducted and confirmed a shortlist of two names. Their records showed they were verbally advised of the client's decision not to go ahead, although Sandi hadn't sent emails confirming it. Not All Class's way of doing things. We documented every client and candidate contact in writing. Follow up emails were standard and important information for our database. Sandi was ignoring our usual procedures. The fact she'd entered information about the interviews, put her appointment with Jason into her official diary and emailed him on the company account showed how blasé she'd become. The hamster was taking advantage, but she was dumb to think she could keep this secret forever.

My finger shook as I hit the speaker button on my private line and dialled the first name on the shortlist, Martine Hobbs. The call went to voicemail. I decided not to leave a message. The idea was to look for evidence, not to leave it behind. The second shortlistee, Dylan Lucas, answered. I introduced myself and asked if he was free to speak.

'Sure. Give me a sec to get into the cab.' In the background, aeroplane engines whined and there were muffled announcements.

'I can call you back if you'd prefer,' I said.

'Now's good. Two tics.' He said something to the cab driver. The two-way radio crackled, then came the indicator's tac-tac. 'Sorry about that. I'm all yours. I've just landed from Perth. Long day.'

I made polite comments about the lack of glamour in frequent business travel before I reached the purpose of my call. 'I'm following up with some of our candidates, to ask about their experience with All Class Recruitment.'

His laugh was all warm, honey tones. 'I've never had any other recruiter ring me to follow up. I'm impressed.'

'Well, I'm sorry your experience with us ended with upsetting news.'

'I don't understand. What news was that?'

'It must have been disappointing to make the shortlist for the Best Breaks Travel job, only to find the client wasn't going forward with the role.'

I could almost hear him thinking during the long pause. The cabbie's radio crackled.

'There must be some confusion,' Dylan said.

My pulse quickened. 'How so?'

There was a pause. 'I did get the role at Best Breaks Travel, but not through your company.'

The first puzzle piece locked into place. Breath held, I waited for him to continue.

'Two days after your consultant, Ms Watson, said the client had pulled the role, another recruiter called me about the same job ...' He hesitated.

I braced for something I wasn't going to like.

'I thought it was odd, but I was assured it was above board. I should've called Ms Watson to check, but this is my dream job. I wanted a second chance at it.'

'Understandable,' I said and cupped a hand over the mouthpiece. 'Dylan, can you tell me which agency?' I held my breath but already I knew the answer – Keene Recruiting. Hearing the name confirmed in Dylan's honey tones didn't make it easier.

'I hope there isn't a problem,' he said. 'But I should let you know that in my dealings with your Ms Watson, she was very professional.'

'I appreciate the feedback. And congratulations on the job.' I hung up, feeling queasy.

Dylan Lucas hadn't done anything wrong. He was an

innocent piece in the jigsaw I was beginning to put together. It painted an ugly picture of how the Watson-Keene scheme worked.

Sandi was channelling candidates from All Class to Jason Keene. First, on our behalf, she'd advertise the position, conduct interviews, and determine the best candidates. I guessed she'd then tell the client some apologetic story about not being able to compile a shortlist – poor candidate pool or not enough interest from the market. The job would be flagged in our system as withdrawn by the client. In turn, the candidates would be told the company decided not to go ahead with the role. They were unlikely to question it because companies changed their minds, or restructured, and everyone accepted it. Afterwards, she'd give Jason all the details of the role and the shortlist names. Once Jason had them, and the candidates were nursing their disappointment, he'd take the opportunity to make contact on the pretext of a headhunting mission. Candidates are flattered by being headhunted, and few ask how their name came up. Besides, the standard answer was that recruitment firms do not reveal their sources of recommendation. Ego is an easy creature to feed in the headhunting world.

With the candidates on board, I could imagine Jason Keene's perfectly timed, on spec call to the client, skirting around the position All Class was recruiting until the conversation hit its mark. Surprise, surprise. He had just the list for the role they were looking to fill. A day or so to get the candidates' CVs, a brief interview for show and bingo. He'd hand over the shortlist, with a candidate or two from his own database thrown in to make it look legitimate. Given he'd done little work to get the shortlist together, he could afford to pitch his fee lower to win the client over. If one of the candidates was hired, Keene Recruiting would collect the fee even though my company had done all the work. Easy money. And, thanks to

Sandi highlighting All Class's failure to perform in the client's view, it was also a further chip off our reputation. Nothing would make the slimy worm happier. Keene was untrustworthy, unethical, and boy, could he hold a grudge.

I was so angry I wanted to throw something. Preferably at their heads. Blood pounded through my veins.

Sandi belonged on my hit list with Rohan.

I'd given her the job when she was desperate for work, trained her and paid her well. She'd worked in the industry long enough to know what she was doing was unethical, if not illegal. The only explanation for her part was the 'thing' she had going with Keene. Sandi was happy to help him exact revenge, and any money she made was a bonus. I suspected she was doing it for love, although I couldn't imagine either of them being capable of that emotion.

For now, all I had was a great theory, but to act I needed concrete proof they were involved in an orchestrated fraud. I didn't have enough yet, but I had a start – their emails, although vague. Further, I had an idea of the income my business had lost for unfulfilled assignments, but I couldn't prove they were connected to deliberate sabotage on Sandi's part yet. And if they were doing what I suspected, it was happening infrequently enough to fly under the radar. Certainly under my radar.

I inserted a USB into the drive and copied the two emails onto it.

I had a great idea of how to test my hypothesis. I buzzed Andrew.

After I'd told him my idea, he squirmed in his seat. 'I don't think you're allowed to bug the office phones, Chief,' he said, smoothing down the Three Stooges print on his tie.

'Why not? It's my company,' I said. 'I'm disappointed, Andrew. You're an intrigue-loving guy. I figured you'd jump at the suggestion.'

While he considered, I scanned a list of emails beeping from my Inbox for attention.

'You'd need a court order or something ...' Andrew's gaze dropped to Mo, Larry, and Curly. They didn't know the answer either. Nyuk, nyuk, nyuk. 'Sorry to disappoint you, Jac. I could get reports on incoming and outgoing calls on the landlines and the company-issued mobile phones. Would that be any help?'

'It might. Also, I want information on who accessed the database, how often, when, and what sections.'

'... when and what sections,' Andrew repeated as he took notes. 'For everyone? It's a lot of data to wade through.'

I gave him a long look. 'Okay. Run them for one person.'

He raised an eyebrow.

'Swear you'll keep this absolutely to yourself.'

He placed a hand over his heart and lowered his voice. 'I swear.'

'Sandi Watson.'

A twitch played at the side of his mouth. 'I'll get onto it, Jac.'

'Are you sure I'm not allowed to bug the phones?'

'Pretty sure. Besides, even if you were, I'd have no idea how to do it. I assume, given the reports, you wanted to bug Sandi's phone. She might not use the bugged phone. She might use her mobile.'

A massive flaw in my plan.

He scratched his head. I didn't see any sparks fly, but his face lit up. 'You could try a spy pen.'

'Spy pen?'

'It looks like a normal pen but has a recording device hidden in it. Does video and audio.'

'How is that more legal than bugging the phones?'

'I'm not sure it is. Anything you record couldn't be used in court, but if you capture something interesting, it'll give you a starting point to investigate further. And it would pick up her conversation no matter which phone she used. It just needs to be nearby.'

Andrew might be onto something. Besides, if the recording didn't work, I had the option to jab the pen into her eye. Either way, I would feel better than I did now.

'We could sneak the pen into her bag or a pocket ...' Andrew rubbed his chin. 'Then you'd have to download the audio when you got it and ...'

'Sounds complicated.'

'It's easier than bugging phones. It'll be a snap. She won't even notice.' Andrew warmed to his subject, jumping to his feet, and pacing the room. 'Pens are everywhere in an office. It'll be hiding in plain sight. I'm sure the batteries would last for ages. I reckon it could work.'

'It's worth a try,' I said, prepared to try anything to do the right thing by All Class. Cute, coming from a woman entertaining murder. 'I'm disturbed you're so well-versed in this.'

'I live on the Net. The natural domain of the socially ill at ease,' he said, deadpan.

'No comment. Where do I get one of these gadgets?'

'Where do you get anything? Online.'

I typed 'spy pen' into the search bar and, in its helpful way, the internet responded with more answers than I needed, including 'how-to' videos.

We played a couple. The footage made it look simple. This might be part of the answer. 'Andrew, you're a genius.'

He grinned like a school kid who'd been patted on the head by the principal.

'I'll give you the money and you buy it. Use your home computer.'

His eyes bulged. 'Me? Why?'

'I don't want to leave a trail.'

'So, you want me to get into trouble?'

'You won't. They aren't illegal to buy, are they? Anyway, you'll be better at figuring out how to set it up.'

Andrew frowned while he considered his options, which took all of five seconds.

He grinned. 'Okay, what the hell.'

After Andrew left, Paulette knocked and popped her head around the door. 'I've printed the candidate records from the database for the Globe General Bank search you've been working on. Do you want them, or should they go to Sandi?'

'I'll take them.' Sandi still assumed she was working on the brief, but I intended to keep a close eye on it.

Paulette dumped the files onto the desk. 'You look like you've had bad news.'

'No. All good,' I said.

Paulette opened her mouth to say something, changed her mind, and left.

I flicked through the reports. The database had identified eight people who fitted the job profile Globe General Bank wanted. It was a good start. All Class would need to determine if any on the list were interested, organise interviews, then an advertising campaign to fill the gaps if needed. The quicker we filled the vacancies, the quicker the money would flow in. It would make the coffers more respectable and lessen my stress about meeting the future payroll. The breathing space would also give me time to gather more evidence of Sandi's fraud. A sudden thought caused me to draw in a deep breath. What if she was running the same scheme with GGB? I had to get onto this.

Fast.

It was after eight at night when I left the office. My rumbling stomach reminded me I'd neglected it all day. Thinking about facing Rohan when I got home worsened my mood. I realised

I didn't know how long his conference was scheduled for, but I hoped to be asleep before he came home.

I lowered the car window, letting in the fresh air as I navigated the tail end of the peak hour traffic. The latest tender draft was in the messenger bag on the passenger seat. I put the seat belt across it, relieved to know there were a few more days in which to tidy it up and bed down the final details. Andrew still had to run supplementary reports for the appendices before it would be complete. It was a considerable part of the task, but I had confidence in him. I liked him even more since he'd come up with his covert surveillance plan. After Draga, he was the most reliable person in my life. Where were the girlfriends a woman was supposed to have? I sighed inwardly. Most of those relationships had withered because of my neglect.

My thoughts jumped between Rohan, and Sandi and Jason's scheme. My problems were becoming urgent. I should call the police, paramedics, or even the fire brigade. But who needed backup? I could handle Rohan, and Sandi, at the same time. I could juggle while walking a tightrope. I was desperate enough to work without a safety net.

My mobile rang. Andrew's name displayed on the screen.

'Chief, I found it!' he said. 'Best spy pen ever. It has no obvious button, no LED lights, and no visible recording hole on the pen body. Looks like a normal pen. And get this – it can record sound up to thirty metres. I'll put a priority request tonight and it should be shipped immediately. Good, hey?'

Andrew sounded like he'd saved the world.

Mine at least.

CHAPTER NINE

I went to bed before Rohan came home and was relieved to find his side empty when I woke. His idea of selling his business rattled around in my head. He might have planned to run off with the old woman after he got hold of the proceeds. But then why reveal his intention to sell?

I dressed and left off my engagement and wedding rings. Rohan was having an affair, which didn't exactly strengthen our marital bond. At this point, I'd rather be a widow than a divorcee. I checked my reflection in the mirror. My makeup had painted my face cheerier, but I wasn't happy.

Downstairs, Ant was in his usual place by the pool, feet dangling in the water. He watched the ripples his movements created while he sucked on a cigarette.

I slid open the door and called out, 'Breakfast, Ant?'

He shook his head. The Mickey Mouse effect must have worn off. This kid was up and down like the stock market.

I made coffee and grabbed a tub of yoghurt. Where was Draga when I needed her?

As if reading my mind, she arrived. She paused by the pool to speak with Ant before coming into the house, banging against the cupboards with the bulging tote in her hand. Today, three French sticks stuck out of it. The scent of freshly baked bread made my mouth water.

'Sorry I late, Missus Jac. Boy not be happy this morning.' Draga tied on a floral apron. 'You go work?'

'Yes, and I'm working late tonight. I'm avoiding Rohan. He'll want to have one of those "let's talk about things over a long dinner" nights.'

'You not need long dinner to talk. You know already what is problem. You can say in time it take to drive through the McDonald,' Draga said.

'Thanks for that pearl, Draga.' I gathered all the paperwork I needed to take with me and slung my bag over my shoulder. 'You're right about Ant.'

'Not worry, Missus Jac. I watch boy.' She called out the open door. 'Ant, I make you breakfast.'

'Nah, I'm good.'

'I make toast. You eat.'

Ant's shoulders drooped in surrender. 'Fine.'

'How do you do that? He listens to you without question.'

'He know I always say what is true. This is how you make trust between people.'

My mobile chirped and the office number displayed. 'Paulette, I'm on my way.'

'I figured you might be, but there's something you need to know. It's urgent.' Paulette paused, and I realised the news wasn't going to be good.

'What's wrong?'

'Globe General Bank pulled the assignment.'

The back of my neck tingled. 'Every position?'

'Yes. All of it.'

'What happened?'

'Maddison Parker only left a voicemail message to say they weren't proceeding.'

'Did she say why or leave a number?'

'No to both.'

'Okay, I'll dig out her card. I might be a bit late, but I'll be there as soon as I can.'

I rummaged through my handbag, unearthing my purse, scraps of paper scrawled with reminders, tissues, hand sanitiser, and a nail file. I scattered everything across the bench.

'Missus Jac, what you do?' Draga asked, eyeing the items.

'I'm looking for a business card. I'm sure it's in here.' I kept searching, finding a hairbrush, a lipstick I'd been missing for ages, and a lint-covered roll of peppermints.

The bag was as full as Mary Poppins's carpetbag but with none of the magic. I was about to give up then found the card in the bag's side pocket along with two paracetamol capsules and an antacid tablet. I took them all.

I dialled Maddison's number with one eye on Ant, who was still mesmerised by his legs in the water.

Two rings and she trilled into the phone, 'Maddison Parker.'

'Maddison. It's Jacqueline Burne.'

There was a pause. A cold one.

'Jacqueline? I didn't recognise your number. There wasn't any need to call back.'

'I wanted to clarify your message. Is there an issue with our services?'

'No. It's …' I could almost hear the cogs grinding as she searched for an appropriate response. 'We're undergoing a restructure in the area we were recruiting for. We can't go ahead until it's decided. We might revisit it when the new structure's bedded down.'

Maddison finished and the cogs ground to a stop.

'It must have taken you by surprise,' I said, knowing restructures never happened in a few days.

'It did.' There was relief in her voice at having found an explanation.

Except I didn't believe the overpaid, underperforming little cow.

In the background, there was indistinct chatter, clinking crockery, and a burst of laughter. Someone called her name.

'I'm sorry, Jacqueline. I'm at a breakfast meeting. I have to go.' She rang off.

I checked my watch, and then dialled the office. 'Paulette,

what time did Maddison leave the message?'

'Odd thing is the time stamp showed it was left last night,' she said.

'Sandi's not there, is she?' I asked, suspecting I already knew the answer.

'She was here for about fifteen minutes, then left.'

'Then get into her online diary and see if you can find anything.'

Paulette's keyboard clacked.

'According to this, there's blanked-out time until eleven this morning. It doesn't say for what.' Paulette must have imagined my anger and disappointment because she added, 'I can tell you where. She's written 'TFA' here.'

'Doesn't help me.'

'I'm guessing it's her favourite haunt. She's been raving about it because she went there on a hot date and ...'

'Paulette!'

'The Fast Anchor. It's in Williamstown. I'll get you the address.'

'Thanks. Can you cancel all my appointments? Tell them I'll reschedule as soon as possible. I'll let you know when I'm coming in.' I had a hunch to follow.

I hung up just as Ant slopped into the kitchen, trailing pool water behind him. His eyes were hooded. I hoped he'd only been smoking tobacco.

Draga tutted and stopped buttering the toast. She went to the laundry and began to rummage in the broom cupboard. 'Where is mop? Bah!'

'Ant, how'd you like to go for a little drive?' I whispered.

'Huh?' He pushed away his fringe. 'How come?'

'Because I'm having a morning off.' To say nothing of an off morning.

While Ant crunched his way through the toast, my impatience to leave grew, but I had to make sure Draga didn't

89

see me take the surveillance kit she'd confiscated. I'd found it in the linen cupboard with a small towel barely covering it.

As soon as she went upstairs, I sneaked the bag into the car then returned.

'Draga, Ant and I are going out for a while.'

'Where you go?' she asked, eyes like two thin slits.

'I promised him a driving lesson. Doing it early before I go to work,' I said.

Draga's face lit up. 'Is good you do for boy, Missus Jac.'

As Ant and I headed to the car he asked, 'You're really going to let me drive?'

'Yes.' I put the L-plates on and we set off.

Ant had a death grip on the steering wheel.

'Relax. It won't detach from the steering column,' I said.

We followed the scenic route along the bay to Williamstown. Ant took instructions well and stayed calm as cars tooted. He wasn't even fazed by a persistent motorbike weaving between us and other cars, although his knuckles were white. By the time he drove through the roundabout into Nelson Place and found a nose-to-kerb parking spot near a park that The Fast Anchor faced, his grip on the wheel had relaxed. He grinned and cut the engine.

'Good job, Ant.'

'It was intense, but your car's easy to drive. Is Dad's?'

'That thing? Super easy. Shove it into drive and go. It moves like a cut cat because of the sports pack. Too fast for me. I prefer this little thing.' I patted the dashboard.

'You reckon Dad would ever let me drive his car?'

'He doesn't let me drive it.'

'Anyway, why are we here?' Ant asked, looking around.

I pointed across the park to the restaurant's front door. 'Over there is The Fast Anchor. Anyone going in or out has to walk or drive past here. The side street leading to it is a cul-de-sac.'

'You mean it's a dead-end,' he said.

'Yep.' I hoped my mission wouldn't be.

Ant smiled, looking so like his dad that I drew back.

'You can be funny,' he said. Before I had the chance to say 'Thanks', he added, 'When you're not complaining. So, what are you looking for?'

'Not what, who. Someone who might be in there.' I grabbed my surveillance kit from the rear seat and unzipped it. Out came the opera glasses. I held them up in front of my sunglasses, demonstrating my poor spying style.

'What the ...?' Ant laughed.

'I don't have any conventional binoculars. I have to do this at a distance. If I go in, they'll see me.'

Ant did a palms-up. 'I'll go in.'

'You can't.'

'Whoever you're spying on won't know me.' He waggled the phone in his hand. 'Besides – camera, video.'

Ant would be less conspicuous and at this point, my morals were developing a lot of stretch. 'That might work.'

'I'll look around and if anyone asks, I'll say I'm thinking of booking the place for my eighteenth birthday party.'

'They won't let you book an eighteenth without a parent.'

'Then I'll tell them I'm looking for a job.'

'Who knew you were so shifty?'

'Me shifty? You're pretty good yourself,' he said.

I reoriented my moral compass to consider it a compliment.

'What does he, she, it, look like?' Ant asked, opening the car door.

'A stuck-up young woman, about my height. She'll be easy to spot because there'll be lots of hair tossing. Another woman, blonde, also not too tall. She'll be wearing a lot of makeup. She still oozes self-absorption under it.'

'Those aren't very good descriptions.'

'They're all I have. Do your best.'

He loped across the grass to the building and disappeared inside.

I focused on the door as though staring hard enough would somehow let me see what was happening beyond it. Fifteen minutes passed, during which a steady trickle of people went in and out. Business-suited people carrying folders, mums with strollers, couples holding hands, and a thickset, beefy guy who pulled up on a motorbike and lumbered through the door.

A passerby did a double-take and I lowered my opera glasses. No need to draw attention to myself, but it was harder to take in all the details with the naked eye.

I rehashed my conversation with Maddison and the plan I suspected Sandi had executed. Bet Maddison transferred the roles over to Jason, spurred on in some fashion by Sandi. They'd all be in it together. The idea of confirming yet another betrayal filled me with dread.

I spent a few minutes scanning the street, watching as people went about their ordinary lives. My life was anything but ordinary. It was chaotic, and I couldn't help thinking things were going to get worse.

The Fast Anchor door burst open. Ant ran out and across the grass, his face contorted with fear.

I gasped. Something was happening at the restaurant door, but I focused on Ant. I jumped out of the car and around to the driver's side and started the engine.

Ant flung the door open and dived in. 'Go, Jac! Go!'

Forced to look over my shoulder to reverse, I couldn't see who, or what, he was running from. There was a break in the traffic, so I gunned the engine as fast as I dared. At the first intersection, I made a right and drove until we were well away from the scene.

Ant kept looking over his shoulder, chest heaving.

'What happened?' I checked in the rear-view mirror. There was nothing extraordinary behind us except a few cars and a

Lycra-clad rider in the bicycle lane.

Ant faced forward and his breathing started to slow as we put more distance between the restaurant and ourselves.

'Ant, you're scaring me.'

'It's nothing.'

'You're as white as a sheet. Something happened in there.' I took the next turn and we coasted along quiet suburban streets.

Ant pulled his phone from his pocket. 'I got some pics. Hope they're what you want.'

'Thanks, Ant, but ...'

He shook his head. 'Please, Jac. I don't want to talk about it.'

We drove in silence. I was protective and curious, but kept my mouth shut, frightened my words would push him into total withdrawal.

Ant checked over his shoulder once more, then settled and scrolled through the photographs. He held up the phone. 'Here.'

I glanced at the images. Some were blurry and revealed nothing. One pic made me pull over. I took the phone from Ant's hand and examined it.

Maddison, Sandi, and Jason. More followed, snapped from different angles. The evidence couldn't be clearer.

Ant took back the phone. 'You thought you'd feel better about this, didn't you? Now I'm kinda sorry I took them.'

'Don't be. You're a very effective spy. I needed to know, even if a part of me didn't want to.'

'I still don't get who these people are.'

'The blonde is one of my senior staff. The brunette is – was – a client. The man is a major competitor who used to work for All Class.'

'I guess they're not supposed to be hanging around together?'

'Correct.' Meeting together wasn't illegal, but I suspected

their scheme might be. Problem was, this picture proved nothing except they all knew each other.

'What next, Jac?'

'Save the images to my computer for me.'

'Easy.'

'Only part of this situation that is.'

We sat in the parked car in silence until Ant said, 'Just goes to show there are heaps of ways to get screwed over.'

Draga fussed when we entered the house. She stood with her broom stretched out in one hand, the other hand on her hip, like a Roman soldier with an apron for a shield.

'What happen? You face much red, Missus Jac.' She waggled a chubby finger at Ant. 'You, too. You look much white. What is wrong? Where you be?'

Ant opened the fridge, took out orange juice, and poured a glass. 'Spying.'

Draga took off her glasses and let them drop on their neck chain. She scowled. 'You take bag again?'

'Again?' Somewhere under his fringe, Ant's eyebrow lifted.

I put my index finger to my lip and shook my head.

Draga tutted and put the broom to work, muttering in Croatian.

'What's she saying?' Ant asked.

'I don't know. I bet it isn't flattering in any language.'

He grinned. 'I'll download the pics to the PC.' Juice and phone in hand, Ant headed to the study.

Draga stopped sweeping. 'And why you not go office now?' She pitched the same look my school teachers did when I spent hours doodling instead of doing my work. 'What photos you take? What you be doing? You mix up boy … in what? He look big.' She emphasised Ant's height by raising a hand above her head and the skin under her upper arm did a tuckshop swing. 'But he still boy.' She attacked the floor with aggressive sweeping.

'It's no big deal. Why are you so angry?'

She resumed her centurion's pose. 'Da, is the big deal. You not can put child in big person place. Be too much for him.'

'What are you on about, Draga?'

'Bah, you no understand.'

'Wait …' I called after her, but Draga and her broom were gone.

I went to the study and stood behind Ant while he saved the last few photos to a folder called 'Special Project' on the desktop.

'Done.'

'Thanks, Ant.'

'I'm sorry I couldn't get more,' he said.

'The way you were moving, I could tell you didn't want to hang around.'

Ant developed a deep interest in his empty glass. 'I need a refill,' he said and hurried from the room.

I sat at the computer revisiting the photographs, wondering what else I could do to encourage Ant to reveal what had frightened him. I'd been staring at the screen for ten minutes when sparkly light began to play at the edges of my vision. An early warning sign of a migraine. Damn my stupid head.

Draga passed the open door. 'Missus Jac. What is wrong?'

'I have a migraine coming on, but I still need to get to work.' I pressed fingers to my temples.

'You not can go to office when you have much headache. You not can drive car. You must go bed. I bring tablets.'

Strong painkillers and sleep were the usual solutions. Today I didn't have time, but already I was feeling sick and sensitive to the light. 'Okay.'

I sent a quick text message to Paulette, telling her I wouldn't be in, and then went upstairs.

Outside Ant's room, I paused. He was on his phone, his back to the open door. I caught a snippet of conversation, his voice urgent.

'No, dude, I'm telling you. Saw it myself. I'm freakin' out, man. I gotta get ...' Ant's voice dropped to an inaudible whisper.

Draga came up behind me. 'Missus Jac, Bed. Brzo! Hurry.'

She hustled me into my room, handed me a glass of water and the tablets.

I slipped into pyjamas, lay down and shut my eyes.

Draga put a cold pack against my neck. 'Be help.'

She threw a light blanket over me and drew the blinds. 'You sleep. I stay here tonight. You not worry. I look after everything.'

'Thank you, Draga.'

'You rest.'

She left me in the quiet. The headache mingled with worry about Rohan, about work, about my messy life.

I wasn't sure which was causing the most pain.

CHAPTER TEN

I dreamed I was falling and woke with a start. Rohan's side of the bed hadn't been slept in. I checked the clock. 2.17am. The air was sticky, and I threw off the blanket.

The migraine had morphed into a deep nauseating throb. I reached for the painkillers and downed two more. Twenty minutes passed before the pain eased. I swung my legs out of bed and went into the ensuite to splash water on my face.

An indistinct sound travelled through the open window. I pulled apart the blind slats and peeked outside. Nothing was out of place. Moonlight shimmered on the pool water. The James Sterling shrubs around the garden perimeter stood like bushy sentries.

Everything was as it should be, except for a shape in a poolside chaise – Rohan with his legs outstretched.

Dressed in chino shorts and a pale t-shirt, he held a glass, swirling the contents; around and around they went. His other hand rested on his forehead, like a holidaymaker relaxing in the sun. He turned his face up to the window.

I sprang back. The slat blinds snapped together. I counted to ten then prised them apart.

Rohan raised his index finger and beckoned.

Part of me wanted to ignore him, but another wanted to know what he was doing. I wondered why he hadn't snuck off to his rendezvous and what time he'd come home.

I slipped on a dressing gown, and padded, barefoot, through the silent house.

Outside, the quietness was punctuated with the sound of an occasional passing car beyond the high wall. In the lull, the breaking waves beat out the hot summer night's restless rhythm.

'What are you doing out here?' I asked Rohan in my best 'don't mess with me' tone.

I drew the flimsy dressing gown around me, aware that him seeing me in my pyjamas suddenly felt too intimate. I needn't have bothered because Rohan's eyes were shut.

A bottle of Chivas Regal whisky was on the ground beside him. Judging by the bottle's level, most of the alcohol was now in his bloodstream.

'You can't sleep either?' he asked.

'Evidently.'

'We didn't get to finish our conversation.' He still hadn't opened his eyes.

'What conversation?' I knew what he meant, but wifely cooperation was in short supply.

His eyes flew open, dark, and angry. 'Forgodssake, Jacqueline.'

His tone made me feel like a naughty child. I bit my lip, breathing in the salty air. Heat pressed my skin. It was the sort of balmy night where we once would have made love.

'This is not the time for a conversation.'

'No time like the present,' he slurred.

'We can't have a serious talk if you're drunk.'

'Not drunk enough. Do you have any idea of how unhappy you are, Jacqueline?'

I put my hands on my hips. 'I'm unhappy? Don't be ridiculous. I'm fine.' I was as much of a liar as he.

'You're so miserable, it makes me miserable.' He emphasised his points by stabbing a finger in the air.

'You're unhappy about your work. That's nothing to do with me.'

'Forget my work.' He raised his glass in a mocking toast. 'I'm talking about you. You don't care about anything except your little business. And look at you.' He gave me an up and down. 'You dress like a ... a ...'

'Like a woman in sleepwear in the middle of the night?'

He waved the idea away. 'A man needs his partner to care about herself. It shows she cares about him.'

'What century are you living in, Rohan?' It didn't make his jibe less cruel and another massive chunk dropped off my waning confidence.

'You've become so boring.' Rohan's mouth twisted, and his voice dropped low. 'You're in love with your job. You work seven days a week.'

'I'm trying to keep the business afloat. I have staff and clients to consider. You're the one who's constantly at meetings.'

'No, no, no. Don't bring me into this. I know you married an insurance policy. Financial support, community connections. You built your business on my reputation.'

'Where is all this coming from? I'd established my business before we met. All through my own resources. When things went bad, I could have asked for support, but I didn't. I did it alone.'

'Your stupid independence is the problem. When we married, I expected life would be different. I figured we'd do more together,' he said.

'That's unfair. We did a lot together. Then you started calling me a trophy wife. Did you just want someone with the right looks on your arm? What did that say about your idea of the marriage? Of me?'

Something unravelled inside as I remembered our early days. Even if I could now tie together every good memory, the knots would never hold. A cool wind sprang up and the night air became thick with the promise of rain.

'You're keeping secrets, Jacqueline.'

'I'm keeping secrets? I'm keeping secrets?' My debating skills were poor and repeating the question didn't make them stronger. 'What about the secrets you're keeping? I know you're seeing someone,' I blurted out.

'Don't be ridiculous.'

'I saw the two of you leaving The Admiral's Retreat.' I pushed away strands of hair that stuck to my cheeks in the humidity and jutted out my chin.

'You can't blame me for getting a little comfort elsewhere,' Rohan said defensively.

'I do blame you. You're the one destroying our marriage.'

There was no positive way to talk about us. No way to make this better. This was my life and it had to change.

I sighed. 'Rohan, this is pointless. Do we have to have this discussion now? I'm exhausted, and I have the remnants of a headache. I need to sleep. Let's talk tomorrow.'

'It's always about you, isn't it? What you want. What you need,' he shouted.

'Shh. You'll wake Ant and Draga,' I said in a voice loud enough to do so.

'Let them wake up. Don't pretend you care about anyone.'

Everything he had held in came to the surface; a massive festering boil that burst, spraying me with a list of my wrongdoings and faults. I was immature. Incompetent. Remote. Self-centred. Unattractive. Banal. Dull. There were other descriptors, but I couldn't take them in. I stood immobilised, stunned by his words.

The wind strengthened, carrying with it the odour of dying seaweed beached on the nearby sand. It stirred something in me. Rohan's verbal onslaught forced me backwards like a cartoon character leaning against a gale.

'Please, Rohan. Stop. Stop!'

'I forgot to add the most important one to the list.' He sneered. 'Frigid. It's such a big one I have synonyms. Unresponsive. Passionless. Ice Queen.' He lifted his glass in a toast. 'To my trophy wife.'

His mouth opened and closed like a fish, spouting more

ugly words lost in a roaring noise, a noise I mistook for the ocean beyond the high fence. Then I realised the sound was in my head, an internal drum roll announcing impending disaster.

'I had a miscarriage.' The wind died, and my voice carried.

At least, now, Rohan would understand my distance, my fear, my loss.

Rohan stared with glazed eyes. 'When?'

'Six months ago. You were so adamant about not wanting to have children. I didn't know how to tell you about the pregnancy.'

'You got pregnant on purpose without telling me?'

'What? Of course not.'

He wobbled to his feet and leaned in enough for his whisky breath to make me turn away.

'I don't believe you,' he spat, his words tripping across one another.

'Why would I lie?'

Rohan peered into his glass, rocking on his heels. 'Well, it's a good thing you lost it. I mean, what sort of mother would you have made?'

White-hot heat radiated from the pit of my stomach, seared through my body and into my face. I stepped towards him and balled my hands into fists.

'What a horrible, cruel thing to say,' I shouted. 'You're the one who doesn't care about anyone except yourself. Go ahead. Sell your business, then get out of my life.'

Rohan smirked and something inside me detonated. My body straightened, my right fist swung wide and across. With a Wimbledon-worthy grunt, I followed through. Stubble pricked my knuckles as I connected with Rohan's chin. A loud crack. Pain exploded into my hand, and along my arm.

Rohan was bug-eyed. After a beat, his eyes rolled back. His hand opened, the glass dropped and shattered. He concertinaed and fell, head bouncing with a thud when it hit the surrounding pool tiles.

The moon slipped behind black clouds and thunder rumbled above. Heavy drops of rain stung through my thin gown as I stood over him.

'I deserve an apology,' I said.

Rohan lay at my feet like a crumpled marionette. Blood seeped from his head. One sandal was still on his foot; the other had flipped off and now bobbed in the pool.

I bent down and shook him by the shoulder. 'Get up.' The smell of alcohol made me gag. 'Rohan?' I shook harder, my voice like a bullfrog. 'Rohan!'

His shoulder flopped back and forth under my hand.

The rain grew heavier. The sound muffled my cries and blurred my vision.

I pushed my fingers into the warm, rough-skinned groove on the side of his neck, searching for his pulse. I pressed deeper. Nothing. I wiped the rain from my face, and I tried again. All the while, I talked to him, pleading, cajoling, then demanding.

It was as if I was outside my body, looking down on a horror scene. I stifled a scream and fell onto my knees next to him in the puddling rainwater.

This wasn't what I'd planned. Not that I'd had a plan in place, more of a wish list; a cosy fantasy, cooked up in anger and pride. I played it out in my head when I needed comfort. I'd thought I wanted him dead, but despite my vengeful fantasies, I wasn't cut out for murder. A few hours of watching crime shows had told me that.

Fate had responded to my fantasy of killing Rohan. It didn't feel as good as I'd imagined. What I'd truly wanted was for Rohan to disappear, benignly. Not lying in a heap at my feet while his blood washed away in the rain.

The storm gathered momentum. I didn't have a Plan B or C, or any plan associated with any letter of the alphabet. No alibi, no escape route and no exceptional lawyer to defend me. I didn't deserve to be defended. I'd done something unthinkable. Violent. Cruel. And irredeemable.

I considered calling the authorities. All Class would close, leaving my clients in the lurch and my staff camping at Centrelink. Draga would have to register with a job network provider to find a new employer and Ant would have to go back to Triple-T. But if I stayed out of prison, they'd be okay. I could never reverse what I'd done, but what happened to Rohan was an accident. Sort of.

I glanced over my shoulder to the house, but no lights came on. I had to get Rohan's body out of open view and the logical place was the room near the pool. He called it the 'utility room', a pretentious title making it sound grander than it was. It was just a small shed, housing the pool filter motor and some gardening tools. The door was less than a metre from the scene of my crime. Not too far to drag him. I edged to the entrance, keeping Rohan in my line of sight in case he rose, zombie-like, to exact revenge. I opened the door and screwed up my nose against a strong odour of chlorine. I didn't turn on the light in case it drew attention. The floor was clear – enough space for a body.

Drenched and shivering, I went back to Rohan, put my hands under his shoulders, and tried to lift him. I grunted with the effort, but I couldn't budge him. He was a dead weight – literally. Body disposal is hard work in low light and pouring rain.

I bent to rest my hands on my knees, panting, working out my next move. Deciding to roll him, I knelt and pushed. It wasn't easy, but once I got the first arc over, the rest of him followed. I avoided looking at Rohan's face. Another roll and he was at the utility room entrance. I angled him through the door and slammed it shut. I couldn't leave Rohan in the utility room for long.

The rain had washed the blood from around the pool. It

would take more than a summer storm to wash my soul clean. Lightning cracked with biblical menace.

I entered the house and slipped, falling onto all fours. Sharp pain speared into my knees, sucking the air out of me. I hobbled up the stairs, water trailing behind like a bridal train.

I'd been so confident I could sort out my life. I was wrong and there was only one option left.

I took a deep breath and opened the bedroom door.

CHAPTER ELEVEN

I switched on the bedside light and shook Draga.

She squinted, then sat up, eyes flicking left to right. 'Missus Jac, what is wrong?'

'It's Rohan.' My voice was squeaky and thin. I put my hand on my throat to stop from screaming. 'I've killed him.'

Draga's eyebrows went up a smidgeon and she laughed. 'Without me?'

'I'm serious. He's dead.' I choked down a sob.

She wriggled herself upright and put her glasses on. She looked at my wet body and searched my face. 'What you do?'

The words wouldn't come.

Draga swung out of bed, revealing a three-quarter length nightgown patterned with large-eyed teddy bears. It rode up to reveal her heavily-veined legs. She placed a finger to the blood on my dressing gown. Her brows made a deep X at the bridge of her nose.

The story blubbered out of me. When I reached the part about the right uppercut, she picked up my hand and examined my knuckles, shaking her head. I was suddenly aware of how much they hurt.

'He fell and hit his head. He's dead.' Confession is supposed to be good for the soul, yet I wasn't feeling any less burdened.

'You sure Mr Ruin be dead?'

I nodded. 'I couldn't find his pulse.'

Draga crossed herself. 'Neka te bog oprosti.'

'I doubt I'll get forgiveness from anybody, Draga.' I wilted to the floor and leaned against the bed. 'It was an accident. We got into a fight. He said cruel things about the baby ...' I wiped my snotty nose with the back of my hand. 'I snapped and ...'

'You explain after.' Draga fetched a towel and draped it around my shoulders while she soothed me. 'Where Mr Ruin be now?'

'In the utility room. I have to move him. Somewhere. Anywhere but here.'

Draga did the cross thing again. This time, she turned her eyes to the heavens. 'I not have much experience move the dead person, but I try my best.'

Much? I wasn't about to ask how much.

Draga patted my arm. 'Not worry, Missus Jac, I find way. First, you get shoes for me.'

I reached for her Homyped sandals.

'No. Other shoe.' She pointed to a pair of sturdy sneakers. 'For heavy work, I must wear strong shoe.'

'I'm supposed to know the appropriate attire when getting rid of a body?' I asked.

Water dripped from my hair onto her skin as I helped her to squeeze a chubby foot into each sneaker. This was crazy. I'd be caught for sure. I imagined myself in prison. It might be like that Wentworth television show about women doing time. Ill-fitting clothing, grumpy inmates.

When I'd finished, she stood and secured her glasses around her neck on their cord. She jerked her head towards the door. 'Brzo. We go see Mr Ruin.'

'Draga, we're not joining him for a cup of tea.'

We went downstairs, me limping and Draga's teddy bears dancing to her waddle. She detoured into the laundry, tied on an apron, and retrieved her favourite broom.

I shot her a quizzical look.

'I must wear apron when I work.' She carried the broom handle like a weapon.

All I carried was a massive load of guilt.

Draga motioned me to keep moving. We stepped into the

night where the rain still fell in sheets.

I led her to the spot near the pool, fighting down a wave of nausea accompanying the memory of Rohan lying there. 'He fell and hit his head here.' The wind carried away half my words, and rainwater ran into my mouth. At this rate, we might drown before we did anything.

Draga squatted using the broom for support. 'No blood. This good. Majko moja! Much broken glass.' Draga proceeded to attack the shards with her broom.

'Not now, Draga. Look.' I pointed to where the wind created waves on the pool and Rohan's sandal bobbed; going nowhere, like its owner.

Draga reached out with the broom handle, hooking the sandal on the tip. She drew it to her and declared, 'Is nice and clean,' before slipping it into her apron pocket.

I followed her to the utility room door. She stood still then held the broom out and stopped me. The handle tip hit my head.

'Ouch.'

'Sorry, Missus Jac. I want be sure no one here.' She scanned around then craned her neck to look over the fence.

'Draga! It's just you, me and the dead man behind that door.'

'And boy. Not forget boy.'

Ant. How would I explain his dead dad? Just when the kid and I were starting to get along. 'I'm a monster.'

Lightning cracked.

Draga yelled back. 'We talk about you after. First, you show where be Mr Ruin.' She waved her hand to hurry me up. 'Brzo, in case boy wake up.'

I hesitated. 'I don't think I can look at him.'

'Bah! We must look so we can know what we must do.' Draga positioned herself at the side of the door and raised the broom handle, on the offensive.

'What are you doing? He's not going to attack you.'

'I want be sure,' she said, then nodded to encourage me to open the door.

I inched my hand forward, gripped the latch and froze.

'Why you wait?' Draga asked.

I pulled up the latch. To my muddled mind, the scene unfolded in slow motion. The door's bottom edge dragged on the ground. I lifted it and pulled it open.

We brought our heads together and peered into the dark interior. Draga's broom remained on high alert.

I eased through the entrance and snapped on the light switch. Nothing. I flipped it several times, but it wouldn't work. I could just make out Rohan's lifeless form in a shaft of moonlight. His t-shirt collar was stained where blood had run down from the head wound, the rain diluting it to pinkish hues.

Draga's head popped over my shoulder. 'He look okay. If we not count blood.' She tilted her head and her eyes became like big blue spotlights behind the thick lenses. 'Missus Jac, we must think where we take Mr Ruin.'

'I don't know where to take him. All I know is he can't stay here.'

'We put him in car and find place.'

'Like where?'

'Maybe forest.'

'There's no forest around here.'

'Okay, bush.' Her face lit up. 'We take him to zoo in Werribee.'

'The Open Range Zoo?'

'Yes, is nice place.'

'We're not taking him on an outing, Draga.'

She gave a one-shoulder shrug. 'Okay, okay.' She tapped the broom tip handle to her lips, then brightened. 'This what we do. We put Mr Ruin in car and go until we find place. We know when we see.'

'Your plan is just to drive around the streets with a body in the boot?'

'You have idea better?' She thrust her chin out and her voice ratcheted up a notch.

I made a 'keep it down' gesture. 'Shh. Remember Ant? And, nope, I don't have a better idea.'

'Then we must put Mr Ruin in car.' Draga disappeared out the door, leaving me with Rohan. I stared at him until she returned. Behind her, she dragged a shag pile rug that had been stored in the garage along with bags of items I'd intended to donate to the op-shop.

'We put him in this.'

'You want to roll him in a rug? Like in a bad movie?'

'Is why they put in movie, because is good idea.' Draga clapped her hands together.

I sighed heavily. 'What's one more cliché?'

We inched nearer to Rohan. 'I don't know if I can touch him again,' I said.

'I not can do by myself. We must do together.'

I strained in the dim light as I spread the rug on the ground, its edges as close to Rohan as I dared.

Draga went to one side and I went to the other. She used the broom as a lever.

We grunted in unison as we gave one mighty push and manoeuvred Rohan onto the rug edge and then rolled it over him. His lower legs stuck out.

'It's too small. It'll come undone,' I said.

'Be enough for now,' Draga said.

He looked like a spring roll. An unhealthy one. I was glad I couldn't see his face.

Draga pointed at his one-sandaled foot. 'He half dress.' She took the other sandal from her apron pocket, put it on his bare foot and gave a thumbs up. 'Much better.'

I wiped my hands down the front of my dressing gown,

wanting to get rid of the feel of Rohan's still warm skin. 'He's too heavy to carry. How will we get him to the car?'

Draga considered the problem before declaring her solution. 'We use wheelbarrow.'

I eyed the barrow that leaned against the wall. 'That little thing?'

'Be big enough.'

Getting the rolled carpet onto it was a feat of engineering. It involved the broom, a length of rope we'd found hanging on a hook, and a tangentially related anecdote from Draga's childhood. The rug hung over the barrow's sides with Rohan's feet sticking out.

Draga brushed her hands together in a 'that's that' gesture. Her expression turned grave. 'You not can bring this small carpet home after. Not be good luck.'

I rolled my eyes. 'I'll get my car key.'

'No! Missus Jac, we must use Mr Ruin car.'

'Why? I hate driving the Beemer.'

'You car small. First, you be make him to squash inside, but after, it not be nice to drive car where was dead body.' Draga grimaced.

Good point. 'I'll get that key.'

'I stay with him.' She raised an eyebrow. 'Just in case.'

The rain eased to a drizzle. Moonlight bounced off the wet ground like a film noir scene. When I returned, we each took a barrow handle and wobbled it through the garage side door, past the op-shop bags, to the Beemer. I took one hand off the handle and dug into my pocket for the car key. The wheelbarrow lurched to the side and Rohan almost rolled off. Draga and I did a kind of two-step as we levered Rohan into the boot, curling him to fit.

'Missus Jac, be careful where is his head.'

'What difference does it make?'

'So we not bump.'

'Bump? Seriously?'

I slammed the boot lid and leaned on it, senses on full alert. 'I can't stop shaking.'

'Is you nerve. You should be nervous. If the police come to get you ...' She put her hands together in prayer and waggled them up and down to emphasise her point. 'Better not to think about police. Brzo! We go.'

Draga threw her broom into the rear seat and waddled to the passenger side.

I slid into the driver's seat and pressed the garage remote. The door rolled up on the deserted street. I pushed the key into the ignition and hovered my finger on the starter button. I was about to cross the Rubicon and there was no coming back.

'Stop. Stop!' Draga said.

I jumped. 'What? What?'

'Look how we dress. We in clothes for the bed.' She pointed at my soaked nightwear. 'I wet, but you much wet like the fish.'

'Draga, it's the middle of the night and we're dumping a body. Style isn't a priority.'

'What if somebody be see us? We look suspicious. Me not much, but you, da.'

'Don't be ridiculous. If we're seen, it'll look suspicious anyway.'

Draga's lips set in a line.

I knew that look. It said, 'I'm not moving until I get what I want.' Draga employed it with tradespeople. Like all those times, there would be no convincing her otherwise.

'Okay. Okay. We'll get changed.'

We went inside, tiptoeing upstairs, where I dried myself, pulled on track pants, a top, and slipped into canvas sneakers.

Draga emerged from her room, wearing a black, elastic-waisted skirt over another nightgown. This one had kittens printed on it. It bunched up like an ill-fitting blouse.

'I put this over my head because shoes make me trouble to

take off. I look nice, da?' she whispered, twirling.

I lowered my voice, one eye on Ant's door. 'Draga, it's not the time for a fashion show. Let's go.'

Draga raised her index finger. 'Shh. Listen.'

'What?' A faint whine. The sound became clearer. A smooth-running engine.

The Beemer.

A beat then I sprang into action, running down the stairs ahead of Draga. I bolted out the back door and raced into the garage. The open roller door was like a wide laughing mouth. I ran into the street to see the Beemer hurtling away, headlights shining off the wet road. The brake lights lit, and it made a left. The sound of its engine faded out across the still night.

Draga came up behind me, panting. 'Bože moj! Where Mr Ruin go?'

'He's not the one driving, Draga. He's in the boot with a great big hole in his head and not breathing. Remember?'

The empty street was quiet again. What the hell was happening? Rohan was dead. His body gone. In a stolen car. Just like the plot of a B grade movie.

The world began to spin. I held my hands to my head then collapsed against the garage wall, catching my calf on a sharp wire sticking out of an open toolbox.

In the background, Draga swore in Croatian, lamenting the loss of her broom.

When I came to, she was standing over me, buzzing like a giant wasp.

'Missus Jac, wake up.'

I leaned onto my elbows. 'God!'

'No, is me.' Draga knelt beside me.

My right leg stung. I reached to where the pain was most pronounced. Through a rip in my track pants, there was the unmistakable stickiness of blood.

The image of the departing Beemer flooded back. 'Rohan ...'

'Bah!' Draga waved her hand. 'He go.'

'He wasn't … Never mind.'

'No matter. He go. My best broom go, too.' Draga's shoulders sagged.

We both sat on the floor. I willed the pain to ease while calculating the odds of finding the car. They weren't good.

Draga's calf socks dragged around her ankles. She tugged one upward. 'That broom good for sweep inside and outside. I like much. Now ffftttt, gone.'

'Who cares about a damn broom? Whoever took the car will find the body and then the cops will slap me in handcuffs.'

'I not think so. They not use the steel. They use plastic string to tie hands. You not pay attention to police television show.'

'Cable ties then. Whatever. Either way, I'll end up in prison.' The cut on my leg was killing me and I was getting queasy.

'If you go prison. I lose the job.'

'Is that all you can think about right now?'

'I lose broom already. I not want lose job, too.'

How was I so stupid to leave the key in the ignition? Didn't I have enough on my plate already? I rolled onto all fours.

Draga rocked back and forth on the concrete, building the momentum to get up. After several attempts, she gave up and extended her hand. 'You help, molim. Pliss.'

Dear old Draga – short and stumpy, and stuck on my garage floor. It was the middle of the night, and she was prepared to help me dispose of a body, no questions asked. I guessed a joint venture in murder brings you closer together. These could be my last few hours of freedom and my lasting memories throughout my life sentence. My life was already a disaster, but now it was also ridiculous. My business was going down the gurgler. I'd killed my cheating jerk of a husband. His body and the car could be anywhere, and my accomplice was beached on the garage floor, bleating about a broom.

I sat up and began to laugh.

Draga's eyebrows arched. 'Why you laugh?'

There was no explanation. I laughed until I wanted to cry, but crying wouldn't help. I pressed my palms into my eyes.

Draga sat beside me and didn't mention the broom once. She helped me to my feet and supported me as I limped into the house. The scratch on my leg was an angry shade of red. She fetched antiseptic and cotton balls and handed them to me, then switched on the coffee machine. 'You want strong coffee?'

My stomach lurched. 'No, I couldn't ...'

'Okay, I make you the camomile tea.'

Blood-stained cotton balls piled up on the floor until my leg was clean. The area around the injury burned and the bruises from my earlier fall were throbbing. I covered the wound in tape. I rested my head on the table.

Once they found the Beemer, it would be a done deal. Already I imagined a forensics team in hazmat suits examining it and collecting evidence. I could see the headlines: Body in Beemer boot. Broom baffles. Beloved wife behind bars.

The kettle rumbled to a boil and snapped off. There was a lot of background noise and grumbling, and then a mug clattered onto the table.

I lifted my head.

'I put much sugar. You need.' A plume of steam spiralled up from a daisy-patterned mug, its bright flowers at odds with my mood.

I wrapped my hands around it and let the heat seep into my fingers.

The oven clock digits showed 4am. Despite the hour, Draga was all business.

'I have plan,' she said.

More trouble ahead.

CHAPTER TWELVE

Draga's car was a maroon 1999 Mazda 121, which she referred to as 'the half car' because of its size. Its identifying feature was a large dent in the right front panel, incurred when she'd failed to give way at an intersection. She'd argued it wasn't her fault because she hadn't seen the other car. Draga had refused to pay for repairs on principle and the damage remained as a permanent reminder of her poor driving and even poorer English. After that, she limited her journeys between my home, her home, the supermarket, and her church. She could do with a few more of those church trips, given her current activities.

I fumbled with my seat belt while Draga checked the dashboard as though it was the cockpit of an Airbus A380.

Draga's plan was simple: drive around, starting with following the route the Beemer took. That should take us to the next corner. After that, we'd have to wing it. I wasn't expecting to find anything, but we could get lucky. At least the drive might clear my head.

'You be ready, Missus Jac?' Draga started the motor and gripped the wheel. She leaned forward, squinting at the road ahead, and pressed the accelerator. We took off, putt-putting down the road. Draga was disinclined to get out of third gear and the engine strained.

'Draga, I could walk faster than this.'

'I not like speed,' she said but moved up a gear. We hit thirty kilometres per hour. At the corner, she swung left then slowed down. 'Which way we go, Missus Jac?'

One block down the road and already the plan had lost momentum. 'I don't know.'

'Then we must think. If I steal car like Mr Ruin car, I go quick to place where no one see me. Then I stop and look at car properly. Da?'

'I'm not a car thief.' I was a murderer. 'Keep driving, Draga. If nothing else, we're getting some fresh air.'

'Good idea. You not thief, but you good make other crime, Missus Jac.'

'Thank you.' The compliment signalled I was beyond redemption.

For the next hour, we navigated the streets, but found nothing. There was only row after row of slumbering houses. Behind their facades, any manner of drama might be playing out.

Draga drove down a lane and into every pothole. Each bounced us around and my stomach wasn't feeling great. 'Draga, take it easy.'

'Is not my fault, Missus Jac. Is council. They not fix holes in road, they put more hole,' she said, hunched over the wheel. Her glasses sat askew.

We travelled along the beachfront, driving to the far end where the road turned into a rough track that wound into an adjoining sprawling reserve. Small trails leading to the wetlands riddled the area. From there, dirt paths went down to the water at a steep angle and the ground fell away a few metres.

Draga pulled up facing the water and left the parking lights on.

'Why are we stopping? We can't find anything sitting in a parked car,' I said.

'I must think.'

We stepped out into the sticky air and leaned against the bonnet.

To the right, a wetland reserve spread into thick shrubbery. A well-known spot for lovers' trysts, it was now deserted. The ground was littered with the contents of car ashtrays: matches, cigarette butts, bottle caps, plus the odd condom wrapper.

'Can't believe this is a lovers' hotspot. Proves romance is dead,' I said.

Draga screwed up her nose. 'Tsk. I not know how people be so dirty.'

The predawn air quelled my nausea. 'We'll never sort this out.'

'We must. You not want go prison. For sure, I not want be stay in prison with you. You make trouble for me in there.'

I leaned my head on her shoulder. 'I shouldn't have dragged you into this, Draga.'

'Not worry, Missus Jac. I give you best help.'

'Why? Why would you help me so much?'

'I not want lose people who important.'

'I'm important?' I wanted to hug her.

Draga waved me away. 'You ask much question.'

'It was one question.'

The moon occasionally peeped from behind clouds.

'We should go,' I said. 'Keep driving around a bit more. We might get lucky.'

As we went to our respective car doors, I noticed a dancing light across to the far side of the wetlands.

'What is wrong?' Draga asked.

'Over there.' The spot pulsed red and gold.

Draga peered into the distance. 'What can be?'

'Idiots lighting fires probably.'

We watched as the glow intensified, then a loud bang was followed by a spire of reds and oranges shooting upwards. It died down to a kaleidoscope of pulsing oranges and reds.

'Aiii!' Draga grabbed the car door, her terrified face silhouetted by the light.

Another blast came. Smaller, but no less effective. A cloud of smoke plumed upward, and the faint crackle of the fire carried in the still air.

Draga watched the flames, immobilised.

I ran to her side. 'It's okay, Draga.'

She trembled and shook her head.

'Draga, what's wrong?'

'Make me to remember war.'

'Come on, I'll take you home.' I took her calloused hand and guided her to the passenger side. She was mute while I fastened her seat belt.

I drove, bumping across the potholed track, copying Draga's driving posture. Every few seconds, I glanced sideways to check on her, almost expecting the jolts would break her. I held the steering wheel in a death grip until we were back on sealed roads.

When we arrived home, Draga went to bed. She still trembled as I pulled a light blanket over her.

'I sorry, Missus Jac. I remember how was for me. For my family. Make me scared. Make me much sad.'

Her strength and humour had always made it easy for me to forget about her past.

'I'm the one who should be sorry. I can't imagine what you've been through. To lose your family ...'

She squeezed my hand. 'You my family, too. I not want lose you. Was accident with Mr Ruin. Things can be fix. We find way.'

Behind the grief in her eyes, there was something else – love and loyalty.

Despite not knowing what the next day held, I wanted to reassure her. 'Don't worry, Draga. Everything will be different tomorrow.'

Draga looked to the window where the first slivers of light had broken through the night sky. 'Is tomorrow, Missus Jac.'

I drew the room's blinds on the dawning day. 'Do you need anything, Draga?'

'I want sleep.' She rolled onto her side and pulled the

blanket under her chin. 'I see you soon, Missus Jac,' she said, as though her traumatic memories were just wisps of small cloud passing across life's horizon.

I slept sporadically until just after 8am, then lay in bed, reviewing my life. I was a heartless, albeit accidental, killer. I'd lost my husband's body, which also made me an incompetent one. My business was in trouble, which I could focus on if I wasn't busy extricating myself from my criminal life. And, I'd been indifferent to Draga's suffering.

I couldn't imagine fixing any of it.

By the time I'd showered, my aches had become a background niggle. I dressed in shorts and a t-shirt, pulled my hair into a rough ponytail, and slipped on my sneakers.

I passed Ant's door. How would I ever tell him what had happened to his dad?

'Good morning, Missus Jac.' Draga's pink blouse was so bright, I almost had to put on sunnies.

'How are you feeling?' I asked.

'I very good,' she said as if nothing had happened last night.

She hummed as she beat eggs in a bowl. The whisk hitting the metal sides reverberated around the kitchen.

'Draga, you'll wake Ant. I'm not ready to face him.'

'Boy can sleep in earthquake.' She gave the eggs a few extra turns and poured them into the pan.

If Draga couldn't have a broom in her hand, a kitchen utensil was the next best thing. But I feared she might develop clinical depression over her favourite broom's unexpected departure.

Mine was developing over the loss of Rohan's corpse.

'Do you think he's been found?' I asked.

Draga shrugged. 'Somebody telephone if they find. We must think what to say.'

'There won't be anything to say.'

I slipped bread into the toaster and set it on high. I watched it until a thin line of black smoke spiralled up to the ceiling. I nibbled the blackened toast, scattering dark crumbs on the bench.

Draga collected them with a damp rag. 'You not be the good cook, Missus Jac.'

She served the eggs. They were like rubber in my mouth and I pushed the plate aside.

Draga hooked the strap of a fruit-print apron over her head and then fumbled at the apron strings while jabbering in Croatian. 'Dođi ovdje! Missus Jac. Pliss, you help.'

She backed up to my chair, her ample backside near my head, and I tied the apron strings around her thick waist. She lifted the apron hem and wiped her brow, ignoring the moisture on her upper lip forming a water moustache. 'We make the new plan.'

I groaned. Please, not another Draga plan.

'It's too late. They'll find the car. They'll find Rohan. They'll find me.'

'You must say car be stolen. Is true.'

'Technically. How do I explain how it got out of a locked garage?'

Draga cocked her head, frowning. 'I not can think without the good broom. Spare one not same.' A few seconds later, she brightened, and her eyes glinted. 'You tell police you not know how happen.'

'Really? It'll be hard to sell. This is a safe house and the car has lots of security features.'

'No, no.' She warmed to her story. 'You must say you open garage door be put rubbish bin outside.'

'I never put the rubbish outside, Draga. You do.'

'They not know that. Mr Ruin know, but he not can say anything.' She slapped her hand onto the table. 'This be good idea. You must say you forget bit rubbish inside house, garage door be up and when you came back, poof, car is gone.' She grinned in triumph. Her glasses slid down her nose a little. Instead of pushing them up to the bridge, she tilted her head back and refocused. 'Is good story, da?'

Maybe. 'How did the thief get the car key?'

Draga frowned. 'Why you always think new problem?'

Visions of sitting in a cell, badly dressed, flashed across my mind. 'I don't think anything will work. I'll be in prison garb before you know it.'

'You not look nice in those clothes.' She scratched her head. 'If you not like what I suggest, you must think better story.'

I couldn't think of anything except that it might be easier to hand myself in. 'If I go on with this, my life will be nothing but lies from now on.'

'But will be good lies.' She scratched her chin. 'I know. You must find where Mr Ruin have meeting. Make sure you say you be somewhere else at same time.'

I hadn't even considered an alibi.

'Where he say he go for the last meeting?'

'If he did say, I wasn't listening.'

'You must look inside Mr Ruin book for appointment.'

'I suppose his diary's in his briefcase.'

'I get.'

If Rohan was going to another conference as he claimed, the details would have to be there. His aversion to technology meant he didn't use a digital calendar, so everything was hard copy. Knowing his penchant for lies, I expected we'd find nothing unless he'd written 'Meet my lover'. But if his scheduled appointments put me a fair distance from him, the diary might help me avoid jumpsuit-clad prison life.

Draga returned with the tan leather briefcase I'd given Rohan years ago as a celebration gift following the success of one of his business deals. He'd loved it. I remembered how he'd hugged me and then kissed my forehead. My forehead. It had become a habit. Right there, I should have taken the hint about the state of our relationship.

I flinched as Draga slammed the briefcase on the table.

Fingers on each barrel locks, I flicked the two latches. Only the left one opened. I frowned and kept sliding the catch, but it held firm. 'Damn. It's half-locked.'

Draga sighed. 'You think wrong. You must think the right way. Is half-open, Missus Jac. We must break other lock. I get hammer for meat.'

'You can't use a meat mallet on it. It'll look suspicious if someone ever sees the damage. I might be able to figure out the code.' I positioned the briefcase to read the open lock numbers. I only needed three. It wasn't Tattslotto, so the combinations weren't infinite.

'If I choose numbers, I choose ones easy to remember. Like my birthday,' Draga said.

'You mean day and month?'

'Yes, for me, fifteen October. Is one, five, one, nothing.'

'That's four numbers, Draga.'

'Maybe not much good idea,' she said and pulled a face.

'No, it is a good idea. See? The open lock fits with Rohan's birthday. He might have used someone else's birth date on the other one.'

I rolled the barrels, trying the dates for my birthday first and then Ant's. No go.

Ant. The sick feeling returned. What was I going to say? Morning, Ant, did you sleep well? By the way, I killed your father, shoved him in the boot of his car, and now it's been stolen.

Poor kid. Sure, his dad was selfish and distracted, but he was all the kid had, which showed how pathetic Ant's life was.

'Well, Ant or I aren't special enough. Our birthdays don't fit.' I shoved the briefcase aside. 'Nothing is important to Rohan except money, some old woman, and ...'

Draga fiddled with the gold cross around her neck. 'What is?'

'... and his Beemer.' The car! He couldn't be so twee as to use the last three digits of the registration number. I rolled the barrels: Three. Five. Two. The lock snapped open. The man's a moron. Correction – was a moron.

Draga picked up the apron hem with both hands and moved it side-to-side, accompanying a little jig. The pear-apple-plum print on it danced.

The briefcase held the finance section from an old copy of The Age, pens, notepads, and, under them all, Rohan's diary. I flipped to today's date.

Damn. He was going to a conference.

'From tomorrow's date, he's crossed out three days for ... it looks like Brisbane. There's a flight time marked here, Virgin at ... oh no, the flight's this morning.'

I imagined the airline staff calling his name over the public address system. Last chance to board.

'This good.' Draga quivered with excitement. 'You must say you not see him leave house to go plane. You must say you believe he go. You tell to everybody same thing. Even boy.' She placed her hands in a prayer position.

'Stop it, Draga.'

'We need much help.'

Her idea might just work. Rohan hadn't been home when we all went to bed. He must have come home when we were all asleep. I could say he left in the morning before I woke, as he often did.

The diary slipped and bounced onto the floorboards. Folded papers inserted between the pages escaped and fluttered onto the ground. I bent to collect the pieces of my dead husband's life: petrol receipts, business cards, and a bank statement that wasn't from our bank. The account was in Rohan's name. The balance made my vision swim. Three hundred and ninety-seven thousand dollars.

How did Rohan have this sort of money? And where did he

get it?

I read through the statement. Each deposit was an irregular amount, designated as 'Internet Transfer Regular Payment'. It didn't reveal anything about the source. All transactions were under the ten-thousand-dollar mark. Rohan had moved nearly forty thousand dollars into the account at the beginning of this month. At month's end, he'd withdrawn nineteen thousand in cash, in two transactions.

Could he be day trading or have a second job?

There was no logic to any of this, but logic currently played no role in my life.

'What you look, Missus Jac?' Draga asked. 'You face white like snow in my country.' She scurried off and returned with two glasses and a large carafe of water.

I waved the statement under her nose. 'I don't recognise this account. Look at all this money. What's he been doing with it? That ...' I yelled. 'That ... cheat! That cunning, deadhead, idiot, cheat ...'

'You say that one already,' Draga said.

'He has almost four hundred thousand dollars in an account. Why? How? A secret bank account can't be good.'

'Show to me.' Draga took the statement, and holding it at arm's length, tilted her head back to read it. She let out a long whistle. 'Majko moja! He can buy much new underpants with this money.'

She ignored the water and took a bottle of Jamieson Irish whisky from Rohan's bookshelf. She poured a glassful. 'I know is early, but sometime is not enough early.'

I reached for it, but she lifted it to her mouth and took a swig.

I'd never seen Draga drink alcohol. This degeneration in her behaviour must be the result of becoming my partner in crime.

She topped up her glass and poured a liberal dose into mine.

Slamming the whisky down in one gulp, it burned down my throat.

I returned to the statement. The page number was twenty-three. So, at one statement per month, the account had been active for at least two years. But this statement was six months old, leaving me wondering what had happened to the account since.

Draga shifted her gaze from the heavens and the bottle of whisky then topped up my glass. 'You must find what Mr Ruin do.'

We rifled every desk drawer in Rohan's study. Paper littered the floor. Draga upended the shredder in the hope of unearthing clues. Tattered paper covered her like confetti.

'There must be a clue here. Maybe he's hidden something somewhere, like behind the artwork, or taped under a drawer.' I lifted a painting off the wall. There was nothing except a faded patch where it had hung for too long.

'You watch too much the old movie,' Draga said, examining the filing cabinet's contents.

I sighed. She was right; this wasn't fiction. This was all too real.

I was a widow of my own making and I was sure I was a little drunk.

'Missus Jac, look!' Draga held up a manila envelope. 'I find on bottom with the stuck tape. Must be the big secret if Mr Ruin hide.'

I grabbed it, noting 'Personal' written in thick black ink across the front in Rohan's handwriting. The envelope edges had lightened in colour.

'Too many old movies, eh?' My hands shook as I ripped open the envelope and pulled out several documents. I shuffled the paperwork then stilled, recognising a life insurance company logo on one. The policy dated back to the time of our marriage; to the days when Rohan cared. I read it. Life insured:

Rohan Anthony Burne.

Insured amount: $1.5 million.

Beneficiary: Jacqueline Camilla Burne.

I lowered the document.

It confirmed me as the prime suspect.

CHAPTER THIRTEEN

With the policy in my hand, I stared at the wall. In the background, the phone trilled. The call went to message bank, chirped the notification tone, and then began to ring again. After the third time, I checked the number on the display and answered.

'Andrew, I can't talk now. I'll call you back.'

'There's a big problem. You have to come in as soon as possible.'

'Can't it ...'

'Chief, the database is gone,' Andrew said.

'Gone? How can it be gone?'

'I'll explain when you get here.'

At red lights, I banged my fist on the dashboard and abused slow drivers. The speedometer soared well above the speed limit. If Andrew was right, everything was blown – the tender and the business.

Paulette was in the tearoom where Andrew was trying to calm her down.

'I did what I always do,' she said. 'I entered the date, I pressed 'save'. I selected the usual report criteria and pressed the print button.' Paulette wiped smeared mascara with a balled-up tissue. She looked like a panda – an angry one. 'How dare you accuse me of screwing it up? I told you I didn't access any files.'

'I didn't mean to say ... but ...' Andrew said.

Paulette stood nose to nose with him. 'I didn't do anything different. I've done the same thing for two years and it's always been okay. You're supposed to be the IT guru, you work it out!' She folded her arms and glared.

'Quiet down both of you,' I shouted. They turned in unison. There was a short silence before Paulette launched into her tale of woe. Andrew tried to speak every time Paulette paused to draw breath.

I caught the gist of what Andrew had warned me about – reports, database, deleted.

The word 'deleted' was never a good one when it came to databases. Death and disaster were all around me. 'Let's go to my office and talk calmly,' I said.

Paulette threw Andrew a filthy look and stormed towards my office. Her ponytail swung like a thick whip.

Andrew sighed, and followed.

'Walk me through the problem,' I said.

Paulette pouted on the sofa, one long leg crossed over the other, her foot waggling, pumping up her anger. Andrew sat opposite, rubbing his palms together. A sheen of sweat covered his brow.

I glanced from one to the other. 'Come on, who wants to go first?'

'He's accused me of deleting all the data,' Paulette said in her 'revealing secrets of national security' voice. 'When I didn't.'

'Paulette, I'm sure you haven't done anything wrong. I can't imagine you can delete the whole database with one keystroke. Are you sure you can't access it?'

Paulette gave an exaggerated sigh. 'Nothing shows up. I ran the reports as usual. The same steps. Suddenly, I'm looking at a frozen screen. I refreshed it, but it didn't work. Then I rebooted, and I got a message I've never seen. Before you ask, I can't remember what it said. Then the screen went black and the PC crashed. I rang Andrew straightaway.' She glowered hard enough to make him sit back. 'He acted like it was all my fault.'

Andrew did a palms-up. 'I was just asking what you did, in case you did something different. Geez.'

'Well, I didn't. Why would I?'

'I wasn't saying you would, I was just saying.' Andrew's hand-rubbing was creating enough friction to start a fire.

Without the database, I didn't have a business. The tender was at risk because I couldn't run the final reports to include with it. I couldn't let my staff see my panic. Image is everything. 'Andrew, is the only problem that it's not generating reports?'

'Not just that. I can't access any data, not on anyone's computer. I checked.' Andrew scrunched his face. 'I can't figure out what the problem is yet. It could be a virus, but that's unlikely given the protections we have. It's similar to what I noticed the other day, only worse.'

'What about the offsite data backup service?' I asked. 'That's done daily. They'll have the data.'

'I rang them. I'm waiting on their call.'

'Then we'll wait.' My voice was shaky. 'We can't do anything else until the remote backup service confirms if they can restore it. At worst, we might only have lost one day's data. In the meantime, check everything again, Andrew. Let's get back to our desks and keep doing what we do best.'

Paulette stood, smoothed down her tight skirt, and shot Andrew a look saying she'd never forgive him. She stomped from the room.

Andrew pulled at his collar. Today, the Marx Brothers beamed from his tie.

'Chief, I didn't accuse her. Honest. It's just so weird.' A muscle in his jaw twitched.

'Let's see what the data recovery turns up,' I said. 'It might be something minor.'

Andrew folded his arms and rocked on his heels. 'You're taking this pretty well considering it might all be dead in the water.'

Dead by the water. My mind flashed to Rohan's body near the pool.

'I'm getting philosophical in my old age.' I smiled stiffly.

'Fair enough. Best get back to it. I'll check if we have network problems, too. I'll let you know as soon as I have anything.' He paused at the door. 'Geez, I almost forgot. The spy pen's been delivered. Let me know when you're ready for the next step.'

He left, taking the Marx boys with him. Even at their chaotic best, they could not create the level of turmoil I had in my life.

Andrew was right. Whatever had happened to the database software was weird. I wondered if it had something to do with Sandi, but she wasn't smart enough for something so sophisticated. Maybe it was just another glitch in a week of terrible events.

I decided to stay at the office until the issue was sorted, but I wanted to find out what was happening with Ant. I dialled home, but Draga didn't answer. I'd try again in a few minutes. This was exhausting. If only I could go to sleep and wake up in a shiny, new life. I was entertaining the idea of taking a nap at the desk when a new email notification pinged. The screen opened to a phone message: Geoff Campbell called while you were in the meeting. Please call him ASAP.

I spent ten minutes rehearsing surprised responses to Geoff Campbell's inevitable question: 'Where's Rohan?' I planned to stick to the story suggested by Draga. Whether he believed me depended on my following the script. If I slipped up, I'd have a long prison sentence to review my mistakes.

I rang Burne and Campbell, hoping Geoff was on another call so that I could leave a message and buy myself more time to refine my story.

After two rings, a lilting voice answered. 'Burne and Campbell Investments, this is Louise.'

'Louise, it's Jacqueline.' My voice quavered.

'Hello, Mrs Burne.'

Her greeting made me want to look around for my late mother-in-law; I'd given up asking Louise to use my first name a long time ago.

'I was returning Geoff's call. If he's busy I ...'

'I'll put you straight through.' A click and Geoff's voice came on the line.

'Jacqueline! What have you done with that husband of yours?' He laughed.

Even though I'd rehearsed, he took me by surprise. 'What do you mean?'

'He hasn't arrived at the conference.'

'I don't understand.'

I imagined Geoff scratching his nose as he did when he was thinking. He cleared his throat. 'I had a phone call from Robyn Scott, in our Brisbane office. She was expecting Rohan for a planning meeting today before the conference kicks off tomorrow, but he hasn't shown up. She called his hotel and so far, he hasn't checked in. I don't want to worry you, but I assumed you'd know where he is.'

I mentally consulted my handbook on Lying 101: mix surprise with innocence, a pinch of concern, stir well and don't volunteer information. 'Maybe he missed his flight.'

'When did you see him last?' Geoff must watch the same police procedurals I did.

'Last night.' A bit of truth sells the biggest lies. 'I didn't see him this morning.' Also true. He was gone by then, in every sense of the word. A slight croak added to my obvious concern – about me, not Rohan.

'You didn't?' Geoff paused, perhaps making an assessment. He was the type who kissed his wife goodbye every morning and wouldn't understand anyone else not doing the same. At functions, they still held hands. Another of life's mysteries – the enduring marriage.

'Some days our schedules get chaotic. We're like proverbial

ships in the night.' Except we'd hit a marine hazard. 'Perhaps Rohan changed his travel arrangements for some reason.'

'In that case, I'd expect he'd have let Robyn know,' Geoff said.

'Have you tried his mobile?'

'Several times. It went straight to voicemail.' There was impatience in Geoff's tone.

'He'd have the phone switched off if he's still on a later flight,' I said.

Damn. Where was Rohan's phone? It couldn't be in the house because Draga or I would have heard it ringing. It could have been in his pocket. If it was found, the only messages would be from Geoff and none from me. I'd have to ramp up my 'concerned wife' routine.

'Do you really think something's happened to him?' My hand went to my throat for emphasis; a wasted gesture, given we weren't on a video call. 'Should I call the police?'

'No, Jacqueline. That's a little premature. I didn't mean to alarm you.'

Luckily, I'd hit all the marks with my panicky wife portrayal.

'I'm not sure what else I can do, Geoff.' My voice was shrill, which worked in my favour.

Geoff rallied, and his tone softened. 'I apologise, Jacqueline. There's probably a simple explanation.'

Simple, but nothing like Geoff could imagine.

What if he knew about the other woman? He might think Rohan ran off with her and was checking to see what I knew. But why would he risk alerting me?

'I'll get the booking checked via the corporate travel agent,' he said. 'I suppose he could have swapped the flights for some reason. He'll turn up soon enough. I'll let you know when I hear he's arrived. Better still, I'll get him to call you.'

'I'd be grateful. And, of course, I'll let you know if I hear from him.'

Like that call was ever coming.

Geoff offered more reassurance and hung up.

My hand was damp on the receiver. My mobile buzzed and the screen lit with the home number. 'Draga, what's up?'

'Boy gone,' she said breathlessly.

'What do you mean, gone?'

'He not in room. Is empty and bed be made like I leave yesterday.' Draga's voice was shaky. 'I not have the good feeling.'

Had he gone out? For what? A newspaper? An early morning run? It wasn't Ant's style. 'Draga, check if his backpack or clothes are missing. Call me back.'

'Okay, Missus Jac.'

While I waited for Draga's call, I took a few minutes to consider my position.

First: Rohan. I dialled his mobile phone and left a message saying Geoff was looking for him. I ended with an anxious, 'Where are you? Everyone's getting worried.'

Second: the Beemer story. I didn't need to report it stolen. It not being in the garage when I left this morning could mean nothing if my 'ships in the night' metaphor held. Rohan could have driven himself to the airport without me knowing.

Third: Ant. Had he overheard – or worse – witnessed the events? If he had, would he keep quiet about it?

I was just beginning to consider the implications of the life insurance policy when Draga rang.

'Missus Jac, you be right. Boy backpack gone. He take half new clothes, too.'

'He might be heading back to Sydney.'

'Why he go so sudden? No, something be wrong.' Draga sounded more nervous about Ant than about Rohan.

'You've been in the house all morning?'

'I go hang some washing, but believe me, I see if boy come downstair. Maybe he go last night when we in garage?'

It was the only time Ant could have gone without one of us noticing. Still, the middle of the night was a strange time to leave. Our body disposing operation may have woken him, but I couldn't imagine he'd just walk away if he'd seen us. There must be something else. Something played at the edge of my mind, then I remembered the phone call I'd overheard. He'd sounded frightened. I recalled his expression as he ran from The Fast Anchor. It must all be connected.

'He has no way of getting anywhere unless he hitchhikes. The same way he got here.'

'Be better for him if he can drive,' Draga said, reviewing Ant's travel options.

'Even if he didn't see us with Rohan's body, he still could have taken the Beemer. We were changing our clothes. We wouldn't have seen him.'

'How he can drive Mr Ruin car?'

'I told him it was easy because it's an automatic transmission.' I now regretted my encouraging driving lessons.

'Bože moi!'

'Calm down, Draga. I'll come home as soon as I can.'

'I always calm.' She muttered something in Croatian, then the phone went dead.

I dialled Ant's mobile. There was no answer. If he had taken the car, he could be out there on a highway, unlicensed, and with his dad's body bouncing around in the boot. There was no way of knowing if he'd discovered Rohan. It wouldn't be a pretty find.

What if the police pulled him over?

I had about half a day – a day, max – before Rohan's disappearance began to look suspicious. It gave me around twenty-four hours in which to track down Ant, locate Rohan's body, and find an undiscoverable hidey place for him to rest in peace. Then I needed to get back the database, work out how to deal with the hamster, and finish the tender.

How hard could it all be?

The intercom buzzed as I was about to leave the office. I ignored it while I searched for tissues. My hands had been sweating all day. The waste paper bin was full of tissues I'd used to wipe them dry. I checked my face in my compact mirror. I hadn't done the fully made-up face today because I was too frazzled to live up to my 'image is everything' credo. I'd gone minimalist – foundation and mascara.

A second buzz jolted me from my seat. The compact slipped out of my damp hand and clattered to the floor. I picked it up. There was a crack in the mirror.

'Jacqueline, there are two police officers here to see you?' Paulette made the statement sound like a question.

Police? They must have found Rohan. I swallowed. 'I'll be right out.'

The desk tidied, I wiped my hands with yet another tissue and brushed down my skirt. I took a deep breath and, feigning confidence, marched into reception. I'd better not slip and refer to Rohan in the past tense.

Two men were in the foyer, their backs to me, looking at the wall art. No doubt taking in everything about my company, already on the search for clues.

'I'm Jacqueline Burne. May I help you?'

The taller one turned. Early forties, with a determined set to his jaw, he was impossibly good-looking. His hazel eyes bored into me. He held a compendium and his black jacket hung open, a lanyard around his neck. He introduced himself and flashed his identification. 'Detective Senior Constable Robert Angel.'

I stepped forward and extended my hand. I detected a scent of Bulgari Aqua.

Rohan's cologne. The scent reminded me to keep my story

straight or risk Detective Angel arresting me for murder. He hadn't stated the reason for his visit and I needed to be careful about jumping to conclusions, but any reason police came to your door must be bad.

His colleague, whose name I didn't catch, was shorter and thin. Skinny's posture emulated his partner's, and he had eagerness written all over him, from his oversized jacket to the high polish on his shoes.

We went to my office. Unbidden, Paulette arrived within seconds with a tray of coffees, her expression one of undisguised curiosity. No one spoke when she entered.

'I'll hold your calls,' she said.

In minutes, the office would be buzzing with news that the police were here.

They both declined my invitation to sit and the coffee.

'Mrs Burne, we're making enquiries regarding the whereabouts of your husband, Rohan Burne,' Detective Angel said. His eyes did a seeing-into-my-soul thing.

Despite what Geoff Campbell had said, he must have already contacted the police. Why so quickly?

'Forgive me, but I'm confused, Detective.' I said. 'Rohan's on his way to a conference. I spoke with his business partner earlier, who said he hadn't arrived yet, but he wasn't concerned. We thought he'd missed his flight.'

'Have you heard from him yet?'

'No, but we don't always know each other's exact movements.' I licked my lips.

Skinny wrote something on a notepad.

I shifted and fiddled with my wedding ring.

'Are you okay, Mrs Burne?' Robert Angel asked.

'Detective, are you suggesting something's happened to my husband?'

I placed my hand over my mouth in what I hoped was a sufficiently dramatic gesture.

'We're just making initial enquiries,' Detective Angel said, his expression unreadable.

I regarded him steadily. 'Enquiries into what?'

Detective Angel ignored my question. 'When did you last see your husband?'

I told him, watching his face for any sign of what he was thinking, but he was better at holding back what was going on in his head than I was. He must watch better quality crime shows.

'No contact since then?'

I shook my head. Unless I included the contact when I killed him. 'But I don't consider my husband "missing", just, shall we say, "late"?' The irony of the term wasn't lost on me.

Skinny scribbled more notes.

'People go missing for lots of reasons, sometimes by choice. They turn up when they're ready.' A look passed between Detective Angel and Skinny then back to me.

I straightened. 'Are you implying my husband's left me and not told me?' The idea might be a useful distracting twist. I held it together. 'That's ridiculous. Just because my husband hasn't arrived at his conference, doesn't mean he's left me. His company is checking his travel details, but I haven't heard back. I've tried calling his mobile. I'm not sure what else I can do.'

'Mr Campbell told us the same thing.'

So Geoff had spoken to them.

'When? I only spoke to him a short time ago.'

Was it suspicion I'd detected in Geoff's voice? He might know about the life insurance policy, especially if the firm brokered it. It might have been set up through the company. If he knew about Rohan's lover, it would add to the weight of suspicion against me. None of it explained why he would jump to conclusions so quickly.

This was getting more confusing and I was conscious of not asking the wrong questions or accidentally giving hints about my role in it all. Crime was hard work.

Detective Angel went on. 'Was your husband troubled about anything?'

'Not at all.' Beneath the desk, my legs twitched. I didn't intend to reveal anything about the conversation with Rohan and his talk of selling his share of the business to Geoff because I wasn't supposed to know. Geoff could tell them those details himself.

'Any financial difficulties?'

'We aren't broke if that's what you mean.' It wouldn't take long for them to discover Rohan's secret stash, especially when Rohan didn't turn up and they started digging. 'I can't speak for the financial status of my husband's business. I'm sure it's fine, but you should ask Geoff Campbell.'

'We've spoken to Mr Campbell on several previous occasions.'

I frowned. 'Previous occasions' meant the discussions had taken place before Rohan disappeared. 'I don't understand.'

Detective Angel wrote something on his notepad. 'Mr Campbell said Mr Burne appeared distracted lately. Do you think he was?'

'No.' Geoff hadn't mentioned that. What else had he kept from me?

'Was all well within your marriage?' Detective Angel asked.

'You're not married are you, Detective?' I nodded at his bare wedding finger. 'If you were, you'd know all married couples have their ups and downs.'

Robert Angel didn't blink. His eye colour was deeper than I'd first noticed.

Skinny kept writing. A novel at the rate he was going.

I shifted in my seat, every nerve in my body on high alert.

'Do you have a recent photograph of your husband?' Detective Angel asked.

'I might have something on my phone.' I scrolled down and

found one snapped at a charity dinner. Rohan, in a tuxedo, was suave and tanned with me smiling by his side. Our arms were around each other's waists, the ideal image to allay suspicion. Looking at it now, my smile appeared insincere, and my pose stiff. I gazed at the photo for a few seconds longer than necessary.

'Mrs Burne?'

'Will this do?' I handed him the phone and he passed it to Skinny, never taking his eyes off me.

I looked away.

Skinny examined the snap and handed the phone back.

I sniffed.

Robert Angel reached for the tissue box propped on the desk corner and offered it to me.

'Thanks.' I took one and blew my nose hard.

The street scene outside my window was the same as every other day. Ordinary people's lives went on; café tables filled with patrons, thrumming traffic. The world was full of women who hadn't killed their husbands. I bit my lip while the time stretched.

'Mrs Burne, is there something else?' Detective Angel asked, his voice a little softer yet still firm.

'You tell me. You turn up here saying you've been talking to my husband's business partner for some time, but you won't say why. You're implying my husband is missing, yet you have no evidence.'

Another Oscar-worthy performance during which I sounded indignant but distraught. My head hurt, and stress was burning a hole in my stomach. I hoped what little mascara I wore had run enough to create a doe-eyed look of innocence.

What did the police know already? And what was going on with Geoff?

I took another tissue and dabbed my nose. 'I don't know anything else.'

'Often people know more than they realise. Any little detail is helpful,' Detective Angel said.

I rubbed my forehead. 'I can't think of anything.'

He lowered his compendium. It was Skinny's signal to put pocket his pen and notepad. 'Thank you, Mrs Burne.'

I stood and hurried to open the door.

'One more thing,' Detective Angel said. 'How does your husband usually travel to the airport?'

'It varies. Cab, or sometimes his car.'

Skinny whipped out his notepad, and his pen scratched up a frenzy.

'Which was it on this occasion?' Detective Angel asked.

'Um ...' I'd already rehearsed this, but my thoughts jumbled. If I said 'cab', I'd have to explain the missing Beemer. If I said 'car', I might trip myself up, especially if they'd already checked cab bookings. I had seconds to decide my answer before it looked as though I was thinking too long.

'I don't know for sure. His car was gone this morning, so I assume it was by car.'

'You're not certain?'

'I'm not. All I know is the car wasn't in the garage. I can't see how it's connected to all your questions.'

'It's our job to make the connections, Mrs Burne.'

'Well, I guess it's one of those "helpful little details" then,' I said, and glared at him.

He stared back, and my mouth went dry.

Skinny unpocketed a mobile phone and stepped outside, leaving the door ajar.

Robert Angel offered his card. 'If you think of anything else.'

'Of course.' I eavesdropped on Skinny's phone conversation and caught the words 'vehicle' and 'possibly missing'. He returned, and a look passed between them.

'We'll be talking with you further, Mrs Burne. Please email

a copy of your husband's photograph,' Detective Angel said.

As soon as they left, I slumped into my chair, rattled by the memory of his gaze on me. The scent of his aftershave lingered. One meeting with Detective Robert Angel and already I knew he wasn't the type to give up.

I checked his contact details.

It was the second business card this week that had brought me a whole lot of trouble.

CHAPTER FOURTEEN

In between trying to contact Ant, I used the day to placate Paulette and partially repair her relationship with Andrew. He'd spent ages on the phone with the database recovery company. Finally, he called the techs in and we were forced to wait for a full report.

It was late when I went home with my hopes in tatters.

The landline phone was ringing as I entered. Somewhere in the house, the vacuum cleaner whined. The phone shrilled on, drilling into my head, and I fumbled the folders I was carrying. They slipped, and I danced the quickstep, trying to balance them. I dropped my handbag then the files, which spilled onto the carpet as I lifted the handset.

'Hello?' There was nothing except the cavernous echo of an empty line. 'Hello?'

'You're gunna pay.' The voice was male and rough as rusted metal.

'Who is this?'

'Ya know who it is,' the voice said.

'I don't. What do you want?' A few beats passed before there was a loud click and he was gone.

I cradled the receiver, my pulse quickening. There was only one explanation. Someone must know what I'd done. I had no idea who, or how he'd found out. Pay for what? Was he going to blackmail me?

I took the phone off the hook and breathed deeply, then scooped to gather the scattered documents. I needed peace to think about my conversation with Detective Robert Angel, and to work out the next steps in developing the tender.

Draga was in the lounge, in a cleaning trance, arms pumping the vacuum cleaner back and forth. It droned while she grunted in harmony, eyes gleaming with frenzied energy. Her grey curls were flat and there was a damp V on her blouse.

The house was already like a display home. A scientist with a high-powered microscope would be hard-pressed to find a speck of dust.

As Draga worked, her gold cross oscillated to-and-fro on its chain. I considered telling her about the weird phone call, but she was already helping me out of a difficult spot so why give her extra stress.

I raised my voice over the vacuum cleaner's whine, 'Hi, Draga.'

She waved and kept going.

A half-hour later, the high-pitched vac sound was driving me mad. I stomped my foot on the vac's power button. It whimpered into silence.

Draga shook the handle a few times, pulled off the sweeper's head, and peered into the tube. 'What happen?'

'Enough with the cleaning. What's wrong with you?'

'With me?' She lifted the apron hem and wiped her neck. 'How you can ask me such thing? We have big problem and when is big problem, I clean. Make me be relax.'

'You've been at it for an hour,' I said.

'Problem not look the clock.' She moved to press the power button on, but I grabbed the vac handle. We wrestled it back and forth.

'Let it go, Little John.' I squeezed the words through clenched teeth.

Draga released it and I stumbled back and landed on the sofa.

'Who be John? You find other man to make more trouble?' Draga made her best school principal face.

'It's a joke. You know Little John from Robin Hood?'

'This not time for joke. I not know anyone call that name. Mr Ruin dead. Boy gone. Somebody try hurt you business. Hurt you. Maybe kill you.' She slapped her hands to her cheeks. 'Or worse.'

'Don't be ridiculous, Draga,' I said, despite the threatening phone call replaying in my mind.

'I scare. Believe me, when I scare mean something be bad.' Draga took her glasses off and cleaned the lens with her apron. Her hands shook as she put her glasses on again.

My actions had made her like this. She wasn't the strong, dependable woman I was used to. The one who cared for me and who I took for granted.

My fantasy about killing Rohan was simpler than the reality. I wished I could go back in time and make this whole mess disappear. I'd file for divorce and bugger the cost. Rohan could have the house; I'd have the housekeeper. Simple.

But it could never happen.

'I'm sorry, Draga.' My voice cracked.

'Is okay, Missus Jac.' She sighed and leaned on the vacuum handle.

'Any sign of Ant?' I asked.

She dabbed her forehead with her apron again. 'I try to call him many times on mobility phone. He not answer.'

'Same here.' I wondered where Ant was and what he knew. More importantly, was he safe? I kicked off my shoes and flopped onto the sofa. 'The police came to my work today,'

'Police? Johi meni! What police say?'

I filled her in on the conversation with Detective Angel, leaving out the bit about his good looks and nice eyes.

Draga clutched the vac handle the whole time, but didn't say a word.

Aside from the fridge humming in the kitchen, the house was quiet. The aroma of polish Draga had layered onto the furniture mingled with the scent of the lavender candles she'd lit. If I could rid myself of my guilt about killing Rohan, the worry about Ant, and my company's woes, I'd almost be on the verge of relaxing.

The doorbell buzzed, shattering the peace.

Draga dropped the cleaner handle. It clattered onto the floor and bounced with a clang.

Our eyes locked in an unasked question.

'Pretend we not home,' Draga said.

'Whoever it is must know someone's here. The lights are on and you're making enough noise to wake the dead,' I whispered, before realising my poor choice of phrase.

'Maybe be somebody want hurt you.'

'They wouldn't ring the doorbell first.'

'Okay,' she said. 'But I not trust you go to door by youself.'

'If you insist, you can tag along.'

'Wait...' She waddled to the kitchen, rummaged in the utensil drawer, and returned with a meat mallet.

I pinched the bridge of my nose. 'What are you going to do with that?'

'My best broom go, remember? I must have something in hand. Help me think.'

We went to the door, butted up against one another like characters in a comedy sketch; me leading with Draga shadowing behind. The doorbell rang again, long, and insistent. I pulled up and Draga thudded into my back. I caught a whiff of bleach.

'Who is it?' I called.

'Police.'

Damn I knew that voice. I opened the door.

'Detective Angel.' I went into my concerned wife character. 'Have you located my husband?'

'I'm sorry to disturb you, Mrs Burne.'

Even at day's end, he still looked smooth; clean-shaven with no creases in his shirt and no evidence of the hours he'd put in

– investigating me, I suspected. Colour flooded my cheeks.

Behind him stood a uniformed officer, a young woman with petite features and an unreadable expression. I found myself staring down at her sensible shoes. Anything to avoid Robert Angel's gaze.

'May we come in?' he asked.

In my peripheral vision, Draga sidled away, the mallet behind her back, her face a portrait of guilt. She slipped her weapon under a scatter cushion on the sofa.

I leaned on the door for support and waved Robert Angel and his companion through.

'What is it, Detective?'

'Mrs Burne, you should take a seat,' he said.

I went ahead of him, imagining his eyes boring into the back of my head, reading my thoughts, and confirming my guilt. I sank onto the sofa and folded my arms as if that would protect me.

Detective Angel remained standing. His offsider took up her position behind him. She scanned the room and glanced down the corridor, sponging up information no doubt.

Draga groaned as she lowered her bulk into a chair. Her face was ashen, and her mouth, tight. The apron she wore was grimy and her cardigan sleeves were frayed.

Everything was wearing thin. Draga, me, life.

'And you are ...?' Detective Angel asked, looking at her.

'This is Draga,' I said. 'Whatever you have to say, you can say in front of her.'

I braced, expecting to hear 'Jacqueline Camilla Burne, I am arresting you for the murder of ...' I couldn't bear to think of the rest.

At least being arrested in a seated position meant I wouldn't have far to fall if I fainted. I waited for him to give the spiel and encircle my wrist with handcuffs, or cable ties – whatever was used these days.

Instead, Detective Angel said, 'This is Constable Petra Evans.'

Petite, with short, red hair and dark-framed glasses, Evans looked around twelve. I'd probably be her first arrest.

'Constable Evans is with Victim Support.'

I blinked. 'Victim support?' If she wanted to support Rohan, she'd need to be psychic.

Evans nodded curtly. She had a stern look for someone who was supposed to provide consolation.

'Mrs Burne, we've located your husband's vehicle,' Detective Angel said.

I swallowed. 'Where?'

'It was located at the Skeleton Creek wetlands.'

I waited for him to reveal Rohan's body had been discovered.

'The vehicle's been destroyed.'

'Destroyed?'

'It appears it was deliberately set alight. Burnt out.'

The wetlands fire. Could it have been the BMW? I threw Draga a look hoping both officers would interpret it as shock. I was in shock, thinking of Rohan's body burning to a crisp. Cremated in his beloved Beemer. I shuddered.

'We suspect it might be connected with your husband's disappearance.'

I straightened. No talk of a body? 'Disappearance?'

'He might have left voluntarily, but it's also possible he's come to harm. He might be a victim of an assault, or someone could be holding him.'

'You think he's been kidnapped?' Who kidnaps a dead man?

I wiped damp palms along the front of my skirt. A network of creases had appeared between Draga's brows and her face was now the colour of alabaster.

Robert Angel went on. 'It's too early to say definitively. We have several lines of enquiry. One is that it was an attempt to get rid of evidence.'

'Evidence of what?'

'We have blood. Subject to DNA confirmation, we believe it belongs to your husband.'

'Blood? Where?' This must be the part where he mentions the body.

'On a section of a rug that survived the fire. We wondered if you could identify it.' He pulled out a photograph, which showed one unsinged corner.

'We had a rug like that.' My voice was a whisper.

'Had? You no longer have it?'

'It used to be in the garage, but I haven't seen it for a long time. I assumed Rohan got rid of it.' If lying was an Olympic event, I'd win the gold medal.

Detective Angel leaned forward and my insides vibrated. 'I realise this is difficult. But I need to ask you a few more questions. It would help with finding out what's happened to Mr Burne.'

I nodded as if that was something I wanted.

'Have you had any communication with your husband since we last spoke?'

'No. I've tried his mobile several times. It goes to message bank.'

'Our inquiries indicate your husband hasn't accessed his personal or work email, phone or bank accounts since he was last seen.'

I wondered if Detective Angel knew about the extra bank account. I put on a horrified expression. 'Then you do believe someone has him?'

'We're looking at all possibilities. Have you noticed any strangers around your property?'

'No.'

He glanced at Draga who shook her head.

'Any other odd events in recent days?'

Rohan dead, Ant missing, nasty phone calls, data missing, scheming employees.

'No.'

'Okay. We'll need something for DNA testing. Perhaps your husband's toothbrush?'

'I get Mr Ruin brush for the teeth,' Draga volunteered. She climbed the stairs slowly.

'That's all for now, Mrs Burne.' Robert Angel said. 'We'll be in touch when forensics has something for us. We might have further questions.'

I had a big one of my own: where was Rohan's body?

He handed over a card and told me to come to the police complex at 11am tomorrow to make a formal statement. My hand shook as I took it.

Evans shot me a sympathetic 'poor wife of a kidnapped businessman' look. Not particularly helpful. She wouldn't have been my recruitment choice.

Draga came with the toothbrush, which the detective bagged. She waved them off at the front door. 'You go, Mr Detective. Bye-bye.'

She snapped the lock shut. 'Who want to steal dead man? You can do nothing with dead man.'

Rohan couldn't be wandering the countryside. Whoever took the car must have found him and dumped him elsewhere. But it made no sense to do that then leave the rug behind. My mind went back to Ant, but he wouldn't have had the strength to lift a dead weight, to say nothing of being in shock on its discovery.

The car thief might be someone Rohan had upset. He would have his fair share of enemies. He'd made a few dud business deals over the years. There was still the mystery of his secret money. There must be a shortlist of other suspects, even if I was still at the top.

I drew in a sharp breath at a terrifying possibility. 'What if Rohan's not dead? What if we just thought he was?'

'He look much dead,' Draga said.

'But it's the only thing that explains what's happened. He must have walked away and burned the car to cover it up.'

'He not burn car, Missus Jac. He die first before he do such thing.'

True. Besides, had Rohan been alive, he would have come back, if only to have me arrested for assault. I had a vision of the blood at the poolside and a wave of nausea washed over me.

'Draga, you have to come with me when I go to the police station. They never tell you anything until you're in the room. They might know about the insurance policy and the bank account. Detective Angel could be lying about not having found the body just to trap me. They might arrest me once I'm there.'

'And what I do if you be arrest?'

'Raise bail.'

Draga rubbed her temples. 'This day be too much for me. I go lie on bed and say my prayers.'

Praying was a definite conflict of interest for someone who was an accessory after the murderous fact. 'Does praying help, Draga?'

'Of course. I like to pray and read Bible, too. It help me lead good life,' she said with a look of satisfaction.

She must be reading from the Book of Loopholes.

After Draga went upstairs, I realised I hadn't eaten dinner and she hadn't offered to cook. Draga deserting the kitchen was a concrete sign that things were falling apart.

I put bread in the toaster, and then checked my phone for any messages. There was nothing from Ant. I debated whether to call Triple-T to check if he'd had turned up in Sydney but decided against it. If he had, I'd look like an idiot for not knowing his movements. At least I'd know he was safe.

Yet there was no logical reason for Ant to go back and there was no logical reason for him to have left Melbourne without explanation. My mind was searching for alternative reasons when the doorbell rang.

Ant! I ran to the door and flung it open to reveal an empty doorstep.

The sound of a muffler further down the street floated over the still air and somewhere a car horn sounded, and then the street went quiet, save for the sea's muted waves. I stepped outside to get a better look. My bare foot squelched into something wet and slimy. I looked down. Dog poop.

The stink hit me, and I reeled. Those stupid kids from up the road. I should go talk to their mother, but at the moment it wasn't a priority.

Screwing up my nose, I hopped to the garden hose and sprayed off the muck. I didn't have the energy to clean the step. It could wait until morning.

In the shower, I sat on the floor and let the water run over me while I listed my options. There weren't any when it came to Rohan, but I should leave a few messages in an extra anxious voice on his voicemail, and I'd keep trying to call Ant.

Escaping a murder charge was my biggest problem, but I still needed to deal with All Class's troubles. If we could recover the database, there would still be time to finalise the tender. As for Sandi, if I could find a way to trip her up, get her to show her hand, I might come up with some ammunition and a full understanding of her scheme.

I mused on the changes in her. She was now sour and obstructive. She didn't care about her job or her co-workers. The only time I'd seen her relaxed and happy was at 'Kmuck' with Jason. She'd been giving him adoring looks like he was her spiritual guru and she'd follow him anywhere. I pictured it in my mind, Jason striding along, Sandi disciple-like behind him.

I wondered what she'd do if Jason went somewhere she

couldn't follow: a long overseas holiday, a sabbatical, a new job. She'd hate that. I imagined the look on Sandi's face if Jason deserted her. That's when it came to me – Sandi's weak spot.

Why hadn't I thought of it before?

I emerged wrinkled, but nurturing a glimmer of hope. I fell into bed, where I slept in short bursts and dreamed Evans was teaching Draga how to cook, Detective Robert Angel was dancing with Sandi, and Jason Keene and Rohan were arguing over who got to run me over in the Beemer. I'd woken with a sharp intake of air.

At 6am, I pulled on shorts and a t-shirt and went into the garage where I stood for a minute staring guiltily at the space where Rohan's car should be. I shook away my thoughts and found the shovel I'd come in for.

In the cool morning, the dog poop was still soft but didn't smell as much. It slid easily onto the shovel's plate and onto sheets of newspaper. I binned the parcel and hosed off the stains with a final spray.

A few minutes later, Draga joined me in the kitchen where I'd made coffee and toasted raisin bread.

'No boy, Missus Jac?' she asked.

'No boy.' I yawned.

'You not sleep?'

'Not much.'

'Me, too. I stay awake think what we do next.'

'And?'

'My mind is like empty cupboard,' Draga said.

'Well, at least I have a plan for my work problem.'

'What be this plan?'

'I'm going to trick Sandi into revealing what she's up to. She won't even realise she's doing it.'

'How you do?' Draga sniffed the coffee I'd made and screwed up her nose.

'I'm going to lie my heart out.' I toasted Draga with my mug.

Draga gave me an appraising look. 'If you can kill somebody, then tell big lie be easy for you.'

Yet another skill to add to my expanding criminal CV.

CHAPTER FIFTEEN

During the drive to work I reviewed my plan to trap Sandi. Confronting her and immediately firing her was the logical option, but I wanted her to suffer first. Someone in this life had to suffer other than me. I wanted Sandi to cut her own throat and this morning I planned to hand her the knife. I swallowed hard, remembering I also had to an appointment with Detective Angel later. Big day ahead.

As soon as I arrived at All Class, I sought out Andrew.

'What's the latest with the data recovery?'

'The techs have found something. Some kind of virus. Sounds positive,' he said.

'But not guaranteed?'

Andrew made a face. 'I wish I had better news.'

'It's a start. Another thing, I'm calling a meeting with all our divisional heads. While they're in there, I want you to plant the spy pen in Sandi's office.'

'Yes.' He pumped his fist in the air, making the Superman on his tie dance.

'Don't get excited. Leave it by the landline phone.'

'Am I allowed to know why she's got a beef with you?'

'I'll tell you if my scheme works.'

Andrew saluted. 'No worries, Chief.'

'And don't tell anyone.'

'As if I would,' he said. He left the office with the coolness of 007.

Fifteen minutes later, I stood at the meeting room door, balancing a stack of files I'd grabbed at random from the filing cabinet. Experience taught me a tower of unquantified paperwork could bring focus. The only real documents I needed for the meeting were an agenda, a sheath of pages containing rough data for the tender, and an organisational chart I'd cobbled together. I was ready.

The metal handle was slippery under my damp palm as I opened the door.

'Thanks for dropping everything for this meeting,' I said, looking at Sandi who checked her watch.

'We were wondering what's going on,' Claire said.

Sandi examined her fingernails.

'Well ...' I dumped the documents onto the table. Thwack.

Claire straightened her spine, Will his tie.

Sandi flinched, a hint of curiosity in her expression.

I stepped to the side buffet and poured coffee. The rattle of crockery jarred against the air conditioning's quiet hum.

'Anyone else?' My fingers were tense around the cup handle.

Once seated, my shaking legs were out of sight. I pressed my feet into the carpet. I gathered my wits while I made a show of looking for something among the documents.

'I realise you're all busy. I promise to get through the agenda quickly.'

I slid copies of it across the table.

The boardroom door opened a crack and Paulette's head appeared. 'This meeting wasn't on my planner. Do you need anything?'

'No, thanks, Paulette. It's an informal get together.'

She made a relieved face and left.

I distributed the tender data documents, which included a copy of an organisational chart. 'I'll give everyone a few minutes to go through the items.'

I feigned perusing the material while I waited for reactions.

Will flipped the pages and tugged his collar. Politically astute, he'd expect a hidden agenda. He scanned and turned over each page, his frown tightening.

Claire sat with perfect posture. She placed each turned page neatly over the previous one before reading.

Sandi swivelled her chair to face the window and crossed her long legs. She sighed, loudly enough for the others to glance at her, and began to read.

A prickling sensation started at the base of my neck. I hoped my face wouldn't turn red, or that I'd say too much too quickly.

Will shuffled. He fished out a folded handkerchief and honked into it then went back to the documents.

Claire finished reading and rested her hands on the neat pile of paperwork. Her frown had disappeared.

Sandi's free hand draped over the armrest. Casual chic, that's Sandi. One stilettoed foot jiggled, the leather sheen catching the morning sun. The shoe stilled.

I suppressed a smile. I'd love to see her expression. I stared at her back, willing her to turn.

Will found his voice. 'Is all this necessary, Jac?'

'The performance figures suggest it's the best strategy, Will.'

'This new organisational structure is ... I mean ... bringing someone in over our heads is unexpected.' He dabbed his forehead with the handkerchief then adjusted his blue power tie.

'Might any of us lose our jobs?' Claire asked without ire. As she spoke, she might have been formulating a list of firms interested in her résumé. If she was, it didn't show.

I didn't intend to lose her or Will. 'Absolutely not. There won't be job losses.'

'That's a relief,' Claire said, and Will pocketed his handkerchief.

Sandi spun around. Her hands stretched flat on the table, fingertips splayed. Her chest rose and fell rapidly. 'Why weren't we consulted about these changes?'

'As CEO, I decide what happens in my own company.' My

knees played an audible paradiddle on the table's underside.

Will tilted his head and frowned.

Sandi didn't miss a beat. 'I wasn't questioning your authority.'

I wanted to say, 'Yes, you were.'

'We have bonuses tied to divisional performance. This level of restructuring affects them.' Sandi emphasised her point by tapping her index finger on the papers. 'It's unfair.'

Now she develops a moral compass.

'She has a point, Jac,' Will said. His Adam's apple made a long dip up and down.

'Yes, the bonuses.' Claire's eyebrows rose a millimetre. 'How will they be handled if this goes ahead?'

'Not if, when,' I said. I should have this conversation privately with each Divisional Head, but I wanted Sandi to squirm publicly.

Sandi scribbled on her notepad, her Mont Blanc pen leaving a black ink trail in its wake.

I'd given her the pen after her first year with the company in the days her loyalty wasn't in question. I hoped she'd written something along the lines of Note to self. Next time I rip off my employer, don't get caught.

Except she didn't yet know I was onto her scheme.

'What's behind this?' Sandi's voice developed a shrill edge. Her rapid breathing threatened to pop the top button of her tight blouse.

'I've been rethinking the best options for our service delivery should we be successful in the tender. I want to make sure we're prepared.' I kept my tone even.

'You still think we have a chance at that?' Sandi asked. 'I mean, there's a database problem, you can't get the final documents together.'

'It's sorted,' I said, clinging to Andrew's brief comment about the techs' work.

Sandi glowered. 'It's resolved?'

'Almost.'

Sandi turned to stare out the window.

'Good to hear, Jac,' Will said, as he fumbled for his handkerchief. 'But given we don't usually tender for this sort of work, it seems overkill to change the entire company. What happens if we're unsuccessful? We'll have an expensive structure for no reason.'

'We have as good a chance as any other recruitment firm. We have the capability, and the tender is lucrative. It would more than cover the additional costs incurred.'

How could I tell any of them that All Class couldn't afford to lose the tender, or that there was no guarantee it would reach submission point.

'Are you sure we could handle the extra workload? We already ...'

Claire asked.

Sandi put her palm up to Claire. The stone in her expensive dress ring flashed.

I bet she bought it for herself with money ripped off from my company.

'Never mind the workload. I still don't see why it means we need a new level of management over us,' she said.

'It'll be a smoother process having someone dedicated to planning and development. Yesterday's database problem shows we need to oversee operations more closely,' I said.

'Why can't one of us manage the workload? All Divisions are on target. I'm sure Permanent Placement is,' Sandi said, her face reddening.

Did she really think I hadn't checked her figures in detail?

'That's not right. Contracting is below target this quarter,' Will said.

Claire made a wobbly hand movement. 'Temporary's a fraction under.'

Sandi shot her a dark look.

Claire leaned back as if she'd been slapped. 'I'm sure it's not news to Jac, Sandi.' She pointed to the files at my elbow.

Sandi's lips compressed into an angry line.

This was the best fun I'd had all week.

'It's ridiculous.' Sandi spat the words out. 'Surely we can make the tender process a one-off project. Why change the reporting relationships? It will affect us in so many ways. After all, we're dedicated to this company.' She pouted.

Dedicated? I wished I could sack her immediately and have her charged with ... something. Sandi in prison, without her makeup bag, was a comforting idea.

Then I remembered I might be in the next cell.

Still, I wanted more than a pound of flesh. The more I looked at her, the more my blood pressure rose but this wasn't the time for hot emotions. I refocused. 'I'm bringing in someone external.'

'You've already decided on someone, haven't you?' Sandi sat up tall, her voice icy.

'There is an obvious candidate, yes.' I swivelled my chair side-to-side and looked up at the ceiling. The only sounds were the muted office noises beyond the meeting room door where it was business as usual.

The group held a collective breath. Thoughts would be racing. I knew because I read people well, even though I wasn't so good at it on the home front. Nobody was going to screw with me anymore, especially Sandi Watson.

'Who is it?' Sandi tapped her pen against her mouth's sticky lustre.

Andrew poked his head around the door. 'Chief, I took care of that matter you wanted me to look into.'

'Thanks, Andrew.' I turned back to the expectant faces around the table.

'Well?' Sandi asked.

'I'm making an offer of re-employment to Jason Keene.' I casually picked a speck of lint from my jacket, glad I chose to wear red today. The colour was right for my fiery mood. 'And I'm confident he'll accept.'

Sandi dropped her pen.

'Really, after everything that happened with him last year?' Will asked.

'He does know the industry well,' Claire said. 'It could be quite good for the business. If we can get past ... well ... past the past.'

'I'm sure we can come to an understanding. Jason has more experience now. Besides, I want to do what's best for All Class,' I said, still watching Sandi.

Through her flawlessly applied spray tan, I swear Sandi paled.

The trap was set. All I had to do now was wait for it to spring.

'Okay, everyone. Please look over the figures and come back with any amendments.'

Andrew was in my office when I returned from the meeting.

'I put the pen on the desk as instructed. It's near the landline phone in case she uses it instead of her mobile. The battery lasts for ages, which means we have a good chance of getting something,' he said. 'We just have to hope she won't notice it.'

'You're gold, Andrew.' I checked my watch. I was due at the police complex. 'I have an appointment. I'm relying on you to keep an eye on her. I want to know everything. How long she stays in her office, what she tries to access on the database, if she leaves the building. Anything.'

'Sure thing.' He couldn't stop grinning.

'You'd wear a superhero cape if I got you one, wouldn't you?' I asked.

'It's like playing online spy games for real. Minus the weapons of course.'

I sighed. The notion of a weapon – a bat, a gun, or a missile – was damn tempting.

Draga was waiting at the front door when I returned home to collect her before heading to the meeting with Detective Angel. I checked my watch. We'd get there just in time. I didn't want to risk a speeding ticket. With my burgeoning list of criminal activity, what did it matter?

'Thanks for coming with me, Draga.'

'I not mind, Missus Jac. I like go new places.'

'It's a police interview, not a picnic.'

'For you, da. For me be something new.'

As I drove, my thoughts pinged. What questions would he ask? And could I answer them without digging myself into a bigger hole?

A diet of television police procedural reruns had taught me cops weren't dumb.

'You not talk much, Missus Jac.'

'I'm saving all my words for the interview.'

I parked and then pulled a tissue out of my bag. In the rear-view mirror, I wiped off most of my makeup.

'Why you take the muckup off you face?'

'The wife of a possible kidnap victim shouldn't be wearing makeup,' I said. 'I'm supposed to be concerned with his disappearance, not my appearance.'

Draga tutted. My clever language was wasted on her. I hoped it wouldn't be wasted on Detective Angel.

We walked to the police complex in silence. The doors slid apart and beeped as we went through. The parchment-toned walls were covered with a mix of old and new posters: local youth initiatives, domestic violence support, and

Crimestoppers. There were pictures with brief descriptions of wanted persons. I imagined my mugshot alongside them. I couldn't be one of those people – a criminal on the run. Yet I was.

Draga used an embroidered handkerchief to flick dust off a waiting room chair. She dropped onto it with a grunt then scanned the foyer. 'Not much clean,' she said as if she'd solved a major crime.

The glass reception booth was unattended. The buzzer summoned a ruddy-faced, due-for-retirement-aged constable from behind a secure door. Folds of flesh, restrained by his shirt, cascaded over his belt.

'Help you?' he asked and scratched behind his ear.

'Jacqueline Burne. I have an appointment at eleven with Detective Robert Angel.'

He checked the wall clock.

'Yes, I'm fifteen minutes early,' I said.

'I'll let him know you're here.' He puffed heavily as he pulled the inner door's handle and disappeared.

'You safe if he in charge,' Draga said. 'He not can run fast to catch you.' She signalled for me to stop, then wiped the chair next to her before I sat.

We waited, with Draga muttering and me fighting down nausea. I fumbled at the bottom of my handbag for a mint. The bag fell, and the contents scattered. We both got down on the floor.

Draga picked up my wallet. It flipped open to the plastic pocket containing a faded photograph of Rohan and me.

My gaze lingered on it. Yes, Rohan was a pig. Yes, he cheated – but the man had a child. At some point, I'd have to face Ant and I still had no idea what to say.

Draga laid her chubby hand over mine. 'Is okay, Missus Jac.'

A side door into the waiting room swept open and Robert Angel appeared. He opened his mouth to speak then stopped at the sight of us on the floor, me quivering and Draga clucking.

Evans peered from behind him.

Her expression said she had her work cut out for her.

CHAPTER SIXTEEN

The interview room was windowless and painted dove grey. A table with recording equipment on it was pressed against the far wall.

'Take a seat, Mrs Burne.' Detective Angel pulled out one of the black vinyl chairs and sat opposite me.

'Thank you.'

He put down a thick manila folder and extracted a notepad.

Evans came in with a glass of water and placed it in front of me. 'There you go.'

It was the most talkative she'd ever been. But then, listening was supposed to be her best skill.

I was glad of the chair's support and the glass of water providing a distracting prop. 'This is like in the movies,' I said.

'Not quite.' Detective Angel removed a pen from his pocket and clicked it. The noise echoed in the room. He scribbled a few lines on the paper until the ink flowed.

Evans took a seat next to him.

I avoided looking at her and wished Draga was beside me. I imagined her in the waiting area, brow furrowed, dividing her concern between the state of its cleanliness and what was happening in here.

Detective Angel fiddled with the buttons on the recording equipment. It lit up and numbers flipped over on the LCD.

'Our conversation today is being recorded. It will be transcribed for your review and signature later. For the tape, please state your full name, address, and occupation.'

'Jacqueline Camilla Burne. Company Director.' I added my address.

'Thank you. Mrs Burne, we've spoken before about the sequence of events, but I'd like you to go through them again. Take all the time you need.'

The air conditioning pumped cold air and goosebumps rose on my arms. How long would it be before I said, 'I killed my husband.' Adding, 'It was an accident,' wouldn't make it any less of a problem.

'Perhaps start with when you last spoke to or saw your husband.'

Robert Angel's voice was gentle. Maybe I had some sympathy on my side.

'The day before he disappeared, should I say the day before I last saw him, he said he was going to a conference.' My words sounded like they were scraping along a pipe, emerging broken and crackling. 'Actually, I'm not entirely sure about that. I might have assumed. He's had so much on lately.' Including the fire-hair lady. 'When I woke up, he was gone – to work, I guessed. Then Geoff Campbell called to say Rohan hadn't arrived at the conference.'

Detective Angel jotted something in his notepad. 'You weren't concerned?'

'As I've said before, I thought maybe he'd missed his flight.'

'Would he normally let you know?'

'We don't report to one another,' I snapped. I clasped my hands in front of me.

'What I mean is, we often miss seeing each other for a few days. So, no, he wouldn't normally let me know he'd missed a plane. I wasn't worried at first, but after Geoff called, I rang Rohan's mobile several times. He didn't pick up. I left messages but didn't hear back.'

I licked dry lips, and eyed the glass of water, but didn't touch it. I'd watched enough television to know it's a sure way to give up your DNA.

'You didn't think to call the police?' Detective Angel asked.

'No. It wasn't a problem.' I must sound callous.

'Go on, Mrs Burne.'

'I didn't hear from Rohan that evening. I left more messages on his voicemail. I figured he'd be in touch when he got around to listening to them.'

'Anything out of the ordinary occur that day or night?'

'I told you last time we spoke, Detective. The only thing I noticed was his car missing, but I assumed he'd taken it to the airport and left it with a parking service. I didn't give it another thought until you arrived at my office.'

I met his eyes, hoping it would make me appear truthful, but it just made me more rattled. The vinyl seat squeaked as the fabric of my dress unstuck when I shifted.

Detective Angel rested his chin in his palm, and I noticed a dimple. 'Tell me again about the vehicle.'

'I'm sure you already know all about it. It's a black BMW 5 series, around five years old. I should say was, seeing it's been burnt out.'

'Is it possible your husband was responsible?'

'Never. The car is like a ... a ... child to him.' He treated it better than he treated Ant, but I wasn't about to tell Angel that.

'Do you drive it?'

'Hardly. And before you ask, I have no reason to destroy it.'

'Sure?' Detective Angel gave me a steady look.

'Why would I?' I glared.

His eyes fixed on mine. He must be the master of some kind of hypnosis technique. Words bubbled to the surface. I held them in, but the pressure built. I bit my lip hard, then blurted out, 'The car was stolen.' I gave myself a mental head smack.

Evans sprang into action and pushed a tissue box towards me.

I took one, blew, and tucked the tissue into my top. They weren't getting my snotty DNA-riddled tissue either.

'How do you know it was stolen, Mrs Burne?' Detective

Angel asked. His tone hadn't changed.

I focussed on the tabletop, mind racing through Draga's suggested explanation. Even though I'd rehearsed, I was in danger of confusing the details.

'There were some items I wanted to take to the op-shop.' I paused. Was it op-shop items, or was it the garbage I was taking out? Too late now, I'd have to run with op-shop. 'I needed to move Rohan's car to get to mine and put them in the boot. I opened the garage door, drove his car out and left it in the driveway. I switched off the engine and went inside. I left the key in the ignition. It was after midnight and there was no one around. I didn't think it would be a problem.'

Angel and Evans stared at me. Did I have liar in neon lights over my head?

'You were going to the op-shop at that hour?'

'I planned to do it on the way to work the next morning.'

'And while you were inside, someone just happened to come by and steal the car?'

'Yes.'

'That's convenient. You expect me to believe that, Mrs Burne?'

'It's the truth. When I came out, the car was heading down the street. Ask Draga.'

Had I told him about Draga's presence in our previous conversation? I couldn't remember. The possibility of Draga being interviewed filled me with dread. It would be a jumble of bad English, bad lies, and a bad result.

'Why didn't you tell us about the theft before? Why lie?'

'I was ... am ... embarrassed. My husband will be very upset when he finds out.' I congratulated myself on my quick thinking although couldn't gauge Robert Angel's reaction.

He rubbed his chin. He might be buying my story. It could even start making sense to me if I kept telling it long enough.

'What were they?' he asked.

'What were what?'

'The opportunity shop items.'

'Um, a few garbage bags filled with household stuff.'

He raised an eyebrow.

'Things I no longer needed.'

Evans blinked a few times and pursed her lips.

The air conditioner droned in the pause before Robert Angel said, 'Could you be specific?'

Why did he want details about household junk?

'Draga regularly cleans out the cupboards, so there was some crockery, bric-a-brac, plus old clothes.'

'What about the rug?'

'I put it in the boot.'

Detective Angel wrote something, then placed his pen in front of him and clasped his hands. 'Mrs Burne is it possible your house was being watched?'

'Watched? Why would someone watch my house?'

'It might explain the opportunistic theft. I'll ask again if you noticed anything odd in the days leading up to this theft?'

It couldn't hurt to tell him a few details, especially if they shifted the attention from me. I swallowed. 'There were a few incidents.'

His expression challenged me. 'You've been loose with the facts so far. So, please, any detail, no matter how insignificant it seems.'

I sniffed. 'Nothing major. Phone hang-ups, and ...'

Evans leaned forward and Detective Angel poised his pen.

'Someone left dog droppings on the front doorstep. But I think that was the kids from up the road.'

Detective Angel put down the pen again. 'It sounds like someone's upset.'

'As I said, kids. I mean, dog poop. Really? Not the sort of thing an adult would do.'

'Anyone have a gripe with Mr Burne?'

'It's possible. Although I don't see the connection between what's happened at the house, the missing car, and Rohan supposedly missing. If he's been kidnapped, as you've suggested, then why steal the car? And wouldn't there be a demand for ransom?'

'Real kidnappings aren't like television scripts, Mrs Burne. It's possible whoever is responsible for your husband's disappearance doesn't want money.'

'What then?'

'Perhaps they wanted to get rid of a problem.'

'You make it sound like he's involved with a crime syndicate. This is insane, Detective. Have you considered he might have had an accident? He could have lost his memory or could be in a hospital somewhere.' Even I almost believed it.

'We've made those enquiries. He isn't showing up anywhere. No use of credit cards. No mobile phone usage.'

Damn. They'd done background work and were taking this seriously.

'There's another possibility. Your husband doesn't want to be found,' Detective Angel said.

'I ... I think that's unlikely.'

'He could be having a crisis,' Detective Angel said.

'What kind of crisis?' I asked, even though I figured being dead qualified as a crisis.

'I was hoping you'd tell me.' He tapped his fingers on the manila folder in front of him.

Maybe I should know what he meant, but I had no idea. If he knew what I'd done, he should just say so. There must be something else.

'Clearly, I'm not here to give a statement. You appear to think I'm keeping something from you. If you have an allegation against me, say so. Otherwise, as I'm not being charged with anything, I assume I'm free to leave?'

'Of course.'

I searched his face for a hint of what he was thinking, but it was blank.

I swung on Evans. 'What sort of support do you call this?'

She had the grace to look down. I stood and steadied myself on the table edge. With as much dignity as I could manage, I went to the door and waggled the handle, struggling to push the door outward.

Robert Angel's mouth lifted in a wry smile. He reached across me to take the handle.

'Pull,' he said.

His hand brushed mine and a zillion volts of electricity zapped me.

'Detective Angel, you're the most inappropriately named person I know,' I said as I strode out.

He followed and used his security pass to open the outer door to the waiting room.

I pushed past him with my nose in the air.

Draga was at the glass window, talking to the big-bellied cop.

'Let's go,' I said.

Draga picked up her bag and scurried after me. 'Goodbye, Mr Bill,' she said to the officer. 'Remember not leave in oven for more than twenty minutes or it burn.'

He dipped his head and flashed a crooked smile. 'Thanks for the tip.'

Draga scurried out after me. 'What happen? What Mr Detective Angel ask?'

I recounted the interview. With each new detail, Draga's eyes widened.

When I finished, she let out an 'Ay-yay-ai!' and lifted her hand.

'Don't even think about crossing yourself, Draga.'

She dropped her hand and pursed her lips.

'There's a problem. Detective Angel suspects I know more than

I'm saying.'

'You do.'

'Clearly. But there's a whole lot of stuff that has nothing to do with me. Rohan could have upset someone. I bet it's connected to the bank account. I'll go through his diary, his files, his life. If he's done something wrong, I don't want to be implicated in it.'

'You kill somebody. I not think you can find more trouble.'

'I can. If the police think I'm involved, someone else might, too. They don't know what happened to Rohan. They might still be looking. I have to find out who and why.'

'We be detective like in the TV? How you say – buddy partners?' Draga's eyes twinkled with excitement.

'Sure, Draga,' I said dryly as I beeped open the car. 'We can be buddy partners.'

Draga clipped in her seat belt. 'Okay, but I want be skinny, good-looking one.'

I rolled my eyes then called the office to tell Paulette I'd be working from home the rest of the day. 'Please let Andrew know. He's working on something for me.'

'Sure thing, Jac.'

Later, after one of Draga's quick lunches that could have fed an MCG crowd, I sat on the study floor surrounded by papers, hoping something in them might reveal clues to Rohan's crimes. I couldn't help thinking about the interview with Detective Robert Angel. How long would it take him to find the body, the incriminating insurance policy, the right size handcuffs?

How long would it take to stop thinking about his touch?

Draga poked her head around the door. 'You find answer?'

'Nope.'

Draga snorted and disappeared. It was quiet for a few minutes then a high-pitched 'Ay-yay-ai, djesi moi?'

I dropped the papers and the screeching ceased.

Draga reappeared, face flushed. 'I have much good idea.'

I groaned.

'You not like we talk about fire-hair lady, but if we look for Mr Ruin, she must do, too.'

If that were true, Rohan's lover might have already reported it to the police, but Detective Angel wouldn't have revealed that piece of information.

'There's no way to find out what she's thinking or doing,' I said.

'Sure we can find out. We go her house,' she said.

'Are you crazy? Knock on her door and say what? Excuse me, I killed my husband, your lover, but I'm not sure, so have you seen him? I don't think that'll work.'

'I think you be wrong.' Draga waggled her finger. She plonked onto the study armchair and mopped her forehead with a lacy handkerchief. 'You not lie so good. You already know where live the fire-hair lady. You think I not know where you go, looking, looking, looking? Bah.'

'Okay, okay. I admit I know where she lives, but what would she tell me? She might realise I'm Rohan's wife. If the police find out I was there, it'll mean more trouble.'

Draga adjusted her glasses. 'You not be one who go. I be one who go.'

'You? And do what?'

'I can find what she know.'

The image of Draga on a solo investigation tied my insides into knots scouts would be proud of. 'How are you planning to do that?'

She pinched a small gap between thumb and forefinger. 'I have the little plan. First, I must telephone to my cousin. Then I make the big plan.' She spread her arms wide as she stood up, then left the room, singing.

I chased after her. 'Your cousin? You can't tell anyone about this.'

Draga sighed. 'You not understand, Missus Jac. My cousin has the muckup.'

'Makeup? For what? To disguise yourself?'

'You not smart today. How you can run business?'

'Not very well these days.' I couldn't even think about what was happening at the office.

Draga let it slide. 'My cousin sell the Avon.'

I raised querying eyebrows. 'They don't sell Avon here anymore.'

'No matter.'

'I'm completely lost.'

Draga sighed. 'Not worry, Missus Jac. I say slowly then you understand. Listen. I say to my cousin I want try the Avon. She give me the sample. You give me fire-hair lady address. I go there. I take Avon with me and I tell her I am Avon lady.' She stabbed her finger in the air to emphasise each point. 'Good idea, da?'

'No, it's terrible. You're nuts.'

'Me be the nut? I not one who kill husband.' She crossed herself. 'I know how get inside house and find out much. You will see.'

'Draga, she won't believe you. People buy Avon online, not from representatives anymore. She'll be suspicious.'

'Woman old like me. We not buy on the line. We like buy from person.'

'Again, they don't have represent … Never mind. Besides, you don't look like an Avon lady.'

'My cousin look same. She sell long time.' Draga resumed her singing as she reached for the phone. 'She – how you say? – ah, da, retire! But she keep much sample.'

'How old and out of date are they? You'll make everything worse,' I said, as she punched numbers into the keypad.

'You must have the faith.'

The ground seemed to vibrate. I needed to sit. I needed coffee, a scotch, a tranquiliser.

When her cousin answered, Draga fired off a rapid torrent of Croatian interspersed with throaty laughter. A few minutes later she said, 'Hvala.' Having thanked her cousin, Draga glowed in her plan's unfolding. 'I go my cousin now. You write for me fire-hair lady address.'

'If you insist on doing this, I'll drive you there. I'll park around the corner.'

She frowned. 'No. Is better I alone. Write where I must go.'

I scribbled down the address.

'You not worry. I not drive car. I have bus card for old people.' She dropped her voice as though someone might overhear. 'I more old than my face say.'

In the early afternoon quiet that descended after Draga's deployment on her mission, I returned to my own sleuthing. I was tempted to call Andrew but held back. I trusted him to contact me once he had any news. No point hassling him. Besides, I had enough to go on with. Within a couple of hours, I'd created two piles on the study floor: documents that might provide clues to my pig of a husband's clandestine activities; and a pile that didn't contain anything helpful. They teetered on an angle, threatening to collapse and bury any answers they held.

I made myself a coffee, then graduated to something stronger to help me scrutinise the 'helpful' pile. I wasn't sure I wanted to know all the details of Rohan's secret life, but I was tired of being passive and at the mercy of every move my cheating husband made. Besides, there wasn't a way out of my predicament without facing and gathering the evidence.

I found two more bank statements in Rohan's name. One from the third month of the account's operation, the other the most recent. There were only deposits on the first and only withdrawals on the latest. For whatever reason, the movement of money into the account had stopped, but the money out had increased.

Was he spending it on his lover? Most outlay related to

romance appeared on his credit card statements. They showed he'd spent at least three nights at The Admiral's Retreat in the last year. There were costs for expensive dinners at fancy restaurants I'd never been to and regular orders for flowers, none of which were delivered to my door.

There was nothing there to account for his secret fortune.

After all this digging, it just reconfirmed how devious Rohan was. When would I stop being a doormat?

'You're a jerk,' I said loudly.

'I know, and I'm sorry.'

I jolted at the voice, knocking over the towering paper monuments to my husband's furtive life. They splayed like a deck of badly dealt cards.

I turned.

Ant, pale and trembling, stood in the doorway.

CHAPTER SEVENTEEN

I scrambled over the papers and pulled him into a hug. His clothes smelled musty and he reeked of cigarettes. 'Where have you been? I was worried sick. I've called and called.'

'I'm sorry. I knew Dad wasn't happy about me being here and ...' He hung his head. 'Then things got weird. I might as well be in Sydney and out of the way.'

'How were you getting there?'

'Hitchhiking.'

Thank goodness he wasn't the Beemer thief. And he wouldn't have returned if he'd seen Draga and I put his father in the car boot. Thank goodness for that. The bad part was that he didn't know about Rohan yet.

'What brought you back?' I asked.

'I called Mum when I was halfway there.'

'And?'

'Big mistake. She said she doesn't want me there,' he said, gazing down. 'Says I'm in her way and too much trouble.'

'I'm sorry, Ant. That's hard,' I said. 'I'm glad you're back.'

'Dad won't be.' Ant shrugged. 'But I got nowhere else.'

'I have to tell you something, Ant.' I struggled to make eye contact. 'Your dad is missing.'

Ant leaned against the desk. 'What do you mean, missing?'

'No one has heard from him since the same day you left. He was supposed to be at a conference, but didn't turn up. He might have decided not to go.' The lie slid shamefully easily from my lips.

'That doesn't make sense. He'd tell you if he wasn't going.'

If only Ant knew how many secrets festered between his

father and me.

'He's been under pressure. He might've taken off somewhere for a break,' I said.

'No! Something musta happened to him,' Ant said, his face crumpling.

I hated myself as I continued to tell him half the truth.

'The police are tracing his movements.' I rubbed his back. His bones were sharp under my hand. 'There's something else. His car was stolen. It was found burnt out.'

'That proves something's happened to him!' He choked back a sob and turned his face away. The bruise on his neck had developed into an array of dark colours.

I put my hand to it. 'Ant, your neck ...'

He jerked back, drawing air through his teeth. 'It's nuthin'.'

'Doesn't look like nothing. Bruises like those don't just happen. I know you're in some kind of trouble. I wish you'd tell me what it is.'

Ant stared at me, then flung his arms around me and buried his face in my neck. He shuddered as he bawled. 'They're going to kill me.'

I stiffened. This wasn't just about me anymore. I owed Ant something. The knots inside me started to untie, replaced by a small fire stoked while holding my fragile stepson. 'Tell me.'

Ant wiped his runny nose with his sleeve. 'I owe money to a dealer.'

'A drug dealer?'

'What other kind of dealer is there?'

'A car dealer, a commodities dealer ...'

'Not in my world.'

'How much dope do you have to smoke to be in debt so deep they want to kill you?'

'Not just dope and not for me. It was for Hannah, my girlfriend in Sydney. I was pretendin' it was for me, but I was scorin' for her. She said she was gunna make some excuse to get the money from her dad, cos she reckons he's loaded. She was supposed to give me the money last month ...' He let me fill in the blank.

'Why would they give you the drugs if you didn't have money to pay?'

'It's how they start. They get you sucked in. When my girlfriend wasn't coming up with the money, I asked Mum to help me, but she wouldn't.'

'Did you tell her what the money was for?'

'Nah, I just said I owed someone money. She didn't even ask for what or how much. Just said "Ask your father", he said, mimicking Triple-T's response with searing accuracy. 'She doesn't care.'

Triple-T knew he was in trouble of some sort and she'd hung him out to dry. The game of ping-pong with Ant's life was never-ending.

'When I couldn't pay, Cruiser started charging interest.'

'Cruiser's the dealer?'

He nodded. 'He sent one of his guys around to beat me up a bit.'

'That's why you came to Melbourne? To get away?'

'I figured he wouldn't find me, but he has.' Ant wiped his nose again.

'He knows you live at this address?' I turned to the door as if I expected someone to burst through.

'I'm sorry.' Ant put his hands to his head. 'I'm an idiot.'

The phone calls, the dog poop; it had nothing to do with Rohan or me. They were warnings meant for Ant. I wasn't sure whether to be relieved or not. On the plus side, the new information could confuse Detective Angel's case. For a while anyway.

'Where's your girlfriend in all of this?'

Ant snorted. 'That ... Hannah's not my girlfriend anymore. It's all on me. Cruiser doesn't care who uses it, he only cares who pays for it.'

'How much do you owe?' I braced for the answer.

'About five grand.'

'You'd pay less for gold.'

'I didn't realise how much it had built up. It gets worse. They said if they couldn't get it outta me, they'd get it from someone close.' His chin trembled. 'I think they mighta done something to Dad.'

'I'm sure you're wrong, Ant. Your dad's disappearance hasn't anything to do with you.' At least I wasn't lying to the kid.

He shook his head. 'Maybe they stole his car. To try and sell it for the money.'

'Then why would they burn it?'

'A warning.'

'It doesn't make sense. The car is worth more than the debt. They could have sold it or rebirthed it or whatever they do with stolen cars.'

'I guess,' Ant said. 'But they don't like anyone gettin' away with nuthin'. I've heard stories. They hurt people because they can.'

Hot late-afternoon sun filled the room. 'When did you last eat?'

'Yesterday.'

'Go have a shower. I'll make you something. But I warn you, I'm no Draga.'

'Where is Draga?' Ant asked as he trudged towards the stairs, dirty backpack dragging behind.

'Visiting a friend,' I said, not daring to imagine how Draga's mission was panning out.

By the time Ant reappeared, I'd whipped us up a late-afternoon snack of toasted ham and cheese sandwiches, cut them into approximate halves, and arranged them in what I hoped was chef-worthy style. I piled grapes, peaches and nectarines on a plate, then poured a large orange juice for Ant and allowed myself a supersized glass of red.

We ate at the table, spreading crumbs while Ant talked in brittle tones about his girlfriend.

'Hannah turned out to be a ...' Ant smacked a fist into his palm. 'Because I've been so stupid, Dad's mixed up in it all.'

He wasn't just skin and bone, he was all wounds.

'Perhaps we should go to the police with this information,' I said.

Ant dropped his sandwich. 'No way. Cruiser will kill me if he found out. Besides, they'll never nail him. He's too smart.'

'Okay. Okay.' My hands rose in surrender, but I still wondered if I should give this information to Detective Angel. Much as I didn't want to be caught, I couldn't risk Ant getting hurt. 'Will they let you have more time to pay?'

'They already have and I'm past the deadline.'

'Do you know how to get in touch with this Cruiser?'

'I do, but what's the point? I haven't got the money.'

'I'll give you the money, Ant.'

He gaped as if the words were in a speech bubble hanging over my head.

'There's a condition. You have to come and work for me part-time as a way of repaying it.' In a business that might go under. I'd jump that hurdle later.

'I can't take your money, Jac. It's not right. Besides, I couldn't pay you back cos I don't know how to work. I'd stuff everything up and make things worse for you. I'm no good at anything, just a loser.' He folded his arms and his shoulders sagged.

'You're not a loser, Ant. Besides, what's to know? The alarm sounds. You get up, you get dressed, and come to the office with me. We'll take it from there.'

'I wouldn't be good at the getting up part.'

'You'll get used to it. Most people do.'

'Why do you want to help me?' he asked quietly.

Why did I? Caring for and about Ant might be the closest I'd get to motherhood, but it wasn't that. I thought about Draga's desire to help me.

A place to put the love. I could do the same.

'No matter what you believe about yourself, Ant, you're wrong. You're a good kid and you deserve a chance at a better life. Now, how do I pay the money to Cruiser?'

'Not with a credit card,' Ant said, trying to smile.

I had some cash in the bedroom safe. Roughly half the amount needed, but it was a start. I'd have to figure out how to get the rest.

'Give me a couple of days.'

'Thanks, Jac.'

'Now, eat up. Draga hates leftovers.' Where was Draga? She'd been gone for hours.

We finished our sandwiches and fruit in silence. I decided against another wine. I might be developing a sense of responsibility, starting with being a good stepmother – if I ignored the bit about lending my stepson money to pay a debt to a drug lord named Cruiser. And not forgetting bumping off Ant's dad.

On the bright side, I'd found my stepson a good job.

An hour later, Ant's thin body stretched the sofa's length. On the television, MTV droned low in the background as he snored.

The doorbell buzzed. I glanced at Ant as I crossed the lounge, but he didn't move.

'Who's there?'

A muffled voice answered from the other side. It might be Cruiser or one of his crew, but I figured criminals wouldn't announce themselves.

'Who's there?' I asked again.

This time the voice was clear. 'Detective Robert Angel.'

This guy wouldn't let up.

Ant twitched and rolled onto his side. How was the kid supposed to rest with all this commotion? I should be nervous. Instead, I was narky.

I flung the door open. 'Detective Angel, you pick the most inconvenient times. Is it part of your police training?'

There was a stifled choke behind me.

The detective leaned to the side and looked over my shoulder.

Ant was on his feet, groggy with sleep.

'I swear I only bought the coke for her.' He ran upstairs. A poor choice of escape route.

The corners of Robert Angel's mouth twitched. 'Coca Cola's my favourite,' he said, stepping into the hallway.

My brain was still scrambling for a response when Draga's voice boomed from the rear of the house. 'Missus Jac, I find something. Johi meni! Wait I tell you. Mr Ruin ...'

I wanted to yell, 'Stop! Police!' Nothing came out of my mouth. I couldn't take my eyes off Robert Angel's. He watched me, no doubt waiting for me to give something away.

Draga's voice grew louder. I caught, 'You never believe ...' then louder, '... when I tell you what I discover ... fire-hair lady ...' She burst into the hallway, wearing a scarf tied under her chin like a 1940s charwoman.

She noticed Robert Angel and stopped with a jerk. Avon booklets and samples cascaded to the floor. She tugged at the knot and removed the scarf. 'You want coffee, Mr Detective?' she asked casually.

'Thanks. Milk, no sugar,' he said and smiled.

'I get for you.' Draga gathered her Avon material and strode out of the room, her head at a dignified tilt.

'Have a seat, Detective.' I sat on the sofa, rubbing my temples.

Robert Angel sat in Rohan's favourite spot. He reached into

his inside pocket and took out his notepad.

He studied me with those Angel eyes I regularly mused on.

'Seems we have lots to talk about, Mrs Burne.'

Draga pouted. She shifted her weight in her chair, keeping her arms folded. Her glare was secured to the wall above Robert Angel's head. She wasn't happy in the underdog position, but she knew the detective had her trapped.

He drained the coffee cup and smacked his lips. 'Nice brew.'

'I always make coffee much good.' Draga sniffed and made a show of picking fluff off her blouse.

I chewed on my thumbnail. There was no getting out of this. Draga had already spilled the beans on the current lover, Ant had outed himself as a drug procurer, and I was fighting a desperate urge to confess everything. I'd already had a taste of it when admitting the true circumstances surrounding the Beemer's disappearance.

Detective Angel didn't ask more about the drug issue. At least, not for the moment.

He poised his pen. 'So Draga, you've become a private investigator?'

He grinned, and his face softened.

How could anyone be that handsome?

'Missus Jac?'

I still had my eyes on Robert Angel.

'Missus Jac? What I must say?'

'Huh?' I felt my face burning. 'Just tell him what you know, Draga.'

I was so over all the drama, a restful stay in a cell was starting to look attractive.

'All?' she asked in a conspiratorial stage whisper. 'You sure you want I tell all?'

She could not have dug a bigger hole if she'd used an

excavator.

'Detective Angel can hear you,' I stage whispered back. 'He already knows we're hiding something.'

Draga slid her gaze to him then back to me. 'If you want, I tell.'

'Thank you,' he said.

'Mr Ruin should be punish.'

'Why?' Detective Angel asked.

'He run with woman. Everywhere. Running, running, running. Missus Jac, she must go looking, looking, looking.' Draga clapped her hands together on every point. 'She think I not know when she cry, cry, cry. I be angry, angry, ang ...'

'Draga, we don't need everything in triplicate,' I said.

Draga humphed.

Robert Angel put his hand over his mouth.

This conversation could be fun if it wasn't for the dead/ missing husband, and the drug thing.

'My husband's having an affair, Detective.' There. I said it. Admitted what I was so shamed by – my failed marriage.

Detective Angel's developing smile disappeared. 'Must have made you angry, Mrs Burne.'

'Angry?' Draga jumped up. 'For sure, I be angry. He long time with this woman. I suspect, but I say nothing. Nothing. I quiet person,' she said so loudly they probably heard her in Dubrovnik.

Letting her speak was turning out to be a bad plan. 'Draga, Detective Angel needs more coffee.'

'I not finish tell story,' she said, but went to the kitchen, mumbling in Croatian.

'She's loyal,' Robert Angel said. 'Is what she said true?'

'Every single word. My husband isn't a model of fidelity.' I hoped he wasn't thinking I was a horrible wife; someone who drove her husband into someone else's arms.

'You know his lover then?'

'Not really.' I sniffed.

He pulled an ironed handkerchief from his pocket and offered it to me as Draga reappeared with his fresh coffee.

'Why you make Missus Jac upset?' she asked. Draga's thick arm went around my shoulder as she intercepted the handkerchief with one hand and slammed down his coffee with the other. She flicked the hanky open and gave it to me.

'I'm okay.' I dabbed the hanky to my nose. The hanky was crisp cotton with a faint Bulgari scent. I glanced at the detective, then thought of Rohan.

Draga held Robert Angel in her death look. 'You men always make the trouble.'

He clicked his pen closed and tucked the notepad inside his jacket pocket. 'Some of us are decent,' he said, a tinge of bitterness in his voice. He smoothed his tie and sat forward, resting his elbows on his knees. His expression softened. 'Tell me exactly where you went and what you did, Draga. I won't write anything down.'

In unison, Draga and I sat up; her grip tightened around my shoulder.

'Why have you stopped making notes, Detective?' I asked.

'I could go back to making them, but I won't if Draga tells the truth.'

'Okay.' She waggled her finger. 'You listen because I not say twice. I get the muckup from my cousin and I go to house of lady with fire-hair.'

Robert Angel pinched the bridge of his nose and shook his head.

'I'll interpret,' I said.

'I'd appreciate it.' There was that eye crinkle again.

'Draga's cousin used to sell Avon. She has lots of leftover samples and brochures. Draga figured she'd use them as a cover to get into my husband's lover's house. She's a badly-dyed redhead.'

He gave Draga a nod. 'Bold plan.'

'I put book and sample in basket. I catch bus. A lady near me, she see them, and she ask me if I Avon lady. Like she not believe, so I ask her why you ask me that? But then we come to bus stop and I must go.'

'How did you know the right stop?' Robert Angel asked.

How was she going to answer without giving me up?

'No important,' Draga flapped a dismissive hand.

'It is to me,' he said. 'Remember, no lies.'

'It's okay, Draga.' I put my hand over hers then turned to the detective. 'I'd seen the woman with my husband once and I followed her home. I gave Draga her address.'

His lips flattened into a line.

Draga continued. 'I go to gate. House not nice. I think be cost much money, but is big house. Take much time to clean. I press bell – tring-trang. I wait long time. Then lady come open door.' Draga paused for dramatic effect.

Robert Angel's body language and mine mirrored each other's as we craned our necks towards her. My curiosity about my husband's lover was like picking at the scab of a healing cut.

Draga beamed. 'I say to her, good morning. I come with Avon for you. I see she not sure, then I say, you friend from hairdresser tell me you like buy. Then she believe me.'

'Wait. How do you know her friend?' Robert Angel asked.

'She doesn't,' I said, 'but I think Draga tricked her into it thinking she did. Everyone's friends with one another at the hairdressers. It's a girl thing.'

'Good thinking, Draga.' He gave her a thumbs up.

'Thank you. She believe me, but she not let me in house.' Draga frowned. 'I must think how I get inside.'

'What did you expect to find?' he asked.

Draga let out a long-suffering sigh. 'I think no one take Mr Ruin like you think they do. Maybe he go this woman house. You detective. You should think these things.'

'Point taken. Go on,' Robert Angel said.

'I say husband will like new perfume. She say she not have husband. She say she have "man friend". I say, that nice. What he be like, you man friend? She give me the funny look. She say she not want buy perfume and she shut door. Bang.' Draga clapped her palms together. 'After, I go bus and come home.'

'After all that, you learned nothing!' I said.

'Sounds like Draga learned a lot,' Robert Angel said. 'You suspect Rohan's been in contact with her. Otherwise, she'd have shown signs of being worried. She didn't act like a woman missing her lover.'

'Good, Mr Detective.' She folded her arms and turned to me. 'I like him. He smart man.'

My potential arrest appeared an irrelevant detail.

'You might be onto something, Draga,' Robert Angel said. 'You need to let me handle this now.'

Draga and I exchanged looks. The more he poked around, the greater the chance he'd uncover things I didn't want him to know. I was trying to think of something to say, when there was a shout and Ant came down the stairs in twos.

He tripped on the last, sprawled face down across the floor and lay motionless.

Robert Angel leapt up.

Draga slapped hands to her cheeks, 'Ai, little Ant.'

I rushed to him. 'Are you hurt?'

He didn't lift his head, only raised the hand in which he clutched his mobile phone.

I took it and read the message glowing on the screen. Just what I needed.

The perfect diversionary ploy.

CHAPTER EIGHTEEN

I stared at the phone screen. 'Dead. Dead. Dead.' I tried to make sense of the three-word text.

'Give me the phone, Mrs Burne.' Robert Angel squatted beside me. His warm persona had disappeared, and he was back in detached investigator mode.

I handed it to him, then stood unsteadily and helped Ant up. Ant sank onto the sofa, his face white. Draga fanned him with her apron.

The detective sucked his lips together and frowned. 'Does this message mean anything to you, Ant?'

Ant didn't make eye contact. 'No, but it's from Dad's number.'

I straightened. Dead men can't send text messages. Damn that missing phone. I'd gone over the last scene so many times, but still couldn't remember seeing it. It couldn't have been in the car, or the police would have found what remained of it. Now I knew for certain whoever stole the Beemer must have Rohan's phone. It meant they saw the body. But why send a message to Ant?

'What message say?' Draga asked, flapping the apron faster.

The detective read the text message without emotion.

'You think ...' Draga cast a quick look at me. '...somebody take Mr Ruin?'

'There'd be no point in sending that message. And, if he was kidnapped, where's the ransom demand?' The detective frowned. 'No. This implies something else.'

I knew exactly what had happened to Rohan, but with all these layers of confusion, even I was beginning to have doubts.

Robert Angel pocketed Ant's phone. 'Sorry, Ant, I'll need to keep this for now.'

Ant looked like someone had pulled the plug on his life support.

'I'll return it to you as soon as possible,' the detective said, pressing a speed dial number on his own phone. He stepped into the hallway and lowered his voice.

Ant rubbed his hands along the dark patches under his eyes. He sighed and slumped. 'What if they've done something to Dad? It'd be on me. I know he's not the greatest dad, but I don't want him to get hurt.'

'I know you don't.' Kids love awful parents all the time, living with the thin hope they might change. How often I'd hoped my father would turn into a warm, involved dad who was proud of me. The sort who came to school functions like the other girls' dads; one interested in my dreams. One who wanted me to do what I loved and be happy. Until the day he died, I'd clung to the belief he might change. Ant and I didn't share DNA, but we both understood the pain of having emotionally unavailable fathers.

Draga pulled Ant into a hug. His face disappeared into her breasts. She mouthed something over his head, but I couldn't make out what it was. Not surprising, given half the time I didn't understand her even when she was at full volume. I screwed up my face and gestured my confusion just as Robert Angel came back into the room and caught us mid-semaphore.

Without missing a beat, he said, 'I'll get Constable Evans to get in touch.'

'No!' Draga and I chorused.

'We'll be fine,' I said.

'If you're sure.'

'We sure.' Draga wiped her brow with the apron.

Angel lingered at the front door. 'I'll be in touch. Call if there's anything else.'

I caught a flash of concern in his expression, but I stepped back in case he could hear my pulse thudding.

'Thank you, Detective.' I shut the door and leaned against it.

My problems had just become bigger.

Draga released Ant. 'I go cook!'

'We ate. I made Ant and I sandwiches earlier.'

'Bah! Sandwich no be enough. We must have the energy. First, I make proper dinner, then we eat and then we must talk, Missus Jac.' She emphasised 'talk' by stretching out the word.

I took her place next to Ant while she went to the kitchen where she clattered utensils, talking to herself.

I put my arm around Ant's shoulder. 'We'll sort it all out.'

'Don't you get it?' he yelled, and the veins in his neck stuck out. 'If they have his phone, they must have him. The message was a warning. Cruiser's got Dad so he can get the money. They're gunna hurt him and it's my fault.'

No, it was mine. There weren't any kidnappers, and Rohan was – I didn't know what Rohan was anymore. 'Kidnapping's a bit extreme for only five grand,' I said.

There was nothing to explain what went on after the car was stolen, but what did I know about the way the criminal mind worked? I was still inexperienced, even though I'd had a good start.

'Do you think they can trace the phone's location?' Ant asked. 'They might find Dad if they do.'

'I doubt it. He never turns on the location.'

Rohan claimed he was a Luddite in these matters, refusing to use any GPS on the phone, or in the car. I suspected it was more to do with not letting anyone know his true whereabouts.

'I just thought of something!' Ant blurted out. 'The cops'll read all my texts. They'll find messages about the deals I did for Hannah.'

'You kept them?'

'No. Yes. Some. I don't know. Some were encrypted, but I deleted that app when all this started.' Ant swept aside his fringe. 'Stupid Hannah used normal texts to me. They can retrieve those even after they're deleted. Could I get into trouble for dealin'? I don't want a criminal record.'

He'd have a long way to catch up to mine. 'You were buying. Wait and see what happens. Detective Angel knows what he's doing.' Unfortunately for me. Not for Ant, though. He deserved to know what happened to his dad.

I might have to step up and take what's coming.

Draga put a platter onto the table. It was piled with enough beef ćevapi to feed the neighbours for five blocks in all directions. She added a massive bowl of mashed potatoes, tossed salad, and a loaf of thickly sliced crusty bread.

Ant wolfed down his share. If Draga kept feeding him at this rate, he might have to join Weight Watchers.

I picked at a single skinless sausage ćevapi and nibbled on the salad. I repeatedly checked my phone. Nothing from Andrew.

'Jedi.' Draga said. 'You must eat.' She heaped more potatoes onto my plate.

Afterwards, with Ant moping nearby, I helped Draga tidy up. She insisted on giving me running instructions on what to do, followed by a critique on how poorly I was doing it. When we finished, the kitchen smelled like lemon blossom, with the customary hint of bleach.

Ant dragged himself to his room.

As he climbed the stairs, Draga whispered, 'I must wait until boy gone before I tell you what I see at fire-hair lady house.'

'You already told us,' I said.

'Oofah! First police be listening, then boy. I not have the

privacy. I not want him to hear in case I be wrong, but if I be right, everything be change.' She sat. 'This time, you make coffee and I tell true story.'

'Draga, you lied after you promised Detective Angel?'

'For sure.' She gave a look that reminded me my crimes were worse.

I put the percolator on the stovetop and fetched two demitasses. The setting sun shone into the room, spotlighting Draga, centre stage, as she launched into her tale.

'I go to door and I ring bell tring-trang. I wait long time. Then I ring again. Tring-trang. Tring-trang. Door open and is fire-hair lady.'

'I've heard this bit.'

'I tell you, Missus Jac, her face only nice from far away.'

'Bless you, Draga.'

'You welcome. I say to her, I am here with the Avon and she look me like I crazy woman. She say, she must go out. But I smart. I say, you friend from hairdresser tell me come see you.'

'And I've heard this bit. Get to the important bit.'

'Patience, Missus Jac. She say, which friend? I say, I not know name, but friend have the short hair, all grey. I think she have many friends with grey hair. She do because she say must be Silvia. I say, da, Silvia. Again, she look me like I crazy. She ask if I sell Avon long time. I tell her not so long, but I am good saleslady. She believe me. We talk, and I see behind her inside house.'

'And?'

'House need much clean.'

'But it's beautiful on the outside,' I said, recalling the house's exterior and manicured garden.

'You not should believe what you see, Missus Jac.'

'What else besides the need for cleaning?' I doled three teaspoons of sugar into my demitasse.

'Nothing,' she said.

I dropped my spoon and it clattered onto the table. 'That's your big discovery?'

'Yes. I see nothing in house, but I see she have clothes on arm. Was much man clothes, shirt, the trouser, and the man jacket. She say, I go dry cleaner. I say, okay, I give you Avon book. Before she can say no, I say, I hold clothes while you look. In book is special product. I push book to her and I pull clothes. I do fast so she not can stop me. I say you take you time, I patient saleslady. She not know how to make me to go so she read book little bit. While she do, I quickly look at clothes.'

She paused as if expecting a drumroll. 'Missus Jac, was Mr Ruin jacket.' She spread her arms wide in triumph.

'How can you be sure?'

'Easy. Is one Mr Ruin make by krojač. How you say? Tailor.'

'I wondered where that jacket went. Damn thing had cost a fortune. But it doesn't prove that he's there now. Maybe he left it there a long time ago.'

Draga almost spat out a mouthful of coffee. 'Missus Jac. You be stupid sometime. Why she clean clothes if he not there? If Mr Ruin be missing, she be worried. She not look like woman who worry. She look like woman who must go dry cleaner.'

Rohan alive? I'd seen him dead, dead, dead. 'Are you sure?'

'Yes, sure. When I give back clothes, I say, you man friend have the nice jacket. She say, he need clothes soon so I must go. Missus Jac, for sure he there. Is the simple logic.' She beamed.

'But if Rohan's alive, why hasn't he called the police? I assaulted him. He could bring charges. It would solve all his problems. I'd be out of the way, and he could go off with ... whatever her name is ...'

'Judy,' Draga said.

'How did you find out her name?'

Draga sighed. 'How anybody find somebody name? I ask her. But I not think Mr Ruin want you out of way. And he not want her. Mr Ruin not know what he want. When he have one thing, he want something else. He zbunjen – confuse. I tell you, Missus Jac, the hard man is good to find.'

'You mean a good man is hard to find.'

'I think my way better. When he mixed up, make you mixed up. Me, too, sometime.'

'Spot on, Draga. Rohan does have the air of someone who thinks there's somewhere better to be or someone better to be with.'

We shared a pause, during which Draga sighed and grunted, 'Oofah' a few times.

She thumped the table. 'Missus Jac, maybe Mr Ruin have – how you say – amnesty?'

'Not from me, he doesn't.' I took a fresh pot of steaming coffee off the stove. 'You mean amnesia.'

'That what I say. You make him bang head, that why he not can remember. He not remember anybody; not you, not boy, not me. Be hard forget me, believe me.'

'He couldn't have amnesia, or he wouldn't have known Judy.' I emphasised her name with a sneer. 'And if his memory's affected, how did he get to her house?'

Draga's theory might have merit, but I couldn't grasp the possibility Rohan might be alive. I rubbed the stiffness in my neck. 'You really believe he's at this Judy person's house?'

'Da. I think we make mistake. Was much rain. Much dark. We not see good.'

'Well, I'm not a paramedic, just an angry, slightly unhinged wife.' In my panic and confusion, I might have misread Rohan's vital signs. The possibility filled me with excitement at not facing murder charges. 'Assuming your theory is right, how would Rohan explain to Judy what happened to him?'

'He can say he have accident. He tell her lie like he tell you lie. He tell you he go conference when he not. Many time he do this. One time I remember ...'

'Draga!'

'Okay, better we not talk about.'

'I wonder if she even knows he's married. When he was here, I bet she believed he was away on business. He couldn't blame me for his injuries without explaining who I am. Judy might be as sucked in as I am.'

'Now you be use you brain, Missus Jac.' Draga poured a third coffee shot and downed it. Her eyes shone with a caffeine buzz.

'And how did he get from a locked car boot to her house? He couldn't have rung her if someone else had his phone. Whoever took it must have seen him in the boot. They wouldn't have left him there.'

'If Mr Ruin have phone, he can send message to scare you.'

'But the message went to Ant. He's not a great father, but he'd never frighten Ant on purpose. There's one more mystery. The incinerated Beemer. He'd never do that. Not in a million years.'

I was suddenly over feeling frightened and intimidated by my inadequacies. This was a chance to set things right. 'Let's sneak into Judy's house and see definitely if Rohan's there.'

I wasn't sure how this would work in practice, but I was prepared to wing it.

'Missus Jac, I not small woman.' She ran her hands down her squat body. 'You see? I not good for sneak.'

'Then you can provide the distraction and I'll do the looking.'

'Is better. You good for looking, looking, looking.'

'I'll take a few hours off tomorrow morning.' Could I really afford to do that? I should be in the office, but what would be the point if I got arrested? My business would be lost, anyway. And my poor staff! What would become of Andrew, Paulette, Claire and Will? I hated being pulled in so many directions, but I had to think of Ant.

'Okay. I ring my cousin and tell her I must keep the Avon

longer.'

I went to Ant's room and picked my way through the discarded clothes strewn over the floor. He was asleep on the bed, headphones in his ears. The new lamp glowed softly, and the light made him look so much younger. I covered him with a blanket and planted a kiss on his head. His curls were soft. He stirred a little then settled.

I turned off the light and pulled the door behind me. Ant was safe for now, but I'd have to get the rest of Cruiser's money together to keep him that way.

I yawned. This day had been longer than most and still nothing from Andrew. I couldn't stand it any longer and sent him a text, asking for an update. He replied, full of apologies. It's been full on, but I'm close to restoring the database. Relief flooded over me. I texted back THANK YOU! You're a genius! What about Sandi and the spy pen? He answered, Not quite there yet. Damn! He finished his text with Pulling it all together. DW.

Easy for him to say, 'Don't worry'.

Have something important to do tomorrow morning. Be in late I texted back.

I took a shower, slipped between cool sheets, and listened to the summer night's sounds drifting in via the open window. As I waited for sleep, I reviewed my 'life lists', mentally inking in all the things that were wrong – Rohan, carnappers, my business problems, Sandi Watson, Jason Keene, a potential prison term. Then I listed the things that were right – Draga and Ant. The smaller list had bigger implications.

I didn't have many clues, but I had two big pluses. I'd discovered a smidge of gumption. I also had a plan. It was a loose one, but still a plan.

If I could muster the courage to tell Detective Angel about my investigative campaign, I bet he'd be proud.

Robert Angel.

I debated which of my life lists I should add him to.

We rose at 6am to get a start on our mission, because Draga insisted 'the bird who is early have much worms'.

For once, I'd slept through and woken with more energy and confidence. Detective Robert Angel featured in my dreams, which might have something to do with it.

At seven, my phone trilled, and Andrew's name displayed on the screen. 'What's up?'

'Sorry to ring so early, Chief.' His tone was upbeat. 'I know you planned on coming in late, but I wanted to show you something before anyone else got into the office.'

My pulse quickened. 'You recorded something on the spy pen, didn't you? I thought you weren't 'quite there yet' as you put it.'

'I'm there now. Is there any chance you can come in before your appointment? I'll explain when you get here. I promise it won't take long.'

Before Andrew had disconnected, I'd grabbed my car keys.

'What you do, Missus Jac?' Draga scuttled after me. 'We must go.'

'Don't worry. I'll be back soon.'

I screeched out of the drive, checked my speed, and forced myself to keep to the limit.

The office carpark was empty except for Andrew's blue Vespa. For a geek, he had a tinge of rebel about him.

'Andrew?' I called, as I hurried inside.

'In here, Chief,' Andrew called from his office. He jumped to his feet when I entered. 'Sorry I didn't get back to you earlier. I left the pen in recording mode on Sandi's desk. I kept walking past while she was in there, to see if she noticed it. She came out after about half an hour and left the building. She didn't look happy. It upset Paulette because she ...'

'Enough with the suspense. Did you get something or not?'

'Sure did. It took me ages to download it. I had to reinstall the software. Then ...'

'Andrew!'

'Sorry. I've edited the file to the point at which it gets interesting.' He pushed a USB into the computer and called up the file. 'I've kept this to myself.'

'I knew you would.'

Andrew's face was solemn as he clicked on the play icon and turned up the speakers. He went to leave. 'You might want to listen to this alone.'

'Stay. You've heard it before.'

I waited as a red line tracked along the bottom of the displayed audio file. It started with a quiet hissing sound, a door opened then slammed shut, and the footfalls grew louder. There was some clattering, which I assumed was Sandi dropping things onto the desk. A tiny screech was followed by the distinct sounds of numbers being keyed into a phone.

'She used her mobile,' Andrew said. 'Pity she didn't use the work one or company landline. I could have traced either of those from the records. Anyway ...'

I made a wait signal and listened. Sandi's voice came on and the red line spiked.

'Did you know Jac the Hack was going to offer you your job back at No Class Recruitment?' she asked sharply.

I rolled my eyes, imagining the number of times she'd called me Jac the Hack and All Class by that name. There was a pause while Jason answered her question.

Sandi mustn't have liked his response because her voice became shrill. 'I don't believe you. Why would she come up with something like that without discussing it with you first?'

Another pause, this one longer.

'Flattered? What do you mean, you're flattered? Why would she ask you back?'

From Sandi's reaction, Jason believed re-employment was a possibility. The guy was a deluded, egotistical idiot if he believed I'd ever let him through the door again.

A gap while Jason replied. Sandi made a choking sound. 'No, of course she doesn't know what we've been doing. There's no way she'd offer you a job if she did. NO way.' Sandi banged something on the desk. She quietened, throwing in a few uh-uhs while Jason talked.

When she next spoke, the high pitch in her voice was gone. 'Yeah, Maddison's cool. She'll keep her mouth shut now I've told her we'll do it for a cut price. It'll make her look good with her manager. What a win! Pulling two GGB jobs from this place then the whole assignment.'

The audio dipped while Jason spoke. Sandi sniffed a few times.

'Honest, Jason, I don't want to stay here. I know we can make more money, but it's starting to feel risky.' There followed the squish of the seat cushion as Sandi shifted. 'I can't divert any more assignments now. She doesn't know about all the earlier ones, but now she and the twerpy nerd ...'

Andrew pulled a face and pointed to himself. I held in a laugh.

'... might have found the source of the database problem. I was banking on the system being down until past the tender due date. It would've stuffed No Class up for good. I should've done it a little later and given them less time to repair it. Still, I couldn't believe how easy it was to introduce the virus, thanks to your instructions.'

Andrew and I high fived. The way I obtained her admission might not stand up in court, but she didn't know that. For now, we had a starting point to follow the trail to hard evidence.

There was the sound of Sandi's nails drumming on the desk. 'As far as I'm concerned, what I'm doing isn't against any law. It's simply healthy competition.'

Andrew pulled a face and gave a thumbs down.

'Jac the Hack might argue it's unethical, but it's justice after the way she's treated you. That's more important than money.'

There was another long pause.

'Sure. I'll meet you there. Say half an hour?'

Sandi ended the call. Rustling sounds followed, then a loud honking as she blew her nose several times.

'And she accuses me of having no class,' I said, grinning.

A jangle of keys, the door opening, and then silence. A few seconds later the door reopened. Heavy footsteps, a scraping noise, and then the file clicked out.

'That's me collecting the pen. Mission accomplished. I'm sorry about the virus, Jac. I should have seen the vulnerability in the system earlier.'

'It was my fault, Andrew. I was too distracted.'

'You're back now,' he said.

'I am. And you deserve a pay rise.'

'I do, don't I?'

'I can't give you one for now.'

He laughed. 'Figures. I'll remind you when we win the tender.'

'If we win. It's still a long shot.'

'What do you want me to do next?' he asked.

'Run reports on Sandi's assignments since she started with us, then reports on all her work since Jason left. I want to compare them.'

'No problem. I'll have them in a few hours. What are you going to do?'

'Research what I can about fraud.' I checked my watch. 'First, I have to be somewhere important. I'll be in touch later. Thanks again, Andrew.'

'You're welcome, Chief. We have to keep going. Lots of people count on this place.'

I drove home, imagining my future conversation with

Sandi.

'Sandi, the need to withhold your talents from the employment market has ceased,' I'd say with flair.

She'd be wide-eyed with surprise. 'Excuse me?'

'You're fired, you thieving, lying cow.' I'd laugh while dramatic music built to a crescendo with a close-up on Sandi's horrified expression. Cut to my satisfied grin.

The fantasy made me feel better than I had in a long time.

CHAPTER NINETEEN

Draga pulled up one block away from Judy's house and cut the engine.

'We late.'

'We don't have an appointment for breaking and entering. How can we be late?'

'I be ready early, but you go office. You make me to wait. Make my nerves jump.'

'What have you got to be nervous about? I'm the one sneaking into the house.'

'I nervous because I must be the actress.'

'I'll nominate you for an Oscar.' I softened. 'Thanks for doing this with me, Draga.'

'For sure I help. You my business, Missus Jac. We go?'

Only nine in the morning and already the heat was making me sweat. The need to keep my features covered outweighed comfort so I'd dressed in track pants, runners, and added a hoodie.

As I stepped from the car, a hot wind picked up dust and stung my face. I pulled up the hood to stop my hair flying in all directions.

Draga's grey curls rose skyward, stiffened into place with liberal hairspray.

I shut my door quietly and Draga slammed hers. I put a finger to my lips. 'Shh.'

'Missus Jac, in daytime we not look like we be guilty people.'

'Doesn't mean we aren't,' I said. We were supposed to be hiding in plain sight, but I was conspicuous in winter gear, although nothing could beat Draga's turquoise blouse with its gaudy floral print. 'Let's get this over with.'

'Wait ... I look good, da?' Draga smoothed down her top and her navy skirt and pointed a peep-toe-sandalled foot. Her toenails were bright red. 'I paint. I show I use the Avon. I must have the confidence in product.'

'Draga, you're not really an Avon lady.'

She sniffed and reached into her basket in which she'd gathered the samples and catalogues. She opened a perfume sample and patted the scent onto her décolletage.

'Now I ready.'

We approached Judy's home as if we were out for a morning stroll.

As I got nearer, a gut kick reminded me the last time I'd seen the house was when I'd followed Judy from The Admiral's Retreat.

'Draga, you have to keep Judy distracted, no matter what. I'll jump the side fence and get in through the back of the house. Give me at least five minutes before you ring the doorbell.' My voice rang with authority as if I was experienced at this caper.

While Draga continued to Judy's front gate, I sneaked up the neighbour's drive, sticking close to the fence. I selected a spot behind a shrub that concealed me from any passersby. I clutched the fence top and pushed my toes against the palings. The rough wood hurt my hands. I hoisted myself up, my lack of fitness highlighted as I pulled my right leg, then my left, over in an awkward manoeuvre. I landed with a feet-jarring thud on the other side.

What if Judy had a dog? Too late if she did. No matter what, I had to stick to the plan. Besides, I was about to commit another crime. A dog bite on the bum was the least of my worries.

The house's sideway was bare, except for two potted plants

either side of a door. A small window and pipes on the wall made me think the door accessed the laundry.

Behind the screen door, the internal one was open. I pressed myself against the wall and listened. Canned laughter from a television show floated through the flyscreen. I tried the handle; the door wasn't locked. I crept into the laundry just as the piercing sound of the doorbell rang through the house.

Draga's timing was exquisite. The perfect partner in crime.

There were footsteps, then muffled voices drifted from the front of the house, but Draga's was the louder.

From the laundry, I peeked down a long corridor of flamingo-pink walls. On one hung a garish, abstract print in a dated frame. Judy had no taste; not in art and not in men.

The corridor broadened out into an open plan kitchen and living area. The murmured conversation continued as I stepped into the kitchen. A dishwasher pumped out water, yet dirty dishes were piled high in the sink. A stale smell of greasy food lingered. Knick-knacks lined the window ledge. A talk show was on the television. In front of a floral sofa was a coffee table littered with magazines and an ashtray full of butts. Something steamed from a mug sitting next to it.

I understood what Draga meant about Judy's cleaning skills. Not that I was such an expert, but even I could tell the place could do with some heavy attention from a cleaning crew.

On a buffet was a laptop on which a screensaver scrolled from one picture to another. Images of a car dissolved and reappeared on the slideshow – gleaming, black duco, mag wheels, sports pack, and distinctive grille. Personalised rego.

Rohan's Beemer.

I clenched my jaw. Gotcha! He wasn't dead, dead, dead. He was here, here, here.

Where was he now, the lying, cheating …?

Water gurgled above me. It sounded like a running shower. To get to the second floor meant passing the front door that faced the staircase and slipping behind Judy's back while Draga held her attention. I crept along the wall until I glimpsed Judy, who was wearing a denim skirt and a yellow blouse. Her hair was in curlers.

I would have to slip into the open hallway so that I could then U-turn up the stairs. The manoeuvre carried a high risk of exposure, but I took a breath and sprang into action.

Draga noticed me and began talking more loudly.

'This beautiful for you,' she said, thrusting something near Judy's nose.

I took the stairs two at a time and reached the top with my lungs ready to explode.

The stale smell lingered on the first level. I checked down the corridor. Five doors fed off it, one ahead, and two on either side. I had to choose fast in case Draga couldn't keep up the charade. My contingency plan if Judy appeared was simply to run.

With all the doors shut, I couldn't hear the running water as clearly as I had downstairs and was forced to open each one.

The first room contained a desk covered in papers, a filing cabinet and a printer on a small unit. The second room was stacked with boxes, baskets of clothes, an ironing board and a beanbag. The third room was empty except for a single bed in the corner. I pressed my ear to the fourth door before I turned the handle and found a bathroom. No toiletries on the vanity and no towels. Lifeless moths caught in clumps of dust were gathered in the tub.

What did Rohan find attractive about this house? About its owner?

The last door opened into the main bedroom. Light streamed in through a large, sliding glass door leading onto a balcony. The bed was unmade. On one side table was a stack of Mills and Boon novels. On the other table, business magazines. Jockettes and shoes littered the floor.

An opening on the right led to the walk-in wardrobe. I edged towards it. Dresses, skirts and blouses hung on one side. On the other, a small collection of men's shirts and trousers. I flipped through them, all brands and colours Rohan favoured.

The door on the robe's left must be the ensuite. I stood in front of it, clenching and opening my fists, squeezing invisible stress balls. An ocean of blood pounded in my ears, along with the sound of gushing water. Sucking in a big breath, I flung the door open. Steamy air met me. Through the hazy shower glass, I saw the outline of a man's body. Mongrel! I slid open the screen door with a sharp clang.

Rohan spun around, peering through the suds covering his face as he tried to focus through the steam. He pressed against the tiled wall and his hands flew to cover his crotch.

It'd been months since I'd seen Rohan naked. He'd developed a paunch and his bum was heading south.

'Who the hell are you?'

I pushed the hoodie off. 'Who do you think?'

'Jacqueline! What the ...?' He fumbled to turn off the water, his face a kaleidoscope of confusion. He looked to the door behind me.

'I'm not letting you out,' I said and stepped up to block his path. There was so much adrenaline coursing through me, I could have lifted a Hummer. 'You idiot. The whole world is looking for you.'

Rohan leapt out and dived for the towel on the rail. I snatched it before he got there and held it behind my back.

'Jacqueline, you don't understand,' Rohan said, his hands returning to shield his crotch.

'Don't bother covering up. I've already seen your goodies. You'd better explain yourself, Rohan.'

He tried to snatch the towel from me with one hand while keeping the other strategically placed. 'Me explain? You're the one who knocked me out.'

He had me there. His forehead still bore the mark of our previous encounter. Purple and olive-toned bruises extended to his hairline. The wound was developing a scab. I shuddered as I recalled the blood.

'Obviously, I didn't succeed. What are you doing here with this
Judy woman?'

'How do you know her name? And how did you find me?' Rohan's deep frown almost hid his eyes.

'Never mind that. The fact is you've been hiding here. Ant thinks you've been kidnapped.'

Rohan's face paled. 'Kidnapped?'

He slithered sideways until he could reach behind the bathroom door and unhook the only item of clothing available – a bubblegum-pink satin dressing gown. He slipped into it and tied the belt around his paunch. He waddled into the bedroom like a rosy penguin and sat on the bed. 'What makes him think I've been kidnapped?'

'Because you're missing, you idiot.'

'I'm not missing. I'm … just … unavailable.' He raised his arms in emphasis.

The damage to his brain must be worse than I thought. 'Unavailable? Is that what you call disappearing? The police are involved, Rohan.'

'Police?' His gaze darted back and forth.

There was a rush of footsteps, then a loud, shrill voice behind me.

'What's going on? Rohan? Are you all right?'

I turned and was face-to-face with Rohan's lover. Draga was right about her features – good from far but far from good. Age-spotted hands gripped the doorframe. Her brown eyes were lined with black liner, abundant blusher highlighted her cheeks, and coral lipstick found its way into the fine lines radiating around her lips. Her red hair was showing distinctive signs of grey regrowth. A strong scent of tobacco wafted around her. What did Rohan see in her?

'Who are you?' Judy demanded, looking from Rohan to me. 'How did you get in here? I'm calling the police.'

'Don't,' Rohan said. 'It's okay, Judy.'

'It is not okay,' I said. 'Nothing about this situation is okay.'

'Who is this woman?' Judy shrieked.

I was right. Rohan hadn't told Judy he was married. He was cheating on his mistress. I folded my arms and raised my eyebrows at Rohan.

Colour flooded his cheeks giving him the appearance of a heavily rouged drag queen.

Grey high-rise curls appeared over Judy's shoulder. Draga strained to see into the bathroom.

Judy spun around. 'What the hell do you mean following me into my house?'

Draga ignored her and gave Rohan an assessing look. 'Mr Ruin, this colour not suit you.'

Rohan rubbed his brow and flinched when his fingers touched the bruise.

'Judy doesn't know, does she?' My voice dripped with venom. I leaned towards him. 'Do you want to tell her, or will I?'

Before the issue was decided, Draga said, 'Missus Jac is Mr Ruin wife.'

Judy backed up, staring at me. 'Wife? Your ... your ... wife?'

'How could you not know?' I asked. 'You've picked him up from our house.'

'That was your house? He said it belonged to a friend.' She glared and took a step towards him as if she was about to punch him. 'You said you'd never been married.'

'Two time he marry,' Draga said, holding up three fingers.

'You've got an ex-wife, too?' Judy's lips pulled together into a circle. One hair curler had come loose and was dangling.

Rohan, Judy and I glanced from one to another, while Draga clapped her hands.

'What I say, Missus Jac? I say Mr Ruin here. I be good for make investigation.'

'You owe me an explanation, Rohan,' I said.

'You'd never understand, Jacqueline.' He held me in a cold stare.

'Try me.'

Judy wailed and turned her tear-soaked face to Draga. 'You're not really an Avon lady, are you?'

Draga raised her arms then dropped them to her sides. 'Why everybody say that?'

Draga had wrapped one of Judy's aprons around her middle like a confiscated flag after an enemy's defeat. Seizing the territory of Judy's kitchen, she dug around in the cupboards without any embarrassment, then busied herself making tea and coffee.

If Judy was concerned about the takeover, I couldn't tell because her face was buried in fistfuls of clumped tissues. Occasionally she emerged and opened her mouth to say something to Rohan, only to burst into tears again.

I demonstrated my empathy by passing her fresh tissues. After all, we belonged to the same 'partners of cheaters' club.

Rohan sipped on a coffee and tugged his earlobe. It was his nervous tell.

In different circumstances, seeing him pouting in pink satin would be comical, but he just looked pathetic. Wiry, grey chest hair poked over the opening of the dressing gown, his eyebrows were bushy, and I noticed ear hairs had sprouted. Definitely not the suave, distinguished man I'd married.

I could still hear my father's words. 'He'll be good for you,' he'd said when we'd announced our engagement. 'I can see myself in him, and you need someone strong by your side.'

He'd considered I needed a man's support to live my life, and worse, a man like himself. As I stared at Rohan, I realised I'd only established another relationship in which I was treated indifferently by a man I'd wanted to love me. My life had become a soap opera – a bad one with me in a starring role.

'No more games, Rohan. Tell me everything,' I said.

Rohan huffed. 'I've had a bit of trouble at work. I just wanted a break. I told Geoff I was going to a conference.'

'You were planning to pretend you were there, then come here to hide?' I asked.

'Yes. I just needed a few days to think.' Rohan adjusted the dressing gown and angled his chin. 'How was I to know my idiot secretary would book the conference for real?'

'You're insane, Rohan. It was an internal company conference. Did you think your absence wouldn't be noticed? People have mobiles and emails and attendance registers. You can't just drop off the face of the earth.'

'I wasn't thinking straight,' he shot back.

'Clearly. And did you think I wouldn't notice?'

'I was going to tell you but then ... well ... the pool thing happened.'

'What pool thing?' Judy asked.

Rohan, Draga and I exchanged looks, but ignored her.

'Everyone was trying to reach you. It's how this whole thing started,' I said.

'I didn't have my phone because you took it.' He glanced at Judy. 'At the pool thing.'

'What pool thing?' Judy asked again.

I held my hand up to stop her while I spoke to Rohan. 'I don't have your phone. All I have is a whole lot of trouble. And that stupid life insurance policy you took out made me look like a prime suspect in your disappearance.'

'Life insurance policy?' Rohan frowned. 'Oh, that. I cancelled it a few months ago.' He waved the detail away then paused. 'Hang on, how did you know about the policy? Have you been digging into my personal papers?'

'You have no right to complain, after the way you've treated your wife.'

'Your wiiiiiiife!' Judy made a wailing noise so loud, even Draga flinched.

Like a well-practised team, I pushed the box of tissues across the table towards the near-hysterical woman while Draga made space next to the pile of used ones and placed a cup of tea beside her. Draga caught Rohan's gaze and squinted, burning disapproval into him.

He straightened. 'You have no idea what it's like in my position, Jacqueline.'

'Enlighten me.'

'And me, and Missus Judy,' Draga said, flicking a finger between herself and Judy.

Judy looked at Rohan, her eyes brimming. She blew her nose so loudly, he winced.

'The business demands got on top of me.' He pulled the dressing gown belt tighter and focussed on the floor. 'I've had some financial issues.'

'Such as?' I asked, as Draga and Judy craned forward.

'I sort of borrowed a tiny bit of money from the business.' He made a pincer with shaky fingers and closed it until there was the smallest gap. 'I ... err ... um ... I forgot to mention it to Geoff.'

Judy slapped a hand over her mouth. 'You mean you embezzled money?' she asked. She placed her forehead on the table. Her shoulders quivered.

Draga tutted while she patted Judy's back and aimed another death stare at Rohan.

'If you insist on being technical, I suppose you could put it that way,' he snapped. 'It wasn't that much.'

'You think three hundred and ninety-seven thousand

dollars isn't much?' I asked.

'How did you know?' The sides of Rohan's mouth curved down, highlighting his dry skin and the white stubble speckling his chin.

'I've been digging, remember? What about all that money?'

'It's not all. It's just what's left.'

'Left? You mean you took more?'

Rohan reddened. 'It was more, but I lost some,' he said.

'Lost some? Where? In the street? On a horse? Down the loo?'

'Of course not. Do you think I'm stupid?'

Draga opened her mouth, but I held up my hand. She sucked her lips together and looked pained.

'I made a few bad investments.' Rohan's face layered with a deeper shade of red.

'You're not the best advertisement for your company's capabilities,' I said.

Rohan's eyes narrowed, but he let my comment slide. 'I started to return it in small amounts ...'

'So, all those withdrawals on the last bank statement were you trying to return the money?'

He nodded and hung his head.

'But before you could, Geoff announced he wanted to buy you out. It's why you were ambivalent about the sale. The audits and due diligence would have uncovered your crime.'

'I wanted out of the business, yes, but I couldn't risk Geoff finding out what I'd done. I needed time. I couldn't put it all back at once. It would've looked suspicious. In the end, it wasn't all there to be put back.'

'What the hell were you planning to do with all the money, Rohan?'

'I planned to use it to get away. Leave everything and everyone.'

Judy's wailing converted to hiccups. She buried her face in a new cloud of tissues.

Draga kept rubbing Judy's back. 'Look what you do, Mr Ruin. You make this nice lady much upset.'

Judy reached up and patted Draga's hand.

I ignored their burgeoning friendship. 'What about Ant, Rohan? Did you think for one minute what your actions would do to him?'

'Who's Ant?' Judy asked.

'Is boy. Little Anthony. Mr Ruin son,' Draga said.

'You have a son?' Judy paled. She sighed, then her eyes glazed.

'I didn't think it would affect Ant,' Rohan said.

'Then you're a moron as well as a thief.'

Rohan rubbed his temples. 'I'm in real trouble now. Geoff will have me charged.'

'He won't if he wants to avoid any negative attention on the company. An investment firm with an embezzler as a partner doesn't exactly boost client confidence.'

'It's possible he won't.' He couldn't have looked more sheepish if he were in the paddock with a flock.

No wonder Geoff was keen to find Rohan. He must have thought he'd taken off with the money. I chose not to tell Rohan his crime had already been uncovered. I wasn't interested in saving his neck. He could go fry as far as I was concerned. I only had to consider Ant and how he would take the news of his father's return.

Draga flung a tea towel over her shoulder, her brow glossed with perspiration. 'Mr Ruin, you tell lie to everybody. You business all mix up. You steal money. You have trouble everywhere.'

'I'm not alone, Draga,' he said. 'You're in this with Jacqueline, I bet.'

'Leave Draga out of this Rohan. This is between you and me.'

'Okay then. Face the consequences alone. I could have you on attempted murder.'

Sweat trickled between my breasts. 'You've got no proof,' I said, feigning confidence.

'I'm the proof. One minute we're arguing by the pool, the next I'm sitting by the roadside with no idea how I got there.'

He didn't mention the car.

I straightened. 'That's all you remember?' How had he worked his way out of the rug, and then the boot?

'For now. But when I remember all of it, I'll have you, Jacqueline.' He stabbed his finger at me.

'Really? It happened in the middle of a storm and you'd been drinking. You could have slipped and fallen. If you were disoriented when you came to, you could have wandered off to who knows where. Here, apparently.' I could almost believe the story myself.

'How did he arrive?' I asked Judy.

'He came in a cab,' Judy said, pulling at her fingers. 'He said someone had mugged him while he was out for a walk. I wanted to report it, but he refused.' She turned to Rohan. 'You didn't mention you'd been attacked by your wiiiiiiife! And you have a s...s...son.'

'See, Rohan? You're causing a great deal of grief. Besides, do you want Ant to hear your crazy version?'

Rohan clasped his hands together and sighed. 'No, I don't want him hurt more.'

'Of course, there's another possible explanation. Whoever stole your car could have caused your injuries. They could have knocked you out and taken you with them.'

Rohan's eyes grew wide. 'Stole my car?'

'You own a car? You always take cabs, or I pick you up,' Judy said.

Rohan waved away her comment. 'My Beemer's been stolen?'

'You own a BMW?' Judy asked.

'Owned,' I said.

Rohan paled. 'What do you mean, owned? Where is it?'

'With the police forensics unit.'

'Forensics? What the hell ...' Rohan's jaw went slack.

'The thief torched it.'

Rohan moaned. 'How did that happen?' He didn't wait for an answer. 'You're behind this. I know it.' His chest heaved rapidly, then slowed. He rubbed his chin. 'I suppose the insurance will replace it. Might go for a different colour when I buy the new one.'

'You've shown more emotion about the car than you have about your son.'

Draga glared. 'Missus Jac be right. Look how you scare boy and you make Missus Judy to cry. You ... you ... you not be nice man. You not deserve family.'

'A wife. A son. A BMW,' Judy muttered. She walked, zombie-like, from the room. The loose curler came off and bounced behind her.

Rohan watched her leave, his expression almost sorrowful.

The kitchen fell into silence, broken occasionally by Judy's intermittent sobs travelling from somewhere else in the house.

'Why her?' I asked after a few minutes.

'She makes my life easy,' he said and shrugged.

'You really are a confused moron.'

I almost felt sorry for him. Still, the man deserved a shallow grave. At least I didn't have to dig it. He'd done enough digging of his own, and he'd soon be buried by the consequences of all he'd done.

Draga patted my arm. 'You do good, Missus Jac.'

'I did, didn't I?' I felt free of him. Life was falling back into place.

Judy reappeared at the door, her face blotchy. She drew on a cigarette until her cheeks imploded and the tip burned bright.

'Rohan, did you take all that money?' she asked.

'For sure he do, Missus Judy,' Draga said.

Judy ground her cigarette into an ashtray until the filter flattened.

'You look bad, Missus Judy,' Draga said. She added in a soothing voice, 'I have the Avon in my bag. Come, we put the muckup on you face.

Believe me, you feel much better. Maybe you like buy for next time?'

CHAPTER TWENTY

It had been a long day. Draga had come within a lipstick's smear of making an Avon sale, and I'd gone from killer to acquittal.

'Ant will be so happy to know his dad's okay,' I said as we drove from Judy's house.

'Da. This true.' Draga sighed. 'But what you be say to boy? Good news – you father not dead, but is bad news, too – he big liar thief.'

'I haven't quite worked it out. I'm sure the words will come.'

'You must say how we find him. He will know his father chase the woman. I not think the boy be happy, but you must say what is true.'

The explanation would be tricky, but I needed to stop applying my newly found protection of Ant to everything in his life. Those unsavoury truths would include some about my part in this saga. Although Rohan had agreed to keep quiet about my role in his disappearance, if I had to explain, I would. Making excuses for anyone, including myself, wasn't my job any more.

By the time we arrived home, I'd decided my best course of action was to tell Ant the facts: his father was alive, his father was staying with a friend, his father had poor taste in bedroom attire. Rohan could explain to Ant details of everything else he'd done.

'I sorry for boy. He not have the good luck with mother and father.'

'He still has us, Draga.'

'Da.' Draga turned the car into the street and cruised to the house. A motorbike was partially parked across the driveway entrance. She stopped halfway through the manoeuvre. 'Bah! Look how stupid people park.'

As Draga completed the turn, I glanced at the bike.

The house was in darkness as we jerked to a halt.

'Wonder where Ant is?'

'Boy sleep. He like sleep when he not eat. Boy have wolf in stomach.'

I guided the front door key into the lock, but before I could turn it, the door swung open. I snapped on the hallway light. It cued Draga's shocked voice behind me.

'Bože moj!'

The sofa cushions were slashed, exposing the stuffing. Storage unit doors were open, books and CDs were scattered on the floor. The vase on the coffee table was in pieces and flowers lay among the shattered glass. Water pooled in a murky blotch on the rug.

I flashed back to the badly parked bike at the front of the house.

New South Wales licence plate.

Sydney.

Cruiser.

A thud from upstairs was followed by a whimper.

I stilled. Where was Ant?

Another thud, harder this time.

'Don't move, Draga. Someone's in the house,' I whispered.

Draga tapped my shoulder and I stifled a scream.

She mimed talking on the telephone, put her hands up in surrender, and crossed her wrists behind her.

'I'm not waiting for the police if Ant's already in trouble.'

I found the flashlight on my phone, turned off the room light and signalled to Draga to follow. We went to the kitchen, guided by the narrow beam of light. Once there, she was in familiar territory and made her way through to the laundry storage cupboard and returned with her spare broom.

How should I arm myself? A knife was too risky if it fell into the wrong hands. I chose a heavy granite rolling pin. All I needed to do was get near enough to whack the intruder. Easier said than done. 'Upstairs and stick close together,' I said.

Draga's hand tightened around the broom handle.

We went up the first flight and paused on the landing. The rolling pin was heavy, and my sweaty hand was slippery on the handle. I stayed ahead of Draga, who hung onto the waistband of my track pants.

At the top of the next flight, I stalled. There was enough moonlight through the window to guide us and I pocketed the phone. The doors were all closed.

Draga bumped into me and then stepped back.

I nudged her, pointing to a sliver of light glowing underneath my bedroom door and mouthing, 'There.'

We took positions on either side of the door. I signalled to Draga to grab the handle.

She did a three-finger countdown and turned the knob. Like a cop on television, I burst through the doorway, rolling pin drawn.

Ant was crouched between the wall and the bedside table. A trickle of blood tracked down his face. He shielded it with a bloodied hand.

I dropped the rolling pin and ran to him.

He shook his head. 'No! Jac, don't come in!'

I was already beside him, stroking his face. 'What happened? Who did this?'

'I did.' The same voice that had been on the phone came from behind me.

I turned.

A man with long greasy hair and a wild beard was half-hidden behind the door. Fading tattoos peeked over his t-shirt collar and a stretching taper was lodged in his earlobe. The feature I noticed most was the gun in his hand.

'Step away or you'll get the same treatment,' he said.

I glimpsed Draga in the hallway behind him. She put her finger to pursed lips.

Please don't let him see her. If I kept him talking, Draga could activate her plan, whatever the hell that was. I hoped it was calling the police. Something I cursed myself for not doing earlier.

'What do you want?' I asked, watching his nicotine-stained fingers around the grip.

The thug smirked. 'I. Want. Cruiser's. Money.' He made tick-tock movements on each word.

'Who's Cruiser?' I asked, doe-eyed.

'He knows, dontcha ya, kid? Almost gotcha the other day. I'm sick of chasing ya.' He levelled the gun at us and grinned, revealing teeth that hadn't seen a dentist in a lifetime.

Ant trembled in my hold. I took his hand to help him up. 'Leave him alone. I'll get you the money.'

The man lowered the gun and took a step forward. 'Isn't that nice? I'll need security until I get it. The kid comes with me.'

'Over my dead body.'

He stepped forward. 'If ya want.'

I twisted around to shield Ant.

Ant pulled me back by the shoulder. 'Don't Jac, he'll shoot.' His voice faltered. 'I'm sorry.'

'Shh. It's okay,' I said.

'Very touching. Now get the money.' Cruiser's thug stepped into the doorway.

Draga was now directly behind him. She gripped the broom shaft with both hands, her mouth hard and eyes fiery. She stepped into the room and slammed the broom down on the thug's arm.

He flinched but didn't drop the gun. He spun to face her.

Adrenaline pumped into my muscles until they burned. I

flung myself at him, grabbing him around his right knee. He was all muscle and his clothes smelled of stale sweat and engine oil.

Draga swung the broom and connected with his torso.

I beat at his left leg with my free arm.

The thug grabbed my hair. A clump tore out and I rolled away, screaming.

'Svinja!' Draga yelled. 'I fix you, pig.' She raised the broom overhead.

There was a loud bang, like a giant cracker.

Thug swore. He jumped over me and ran.

Ant shouted, 'Draga!'

Draga lay on her side. Blood poured from a wound on her head. One Homyped sandal was across the room.

No! No! NO!

Heart thumping, I crawled to her, checked she was breathing and searched for her pulse. 'Draga, speak to me.'

For once, Draga had nothing to say.

Blood pooled onto the carpet. I ripped off my t-shirt and pressed it on the wound.

'Ant, get the phone out of my pocket and call an ambulance.'

He punched in the numbers and spoke to the dispatcher in breathless gulps. He hung up. 'They're on their way. Cops, too.'

'Get some towels.'

He returned with my best white ones.

Draga's face was grey and my tears dripped onto her as I held the towels over the wound. Blood spread into them until its stickiness seeped beneath my fingers.

Ant rocked back and forth. 'What should I do? What should I do?'

'Go wait for the paramedics. Hurry!'

Draga's blood was all over my hands. I wiped my tears and blood smeared my face. The metallic scent stayed with me.

'Don't die, Draga. Don't die. Please don't die.'

It seemed an eternity until the windows filled with flashing lights and the staccato of two-way radios burst into the house as emergency personnel swarmed inside.

A paramedic knelt beside me and insisted I let Draga go, but I couldn't.

She prised my hand off the wound. 'Please, ma'am.'

'Help her. Please help her.' I was already on my knees, I might as well beg.

The gloved paramedics worked on Draga. I wanted to scream at them to hurry, save her, but there was nothing left inside me. Draga's blood dappled my skin. In only my bra and track pants, I shivered. I picked up the lone Homyped and hugged it.

My field of vision covered the crowd of legs filing into the house: police boots, police uniform trousers, suit legs and a pair of polished shoes.

A strong hand reached down and helped me to my feet. Someone draped a jacket around me, the silky lining still warm with body heat and a familiar scent. Reassuring hands rested on my shoulders.

'I'm here, Jacqueline.'

I clung to Robert Angel and he cradled my head.

'Is she breathing?' I asked between sobs.

'They've put a mask on her so that's a good sign.' He placed a hand at my elbow. 'You need to come away.' He ran his gaze over my face. He was about to say something else, but I broke from his hold.

'I'm staying with her.'

'I know you're frightened, but the best thing you can do for Draga is to give the paramedics space to do their job.'

I sagged. 'But ...'

'And Ant needs you too,' he said.

I remembered the blood on Ant's face; his look of terror;

his attempt to protect me.

'Where is he?'

'He's downstairs with one of the uniforms. He's shaken up and has some cuts, but otherwise unhurt. We need to get you checked, too.' He guided me to the stairs.

I almost missed my footing twice on the way down. Each time Robert Angel caught me, and I wished I could stay in his arms.

He left me with Ant. 'I'll be back.'

I sat on the sofa next to my distraught stepson and put my arm around him. His pale face and red-rimmed eyes made me feel even more helpless.

Another paramedic team entered the house and came to him. They cleaned and dressed his facial cuts and put a pressure bandage around his wrist.

'The guy who shot Draga ... he was ...' Ant said.

I pulled him to me. His bony body shuddered.

'He's who you saw at The Fast Anchor, isn't he?'

Ant nodded. 'I recognised him when he came in. He nearly got me once, back in Sydney, but I got away.' He swallowed. 'How's Draga? Is she ...?'

'She's alive but ...' I wished I could say, She'll be right down.

Ant broke away and put his head in his hands. 'This is all my fault.'

'No, it's not, Ant.' My earlier feelings of being back in control of my life suffocated under the weight of his distress and Draga's injuries. Rohan, the business, every other problem paled in comparison.

Robert Angel returned with two blankets.

I pulled my blanket tight and tried to take deep breaths, but my chest wouldn't expand. I dripped with perspiration. I could smell the blood, feel its stickiness. Suddenly, I realised how much my body hurt, and my scalp still stung where Thug had pulled my hair.

'You okay, Jac?' Robert Angel asked. He grabbed me as I wilted sideways.

I vaguely heard Ant call my name.

The next thing, I came to with someone holding my hand.

'Jacqueline, my name is Adele. I'm one of the paramedics. This is my partner, David. We're going to check to see how you're doing.'

There was a rasping sound. I realised it was me, gulping air. Was I dying? I grabbed the paramedic's arms, unable to speak.

'It's okay. You're hyperventilating. Concentrate on my eyes and breathe with me.'

It was difficult, but slowly my breathing evened out.

'Good,' Adele said. She strapped a blood pressure cuff around my arm. I winced. Bruises from the fight with Thug were beginning to appear and they pinched when I moved.

'Your BP is a little high. It's normal in the circumstances,' Adele said. 'This is oxygen to help with your breathing.' She slipped the elastic over my head and secured the plastic mask. 'I'll get you to lie down for a few minutes, and then I'll recheck you.'

'I want to see Draga.' I tried to get to my feet.

'Do as she asks, Jacqueline,' Robert Angel said, his voice was terse.

He must blame me for all of this. I slumped down again.

'Stay with her, Ant. I'll be back.'

'Please be okay, Jac. I don't want something to happen to you, too.'

Ant sobbed.

I curled my hand around his. 'Everything will be okay,' I said, but my words fogged in the mask.

I wanted to filter out the noise and horror. The sound of Thug's voice, the stink of him, Ant's terrified face, Draga's blood on the carpet, Draga lying still.

Please let her live. Let her live and yell at me all she wants.

Robert Angel returned. I couldn't look at him. What if I saw bad news in his eyes?

'Draga's stable but she'll need surgery. They're taking her to the trauma unit.'

Ant moaned and let go of my hand. I ripped away the oxygen mask.

'You'll need to leave it on a little while longer, Jacqueline,' Adele said.

'I need a moment with Ant.' I threw her, then Robert Angel, a pleading look.

The detective said something to the paramedics and they stepped aside.

'I'll be over there keeping an eye on you,' Adele said.

'Listen to me, Ant. Draga's tough, she'll pull through this. We both need to stay strong for her.' It sounded trite, but I wanted both of us to believe it.

Ant bit his lip and nodded. 'I'll try.'

'There's something else. It's about your dad.'

'Did they find him? Is he okay?' he asked, breathing rapidly.

'He's fine.' I held his hands. 'Draga and I found him today. We'd just come back from where he's been staying when we walked into all this. It's a long story, and most of it he'll have to tell you himself. I'll call him and tell him about Draga. Then I want you to go and stay with him.'

'But I want to stay with you.'

'Please, Ant. You need time with your dad to sort things out, and I want you somewhere safe. That mongrel's still out there. He won't find you if you're with Rohan. I'm going to the hospital. I promise I'll let you know as soon as there's any news.'

Ant opened his mouth, but Robert Angel stepped up.

'Ant, buddy, are you up to talking with my colleague, Sam Villacorta? We want to get your story. Best to do it while it's fresh in your mind.'

Skinny came forward, still in an oversized jacket, still eager. Our eyes locked and he nodded.

Ant went with him to the dining table, where Skinny took notes.

Ant kept swiping the back of his hand across his eyes. He rested his forehead onto the table. Skinny put down his pen and leaned forward, his hands clasped. He said something, and Ant lifted his head and nodded.

Even though there was nothing I could do for Draga for now, I could help Ant.

'Detective, I need to make a call.' I met Robert Angel's questioning eyes. 'To Rohan.'

He raised an eyebrow. 'Your missing husband, Rohan?'

I straightened. 'I'll explain everything later. First, I need to make sure Ant's safe.'

'Fair enough.'

'Um ... also, I'll need police resources to find a landline number. It's the house where Rohan's staying.'

He gave me the assessing look that was fast becoming a feature of our relationship. I hated him thinking I was a bad person, but what did I expect? All Detective Angel had seen was the lying, nasty side of me.

I called Rohan, then an officer drove Ant to Judy's house. I let him go knowing he was in for more pain. Robert Angel didn't ask anything further. We'd have that conversation later. I swallowed hard just thinking about it.

'The paramedics are about to bring Draga downstairs. I want you to be prepared. She's rigged up to a lot of equipment,' he said.

Just then, Skinny approached. 'Mrs Burne, we need some details about the attacker.'

'Not now. I'm going with Draga. Can't I do it tomorrow?'

'We need to confirm if Ant's description fits with yours. We can't look for him without a full picture.'

'About as tall as Detective Angel. Bearded and built like a brick wall. Wearing jeans and a black t-shirt. Tatts all over him; skulls and thistles. He has piercings. He rides a motorbike. No idea what make, but it's registered in New South Wales.'

'Anything else?' Skinny asked, scribbling down the details.

Voices at the top of the stairs made me turn. The paramedics deftly angled the stretcher around the awkward landing turn. Draga was covered in a blanket, her head immobilised by a neck brace. Her eyes were closed, and the wound area was covered with a bandage. Drips attached to a stand curled their way underneath the blanket.

'I'm going with her,' I said.

'I'm sorry. You can't go in the ambulance,' Adele said.

'I'll drive myself then.'

'What about ...?' Skinny asked.

'I'm not doing this now.' The night's events flashed across my mind, vivid and unforgettable. 'Don't worry. I'll remember every single detail tomorrow.'

Robert Angel gave a tiny nod and Skinny took a few paces back.

I pushed myself up with more bravado than energy. 'I have to find my car key.'

'You're not driving anywhere, Jacqueline. I'll take you,' Robert Angel said. 'There's nothing more we can do here until the forensics guys have finished. The photographer is on her way. Villacorta and the uniforms will be here until it's all done.'

Outside, the air was cool. Curious neighbours were in the street, but a cordon kept them back. They huddled in groups, pointing and talking among themselves. The ambulance door slammed shut and it pulled away, flashing lights alternating blue and red.

With siren wailing, it carried Draga into the black night.

CHAPTER TWENTY-ONE

Forty-five minutes had passed since the emergency team had wheeled Draga into the hospital. The hands of the wall clock circled the face in jerky movements. I watched them, counting the minutes.

Robert Angel and I sat in the last two available chairs in the Emergency Department waiting room. Phones rang, and staff answered in loud, brusque voices. Those waiting paced around, some with obvious cuts, some on crutches, some slumped against carers.

It threw me back to childhood memories of my mother's last illness. She'd faded slowly, cancer devouring her until she was a pale covering of skin over small bones. The image had burned into my brain. I felt as powerless now as I had then.

Draga's dried blood flaked on my fingers. I clasped my hands as though in prayer, but really to stop them shaking.

The doors through to the treatment area slid open with a hiss. My shoulders drooped as a man with his arm plastered and in a sling came out supported by a harried-looking woman. He had stitches across his forehead and a black eye. She wore a sequined party dress with a large rip in the front panel and held black stilettos in her hand. Someone else's night had ended badly.

'I wish they'd hurry up,' I said. I pressed my hand over my heart as though I could stop it racing.

Robert Angel checked his watch.

One staff member, a stout woman with a severe haircut and an air of efficiency about her, caught my eye and sent me a taut, understanding smile. 'The doctor will be out as soon as possible.'

'Thanks,' Robert Angel said.

'I can wait alone, Detective,' I said, although I didn't want him to leave. His presence kept me from collapsing in a screaming heap. Besides, I liked the way his shoulder sometimes brushed against mine when he shifted in his seat. Not that he'd notice. 'Or are you staying to ask more questions?'

'Not for now. Draga's the priority.'

'Thank you.' In the past week, he'd become part enemy, part moral support and definitely someone whose presence changed my breathing pattern. I pulled his jacket tighter around me. I felt protected, which was crazy, given my emerging criminal curriculum vitae.

The speaker system announced a 'Code Blue'. Behind the scenes, a medical team would be galvanising into action, ready to resuscitate. Had it been called for Draga? I stared at the doors of the treatment area, but no one came out.

I scanned racks of pamphlets outlining the illnesses that could affect one's body. Alongside was a notice board, overladen with community announcements. I made a mental note of an Anxiety Support Group's meeting times in case I needed it for future reference.

Nothing could distract from the queasy feeling left by the image of Draga on the floor, her blood pooling. Every time I visualised the scene, tears threatened to escape. I pushed my palms into my eyes to stem the flow. What would I do if Draga didn't get better? I wouldn't allow myself to think about the worst outcome. I stifled a sob with a blood-covered hand. The sharp, metallic smell sent a surge of nausea through me.

'Jacqueline, do you want to wash your hands?' Robert Angel asked. 'I'll be here if the doctor comes out.'

I shook my head, sensing him still watching me.

He went over to the water fountain and returned with his

handkerchief dampened.

'It's clean,' he said, as he squatted near me. 'Do you mind?' He took my hands and wiped the blood off them. I wanted to close my fingers around his. 'Try not to worry. She's in the best place.'

'I know, but it's my fault that she's here. I let her down.'

'I've seen you two together. I know how much you mean to each other. I like her, too, even if she is a terrible liar.' He gave a gruff laugh. 'There must be someone we should call for her?'

'She doesn't have much family. There's a cousin, but I don't know her name or how to contact her.'

What sort of person was I? Draga had worked with me for more than four years, and I knew only what I needed to know about her to make my life better.

The doors opened, and a doctor emerged. 'Family of Draga ...'

Before she finished, I jumped up. 'Here.'

Robert Angel stood beside me and put a steadying hand on my back. I breathed deeply against it.

'I'm Doctor Chen,' she said. 'Draga is stable. The damage wasn't as extensive as we'd anticipated. She's lucky, but she'll need further attention to the injury. We've scheduled her for surgery shortly. We expect it to be routine. Then it'll be a few days in hospital after which we'll assess for rehabilitation. We anticipate a good outcome.'

'Thank you.' I slumped against Robert Angel and his hand on my back pressed in to support me. I straightened reluctantly. 'Can we see her before the surgery?'

'It's not possible. She's already gone to theatre. It will be three to four hours before she's out. She'll need time in recovery, and then we'll transfer her to the neurology ward. There's nothing else you can do here. I suggest you go home and get some rest. Come back tomorrow with some personal things for her stay. We'll be able to give you more information then.'

'Thank you, doctor.' I wanted to hug her.

Dr Chen spun on her efficient heels, and the treatment area doors hissed together behind her.

I wanted to hug Robert Angel, too. 'She's going to be all right!'

'That's excellent news. I'm relieved for her, you and Ant.' He dropped his hand from my back and it felt like I'd lost something.

'Do you feel up to getting Draga's things?' he asked. 'We can pick them up and I'll bring them back here if you like. You look like you need some sleep.'

'There's no need for you to ...'

'Consider it a police directive. I think you've been toughing it out too long.'

'I appreciate your kindness, Detective, but I don't understand. You were investigating me a few days ago.'

'Let's just say I've seen too many women stuffed around by men doing the wrong thing. Sometimes they need someone to let them know they can change things.' He paused and regarded me steadily. 'You're stronger than you think.'

'I doubt that,' I said, looking away.

'Don't be so sure. Think about what you've dealt with in the last few days. You need to see yourself in a different light. The way others see you.'

'Like who?' I asked. Him?

Angel smiled. 'Come on. We'd better go.'

Outside, the air had turned cold. I shivered and slipped my arms into the jacket.

At the car, Robert Angel opened the passenger door for me.

I sat, and he reached across me to pull the seat belt and snap it into place. My breath caught, and I only exhaled when he sat back.

'What's Draga's address?' he asked, starting the car.

'Unit four, seventy-three Temple Street.'

'Have you been there before?'

'Never,' I said in a small voice. 'I only know her address from the employment documents.'

'You won't have a key then?'

'There'll be one hidden somewhere. Draga's always prepared for contingencies.'

But nothing could have prepared her for tonight. I imagined Draga in the operating theatre and silently repeated She's going to be all right like a mantra while we drove.

Robert Angel didn't need directions. Chasing criminals must make the city's layout familiar.

In Temple Street, we slowed until we came to the right number. The neat set of units was fringed by drought-resistant plants. Draga's unit was at the rear. Pebble borders ran along the path to her door. A security light flared on and a dog in the next yard barked. On her doorstep were several garden gnomes and a jade plant in an orange enamel pot. Next to them, a large plastic bag of goods she'd left out for a charity collection.

Robert Angel found the house key inside the hollow of a gnome.

'This is why I get the big detective bucks.' He held up the key and jiggled it.

There was that kick in my gut again. Stronger than all the ones before.

The door opened and I caught a scent of lavender. I switched on the light and it spilled onto my first glimpse of Draga's private life.

The interior colour palette was like an explosion in a paint shop. The entrance hallway was painted daffodil. Beyond it, a fuchsia feature wall in the small lounge room. The vivid hues contrasted with the bland neutral interior of my home.

In the lounge, knick-knacks on crocheted doilies filled every available space: trinket boxes, angel statuettes, little vases filled with artificial flowers. A small television in the corner faced a two-seater sofa. How many nights had she sat there alone with her memories?

Framed photographs covered a sideboard. In one, a young Draga was held in a hug by a handsome man. They both wore wedding rings, and happiness radiated from the photograph. In another, Draga held a newborn in her arms, her face lit with joy. Beside those was a series of snaps of a boy at various ages, sometimes alone, sometimes with Draga or her husband, sometimes as a family group. In the last, he was around ten years of age.

'I'll check everything's secured,' Robert Angel said from behind me.

'Okay.' I wiped my cheeks, hoping he hadn't noticed my tears.

I went to the kitchen. Everything smelled of mild disinfectant and, of course, Draga's favourite domestic weapon, bleach. The pantry door was open. As I closed it, I glimpsed the shelf contents: canned Borlotti beans, tuna, rice, varieties of pasta, flour, sugar, long-life milk. There were assorted preserved foods, plus tins of olive oil, large jars of dried herbs – at least six of each item, all lined up. I should have expected these indicators of siege mentality in someone who'd lived through a war. An experience I should have been more sensitive to. I knew how hard it was to carry a painful loss alone. I was a lousy friend to many people, but especially to Draga.

In her bedroom, a neat single bed was set against the wall, a picture of a haloed saint above it. On the bedside table was a tattered prayer book, the spine secured with sticky tape. I picked it up. Draga had inked her name in spidery handwriting on the inside cover. A photograph slipped from between the pages. The same faces that were in the other pictures – her husband and son. On the reverse, she'd written Petar, Jovan (10 godina). I took these to be their names and her son's age.

I went through Draga's wardrobe, feeling like an intruder.

There weren't many clothes. I selected a week's worth of cotton underwear, a bra, and two nightgowns. I could always come back for more. I unhooked a dressing gown hanging behind the door and collected a pair of well-worn slippers near the bed.

Robert Angel entered with two bags. 'I found these in the other bedroom.' He held the larger one open and without embarrassment, he took Draga's clothing from me and packed it.

'You okay?' he asked.

'I'm a bit overwhelmed,' I said. It was an understatement.

Robert Angel saw the prayer book in my hand. 'That looks like it's important to her. We should take it.'

The way he said we filled me with warmth.

I added the book to the bag, making sure the picture of Petar and Jovan was secured between the pages. 'I think this picture's important to her.'

He showed me the contents of the other bag. 'Toiletries. Have I missed anything?'

He'd packed a toothbrush and toothpaste, deodorant, face cream, and a container of talcum powder.

'Well done,' I said. 'Most men don't know their way around the contents of a woman's bathroom.'

'I've done this before.'

Damn. Of course there must be someone in his life.

'We used to go away on weekends. I was the packer for my partner and me.'

I imagined him with someone and turned away. 'Sounds nice. Did you go away often?'

'We did. Then she went on a solo weekend and never came back. After that, someone else was packing her bags.'

'I'm sorry.' I hated thinking of him broken-hearted. Get a grip.

'I'm not. Not anymore,' he said without bitterness. 'Been on my own now a couple of years and I'm used to it. Sometimes it's not worth hanging on.'

I was beginning to see that. Robert Angel not only raised my temperature, but he seemed like a genuinely decent man, even though he might still arrest me.

'I should close all the curtains if the place is going stay empty for ...' I choked.

How long would it take Draga to recover? Would there be permanent damage?

Robert Angel put down the bag and took my hand. My power grid went into overdrive.

'Draga will be fine. She's a fighter and a strong character. She isn't the type to give up easily.' He stared at me.

I tore my gaze away, wondering if he knew the firestorm he'd started in me.

'I'm sure you're right,' I said and took a small step back, forcing Angel to release his hold. It wasn't what I wanted but it was crazy to have feelings for the investigating officer. Nothing could come of it. 'Um ... anything else?'

'Throw out anything in the fridge that won't keep.'

'I hope she gets well quickly,' I said, as I bundled perishables into a rubbish bag. 'I can't stand to think of her being in pain for a long time.'

'Draga's feisty. She'll be putting all her effort into getting better,'
he said.

'Yes, she's come through a lot. Those photographs in the lounge room are her husband and child. I believe she lost them in the war.'

'I noticed they weren't recent,' he said.

'I'm ashamed how much I didn't know about Draga's life, and how alone she'd been.'

'She has you.'

'Thank you, Detective.' I wanted to hug him for his confidence in me and for not blaming me for Draga's predicament. Mainly, I wanted to feel him against me.

He opened the front door. 'Ready to go?'

'Sure.' As I walked past him, his scent wrapped around me and held
me tight.

While I mused on that, Robert Angel shut the door on Draga's
modest world.

CHAPTER TWENTY-TWO

From the outside, my house appeared normal. The police vehicles were all long gone, and the street was quiet. As if nothing had happened.

Robert Angel walked with me to the front door. 'I don't like you being here alone, Jacqueline. Cruiser's heavy might still be around. If the forensics team hadn't finished, you wouldn't be allowed near the place.'

'I'm sure he's long gone. I'll be fine. The doors have heavy duty locks. I just need a few hours' sleep and I prefer my own bed. I'll visit Draga in the morning, then go to work. I need things to be normal.'

I slipped the key into the lock. After everything Robert Angel had done for me, I wasn't sure how to say goodbye. Shake his hand or high five him? I wanted to kiss him, but I kept my head down.

'Thank you, Detective. I appreciate everything you've done tonight. I'll give a full statement tomorrow, I promise.'

I took Draga's overnight bag from him and our fingers brushed. I pulled my hand back quickly, putting the bag beside the door, ready for tomorrow's hospital visit.

'Good night, Detective,' I said, starting to push the door closed.

He put out his hand to stop me. 'I'll get the uniforms to drive by and ...' He reached into his pocket. 'In case you can't find the last card I gave you, here's my mobile number. Call me. Anytime.' He stifled a yawn. 'Sorry, it's been a long day.'

As his car drove away, my confidence ebbed. Standing in the

quiet, I wasn't so sure about staying in the house alone. In my pride, I thought I could. I considered calling him immediately, but that would be embarrassing. Besides, police had crawled over this place all day and Cruiser's henchman wouldn't risk coming back. I was being an idiot.

What was it Angel said? You're stronger than you think.

I switched on all the lights. In the kitchen, I almost expected Draga to barrel through the door, ready to admonish me about something I'd done wrong. I missed her chatter and rowdiness. I missed the ordered chaos she brought to my days. I made cocoa and spooned in more sugar than was good for me.

The silence was unsettling, and the house was thick with the memory of Ant and Draga being hurt. I stood in the lounge, head filled with images of Draga with tubes hanging by her side, eyes closed and unable to speak.

I couldn't face going upstairs. Instead, I stretched out on the sofa and pressed the television remote. A shopping program popped up in which an exuberant presenter prattled on about jewellery, holding up a gem-encrusted cross. I thought of Draga's plain gold one. How was the surgery going?

I pulled a throw over myself, tucked a cushion in the crook of my arm and shut my eyes. The television presenter's enthusiasm droned in the background. My mind raced as the night's events replayed in my head. Eventually, I drifted into a dream where I stood at the bottom of the stairs, looking up at Draga on the landing. She fell forward, soaked in blood. I woke up sweating. I told myself it was just a dream, yet the sick feeling stayed with me.

I checked my watch: 3.15am. Draga must be out of surgery by now. I'd call the hospital and enquire.

The television program had changed to a black and white movie, dramatic music peaking as a gun battle ensued. I muted it.

There was a scraping sound. It came again, louder.

The hairs on my neck stood. I sat up, ready to run. A thud resonated behind me.

Cruiser's heavy stood in the doorway, all bushy eyebrows, and arms like big hams.

I looked past him to the open back door.

He followed my gaze and turned back, sneering, 'Locks don't bother me.'

Thug positioned himself between me and the back door. 'Ya ain't getting away. Did ya think I wouldn't be back? I want the five grand.'

'There's a cop outside,' I said, voice scratchy.

'No way. I've been watching this joint.' His raspy laugh was honed by years of smoking and too many alcohol chasers.

Could I get around him? I had the home ground advantage. I knew the house's layout and could use that knowledge to get out via the laundry, or out onto the upstairs balcony and down the drainpipe to the street, or ...

The thug pulled a gun out and pointed it at me.

Or I could stand here in the line of fire. I raised my hands in surrender.

'On ya feet.' He snarled. It made him even more ugly.

'Come on, hurry up!' His face was so near mine, his spittle hit me. I gagged and wiped my face with my sleeve.

The movement made Thug jump, and he thrust the gun closer.

I stared down the dark barrel.

'You and that kid already caused me enough trouble. I got cops all over me, and still no money for Cruiser.'

He pushed the gun against my temple; the metal was cold on my skin. Not daring to breathe, I thought of Draga and Ant.

'Get up.' Thug stepped aside. 'Ya said ya had money. Where is it?'

'Up ... upstairs. In the safe.'

He lowered the gun and shoved it into my ribs. 'Let's go!

Don't try anything dumb.'

Hands raised, I pressed against the handrail as we went upstairs, but I stumbled.

Thug shoved me.

I fell forward. Pain shot through my kneecap.

'Get up!'

I couldn't move fast, and he punched the back of my head. I hobbled to the top of the stairs, Thug clomping along behind.

At the open bedroom door, Draga's blood on the carpet had dried to almost black.

I couldn't get the pictures and sounds out of my mind.

Draga moaning as she hit the ground.

Ant screaming.

Me screaming.

Blood. Everywhere, blood.

From behind me, Thug's foul breath fell on my neck. He cleared his throat of phlegm and hacked his deep cough. 'Hurry up!'

I mustered the courage to step over the bloodstain and into the room. Draga's broom still leaned against the bed where it had landed after the bullet hit her.

'Haven't got all night.' Thug jabbed the gun in my ribs.

The safe was on the floor inside the wardrobe. I pushed aside the clothes to get access, knelt, my sore knee jarring. I keyed the numbers on the keypad. My hand shook so much, I blundered. The error tone pierced the air.

'What was that?'

'I made a mistake. I'm nervous.'

He swung at me, catching me hard on the cheek. Lights sparkled at the side of my vision. I put my hand to my skin. It was sticky with blood.

What would happen after I handed over the money? Would he shoot me?

Vision fuzzy, I pressed the combination numbers. The lock

released with a click.

Thug shoved me aside. I bumped back onto the floor. He kept the gun pointed at me, while he crouched and opened the door. He rummaged around, pulling out my jewellery, grabbing a couple of handfuls without looking at it, and shoving the loot into his pocket. He scooped out the documents I kept in the safe.

They scattered. My will landed at my feet. I swallowed and crawled backwards until I came to the bed and couldn't go any further.

He found the envelope in which I kept my 'mad money'. It was money I'd saved over a few years, setting it aside in small amounts for a rainy day. I'd never expected monsoon season. I wasn't sure exactly how much was there, but I knew it wasn't enough to meet Thug's demands.

He saw the notes sticking out of the envelope and thrust it at me. 'Count it.'

I counted aloud, my voice brittle. It took forever. 'Two thousand, seven hundred and seventy-five dollars,' I whispered as I finished.

'It's short.'

'I ... I can get more. I can go to the bank tomorrow.'

Thug laughed, triggering a hacking attack. When he finished coughing, his mouth stretched into a psychopathic grin, displaying his crooked teeth. 'No way ya gunna go to a bank. Not tomorrow, not ever.' He cocked the gun.

I waited, not daring to blink, pressing hard against the bed.

Thug drew nearer, pushing the gun forward. I lifted my sight from it and into his almost black eyes. They gleamed with crazed power.

'Killing me won't get Cruiser his money,' I said.

Thug grabbed my arm. Pain shot down to my fingers as he pulled me to my feet. I yelped. It felt like it would tear out of its socket. He twisted my arm behind me. My legs buckled. I placed a knee on the bed for support.

I glanced at Draga's broom leaning there, remembering the courage and determination with which she'd thrown herself at him.

'Ya been trouble since I took ya car.'

'It's not my car.'

'I don't care.'

He pushed me, and I fell back onto the bed.

'This shoulda been easy. Nick the car, rebirth it. Get Cruiser's dough.' He took a step forward, making a metronome motion with the gun to emphasise each point. 'But whadya think I find in the boot? Some old dude, half wrapped in a rug. What were you and the fat, old bird up to?'

I inched back on the mattress. 'You were going to torch the car with him in it?'

'Do I look stupid?' He paused.

Was he expecting me to confirm the fact?

'I pulled him out and left him asleep on the ground. I got the hell out of there.'

That's why Rohan didn't know about the BMW. He didn't know he'd been in the boot. By the time he'd come to, the car was gone. I imagined him waking dazed in the middle of the wetlands.

'You still could have got Cruiser's money by rebirthing the car.' I prattled on, buying time. 'It would've been more than he was owed.'

'Couldn't rebirth the car. Got some kinda smartarse GPS, hasn't it? They can track it once they know it's missing. The boss wouldn't like that.' He steadied his aim.

No point telling him that even if the car could be tracked, Rohan would have disabled the function.

'Why didn't you just dump it? Why set fire to it?'

'To teach you a lesson.'

'It's. Not. My. Car.'

'I know … now. But it's not pretty when Cruiser's angry.' He bent and placed the gun on the floor behind him and made a fist. 'Consider this interest for being short on the money and the hassle ya gave me.'

'Meaning?'

'I'm gunna beat ya before I shoot ya dead, dead, dead.'

'It was you. You took Rohan's phone and sent a message to Ant.'

'Wanted to let the little turd know I was onto him.'

'From his dad's phone?'

Thug stepped nearer. 'I warned him once before. Didn't work. The kid must be thick.'

'The dog poop. That was you, too?'

'Saw it on TV. The kid didn't get the hint. He mustn't watch the same show.' He frowned, trying to figure that one out. The guy had a PhD in stupidity.

I checked the gap between him and the door. Too small to get past him, and no escape behind me.

'Ya got nowhere to go.' He lunged at me, catching me on the nose. My eyes watered, and blood ran into my mouth. Everything turned misty grey and I thought I might faint.

Thug sprang at me again, snarling.

This was it. I was going to die.

I twisted away, but he punched me in the stomach. Pain shuddered through me. Gagging, I rolled across the bed towards Draga's broom and grabbed the shaft.

'Whadya think ya gunna do with that? The stupid old cow couldn't scare me with it.' His mouth twisted in a cruel laugh. 'Shoulda put more bullets in her.'

Should have put more bullets in her?

Should have put more bullets in her?

Thug was a lunatic and, if he was going to kill me, I might as well go down fighting.

Adrenaline strengthened my arms and legs. Every muscle

screamed in expectation.

My face burned as blood rushed to my head. I gripped the broom handle until my hands drained of colour.

I twisted suddenly and whacked the broom's head straight into Thug's groin. His mouth pulled into a large zero and his eyes crossed. He yowled and doubled over, grabbing his crotch and then fell to his knees.

I scrambled off the bed and swung. This time, catching his neck.

He toppled forward. 'Arghhhhh.' His hand fumbled for the gun.

I stomped my foot down on his fingers and there was a crack.

He howled. I kicked the gun and it skimmed just beyond his reach.

Thug wrapped his uninjured hand around my ankle. He pulled, forcing me to use the broom as a tightrope pole.

He raised himself to one knee.

I planted my free foot and scrambled to a legs apart stance, balanced stance, following his every move.

He got to both feet, his stomped-on hand hanging limp. Blood trickled off it. The other hand reached for my throat.

I steadied myself. The gun lay between us, too far for either of us to reach. Even if I did manage to pick it up, I had no idea how to handle it.

Thug flicked his gaze between it and me. He dove forward, grabbing the broom shaft with his good hand. I drew back with all my strength, but he clung on.

'I'll kill ya.' His tone warned he'd make good his threat.

We both pulled on the broom. I kicked and connected with his arm. He still wouldn't let go. My strength was waning. He was bigger and, I expected, used to this kind of fight. I called on all my reserves, but couldn't prise the broom away.

I changed tack. Instead of trying to jerk the broom handle

away, I pushed my weight onto it.

The shift caught Thug off guard. His grip loosened enough for me to pull forcefully.

The shaft slipped from his hands and into my control. I brought it down on his skull.

He grunted and collapsed, landing over the gun. He moaned then
went quiet.

Panting, I kept the broom raised and poked him with my foot.

His eyes sprang open. He rolled off the gun and reached to grab it.

In one smooth movement, I flipped the broom over and swung it like a golf club.

Straight into Thug's skull again.

The blow reverberated through me. He fell onto his back and lay still. I continued standing with the broom raised, watching his chest rise and fall.

One eye opened. His lips curled into a snarl.

I brought the broom down on his head so hard, the shaft snapped.

Thug grunted and went limp.

I stepped aside and waited until I was certain he wouldn't move.

Hair was stuck to my face with sweat. I raked it off. I picked up the gun, pinching the grip with my thumb and forefinger and locked it inside the safe. I grabbed belts from the wardrobe and strapped two around Thug's ankles and one around his thighs. I raised both his arms and strapped them together with two more belts, then threaded another through those and looped it around the slats of the bed base.

There was a gash on the side where blood streaked down his face and neck. Not as bad as the injuries he'd caused Draga.

Thug groaned. He opened one eye a sliver and strained to

move, and then he raised his head and struggled against the belts. 'Fuck you.'

I pulled myself up tall and stood over him.

'No, fuck you! You and your boss, Cruiser, owe Draga a new broom.'

CHAPTER TWENTY-THREE

Police vehicles lined the street. The same neighbours who'd watched the action when Draga was shot were again outside clustered in groups.

Thug was loaded into an ambulance and left under police escort.

'He'll be fine,' Robert Angel said.

'That's unfortunate,' I said, swigging Jameson Irish whisky. It burned down my throat and warmed my stomach. 'Want some?' I raised the empty glass.

'No, thanks. Not sure alcohol is good for either of us. You look like you're in pain. Those cuts and bruises are pretty nasty.'

'The paramedic said I'll be fine. Nothing's broken.' I put my hand to my face. It ached and was tender to my touch. 'I should've killed him.'

'I'll ignore that.' Robert Angel's eyes were bright. Arresting criminals must give him a boost. He sat opposite and loosened his tie.

'Do you live in that suit?' I asked.

'Almost,' he said, regarding me steadily. 'I know there's a lot of background to all of this you haven't told me. I want to clear up your story as soon as possible. We'll take a formal statement, but let's just chat now.'

'You want a woman recovering from an assault to talk about the trauma?'

'It's up to you.'

I blushed. 'All I've kept back is information about Rohan.'

He drummed his fingers on the table. 'Jacqueline, I didn't get to where I am because I'm stupid. You must be straight with me.'

If Robert Angel kept up this incessant pushing, I might decide he wasn't as nice as I'd started to think. I might be able to talk my way out of this, but I was sick of keeping track of all the lies I'd told about Rohan. Now he was 'alive' again, it would come out anyway. I was also tired of all the hurt I'd brought into every life I'd touched. I'd ignored Ant's problems for years and, because of that, Cruiser's lot nearly cost Draga her life.

There was only the background hum of household appliances. Then, as I increasingly acknowledged the extent of my predicament, the hum became a deafening sound like rushing water flooding my head.

I looked at Robert Angel, and my insides tumbled. After I confessed all, I expected it to be the last time in which I'd see some level of support from him. Damn it. I wanted Robert Angel to like me; really like me, because, damn it again, I really liked him. I was crazy. The circumstances were all wrong. All my thoughts of another time, another place, were swept aside by reality.

I sighed. 'Where should I start?'

He switched to his deadpan detective face. 'Wherever you want to.'

'I've already told you Rohan was having an affair. We argued. He was drunk, and I was angry.' My words stumbled against one another. 'The argument escalated. He said something terrible about ... about a miscarriage I had.'

'I'm sorry. That must have been a difficult time,' Robert Angel said.

'It was. Anyway, I lost my temper and slugged him. He fell and hit his head. I thought I'd killed him.' I paused but it was hard to swallow the lump in my throat. 'I'm not proud of what I did next.'

Robert Angel leaned back. 'Take your time.'

'I put him in the boot, planning to dump the body.'

'How did you get him into the boot?'

'It involved a wheelbarrow and a broom.'

He scratched his temple. 'So Draga helped?'

I gave myself a mental slap. I didn't want to cause her more trouble. 'Not really.'

'Don't lie, Jacqueline.'

'She helped a little,' I said, making the tiniest pinch gesture with my fingers.

'I suspect Draga doesn't do anything in small doses. Then what?'

'We went inside, left the garage door up and, stupidly, the key in the ignition. When we came back out, the car was almost at the end of the street. I didn't know who took it until tonight. That's when I learned it was stolen by the thug who shot Draga.'

'How is he connected to Rohan?'

'He's not. He's connected to Ant.' I sighed. 'Thug's a henchman for a Sydney drug dealer who Ant sourced drugs from. They were for his now ex-girlfriend and she had to come up with the five grand she owed, but she didn't. So Cruiser – he's the dealer – sent that animal after Ant. Wait! By now you must've have seen messages on his phone from her about it all.'

'We're still exploring that. But didn't Ant tell you anything about this when he came down from Sydney?'

'No, but I knew something was wrong. He was depressed, and I noticed bruising, so I figured he was in trouble, but I couldn't get anything out of him. Look, the kid's made some poor choices. He was stupid, yes, but he's young and his life's been tough so far. He just needs a chance.'

'I understand. When did he tell you about the drug money?'

'When Rohan ...' I cleared my throat. '... went missing. I couldn't tell Ant what I'd done. Then, when Ant got the text message, he thought Cruiser had Rohan, so he could get money out of him to repay the debt. Anyway, after the car was stolen, strange things started happening at home.'

'I remember you mentioned the hang-up calls, and dog droppings on the doorstep,' Detective Angel said.

'Yes. I didn't connect them with Ant. I figured whoever took the car knew what I'd done to Rohan and was trying to get to me. Possibly to blackmail me.'

'I can see how you might think so.'

'I was wrong. Thug was sending a message to Ant. The night of ... the incident ... he was watching the house, saw the garage door up and the car idling. He decided to cash in for Cruiser, but when he found Rohan in the boot, he freaked out. He dumped him, and then the moron drove the car to the wetlands and torched it. He still needed the money for the debt and came back to get it.'

I shuddered, remembering him standing in the doorway.

'You knew Rohan was alive all along?' Angel's brows lifted.

'No. It was a misdiagnosis.' I shrugged. 'I only knocked him out. In fairness, he looked terrible. There was blood everywhere. It was dark, and there was a lot of rain and wind. I couldn't see properly. In my panic, I assumed he was dead.'

'Good thing you're not in medical practice.'

I sniffed. 'When Rohan came to, he somehow got to his lover's house. We found him there.' Another mental slap. I hadn't meant to say 'we'.

'We'll get to Draga's part in a minute,' Robert Angel said. 'Rohan was never missing?'

'Yes and no. I believed he was dead, so he was kind of missing. Besides, I never reported him missing. That was Geoff Campbell being zealous. I honestly didn't know where Rohan was at the time.' I poured more whiskey.

'Enough.' Robert Angel took the glass away.

'He was still out to it when Cruiser's thug left him by the road. Turns out he couldn't remember a thing when he came to. He used the conference as a cover for getting away for a few days. He didn't have his phone, because Thug took it, but

Rohan thought I had it. Anyway, he had no idea people were looking for him.'

'What did Mr Burne want to get away from?'

Calling Rohan 'Mister' made me feel I was in a formal interview.

'He was unhappy with his business life. He was having financial problems with Geoff Campbell. Look, if you want any further information, you should ask Rohan.'

He nodded, tight-lipped, and rubbed his temple.

'Detective, what else do you want me to say? I believed I was a murderer. You can't blame me for trying to cover my tracks.'

'And Draga?'

'Anything Draga did, she did to protect me,' I said. 'Come after me if you want, but not her, or Ant. They were just caught up in my trouble.'

'I admire your loyalty.'

'I'm not sure I admire your persistence. Why all these questions all over again?'

'I need to know if you knew about or were involved in Rohan's crimes.'

He had been testing me. 'You already knew about the money he'd embezzled. That's why you'd spoken to Geoff Campbell before Rohan went missing. I swear on Draga's life I knew nothing, but I've since found out.'

Pain was spreading through my body. I was too exhausted to care if I passed his test.

What did it matter what he thought? He was doing his job and just being kind. He was never going to think of me the way I wanted him to.

'Detective, I've told more lies this last week than I have in a lifetime. Lies haven't got anyone in this family anywhere,' I said. 'I'll never be so stupid again. Please, can we finish this tomorrow? I'll come to your office and be as formal as you like.

I'll sign a confession, sit in your cells, whatever you want. I'm too tired to go on.'

'Of course.'

'And what are the chances of finding Cruiser?'

'Shouldn't take long.'

I clasped my hands and hung my head, trembling. Was it all over?

'Jac, you might need help to sort through this. We can put you in touch with a counselling service.'

'It won't make a difference. How can I unsee any of it?'

'I don't know you can, but talking to someone will make a difference. You're a strong woman, but everyone needs support.'

'I'll think about it.' I wondered if they offered those services in prison. Residence there was still a possibility. Rohan wasn't going to make a complaint, but now I'd admitted my role, I had no idea what the police might do.

I stood, wobbled and fell back onto the sofa.

Robert Angel paused then pulled his tie from around his collar. 'I'm not leaving.'

'Excuse me?'

'I made the mistake of leaving you alone once already. Until I'm sure they have Cruiser, I'm not leaving you. I'm staying right here on this couch.'

Heat spread up my neck at the thought of Robert Angel in my house for the whole night. With little energy left to fend off my guilt or my attraction to him, I wanted him as far from me as possible before I did something stupid. 'That's not necessary …'

'No argument. You look exhausted. Let me help you up.' He offered me his hand.

I wanted so badly to take it, but another jolt of Angel electricity would do me in.

I knew what I felt – hold me, kiss me – but what was going on in his head? He was just doing his protective police person thing. Besides, nothing could happen between us – the cop and the criminal.

I rubbed my eyes and stifled a yawn. 'If you insist. I'll get you a pillow and blankets.'

Angel cast his eyes down and rolled his lips before he dropped his hand. 'Cheers.'

When I returned he'd removed his jacket and his watch lay on the coffee table.

'Here, Draga keeps a supply of these.' I handed him a new toothbrush and a tube of toothpaste. 'You know how she is about backup supplies.'

'I've seen her in action.' He smiled.

My insides fluttered. Damn those eyes.

'There's a bathroom through there.' I pointed. 'You'll find fresh towels in the linen press. The kitchen's – well – you know where the kitchen is.'

'I track down crims for a living. I reckon I can find the kitchen.'

'Good night, Detective,' I said, still not making eye contact.

Angel leaned in and his scent sent a little arrow into my gut.

'I'll be right here if you need me. Sleep well. Good night, Jacqueline.'

Why did it sound like a song when he said my full name? Damn him.

I mumbled, 'Good night', then went upstairs as fast as my aching body let me. I felt better with Robert Angel in the house, but it wasn't the only reason my heart was dancing.

I showered and crawled into the bed in the spare room, leaving the bedside lamp on. I wondered what Detective Angel was doing. Had he turned on the television? Was he sending text messages to someone? Reading one of the magazines stacked on the coffee table? Was he thinking about me? I lay there deep breathing, but still, the day's images played like a series of video clips, rough-cut and unedited.

Maybe I should ring a counselling service. Talk about this, the miscarriage and the sense of loss I'd dragged around with me my whole life.

One thing was sure. Today I'd learned I was capable of doing anything to protect those I loved. As Robert Angel kept telling me, I was stronger than I thought.

That was a damn good thing.

'Dragaaaaaaaaaa!'

'Jac! Shh ... It's okay.'

The image of Draga faded as I heard the smooth voice again.

'It's okay. You're okay.'

I opened my eyes. Robert Angel sat on the edge of my bed, pushing strands of hair away from my face. 'It was just a bad dream. You were screaming for Draga. She's safe. You're safe. Everything's fine.' He ran his thumbs across my cheek and pressed away my tears.

I shook as wave after wave of panic spread over me until I thought I would die. I didn't want to be afraid anymore. Mostly, I didn't want to be alone.

My arms flew around Angel and I pushed my face into his warm neck and sobbed. His arms encircled me and he pulled me to him, rubbing my back with a smooth, strong hand. For the first time in a long time, I felt safe. Safe enough to let myself cry about everything that had happened. About Draga, about Ant and about the end I knew had come for my marriage. Anything I needed to face, I could, as long as Draga and Ant were okay.

Lulled by the rise and fall of Angel's chest and his steady heartbeat reverberating through taut muscle, I slackened into his hold, wanting to stay there forever. My breathing fell into a rhythm with the movement of his calming hand and my crazy, tumbling world finally stood still.

Angel moved his hands to my shoulders and drew back. We stared at each other, his eyes blazing. Maybe because they were burning into my soul.

My body pulsed. It had been a long time since a man had touched me. And this man was – well – Robert Angel was like no man I'd experienced before.

'Detective ...' My voice was barely a whisper.

Angel put his finger to my lips and left it there. He needn't have bothered. I'd already lost all my words.

'I think we're past formalities, Jac.' He lowered his gaze and mine followed his downwards. I remembered I was naked. My breasts had pressed against him while he'd rubbed my bare back. We were definitely past formalities.

And we were past words.

Angel slid his hand to the back of my neck and pulled me towards him. His mouth covered mine in deep kisses and I fell effortlessly into them. Soft, moist lips brushed my bruises, then along my neck, each kiss waking my body a little more. Propelled by desire so urgent that I'd not felt before, I ran my hands along the strong sinews of his back, his arms, the tingling stubble on his cheeks. I breathed in his scent and the warmth of him. I took his weight effortlessly, my cries mingling with his rapid breathing.

My name like music.

This is what it felt like to be alive again.

Hours later, tangled between the sheets and his body, I dozed until sunlight streamed into the room and lit the reality of my situation. I propped onto my elbow.

'Robert, will you be in trouble?'

'What do you mean?'

'Sleeping with the enemy.'

'You're not my enemy.'

'Okay, maybe not yours, but ... Please believe that I'm sorry for the problems I've caused. But how deeply am I in trouble? Be honest. Will I be arrested?'

I held my breath, waiting as his mouth, which had been so soft all those kisses ago, set in a tight line.

'I'm sorry to tell you this, Jacqueline ...' He held the moment.

I caught the twinkle in his eyes.

'... you're not worth the paperwork.'

Then Robert Angel reached for me and kissed me again and again
and again.

As I walked into the All Class offices the following Monday, everything
felt different.

More importantly, I felt different.

'Jac! It's great to see you,' Paulette said, looking up from the reception desk. 'We were all shocked about the shooting. Oh, my, your face! Are you sure you should be here?'

'I'm fine, Paulette. I feel pretty good, all things considered.' My constant tension was gone, and I could live with my healing cuts and bruises.

'How's Draga?'

'The specialist said she's doing well.'

The knowledge tempered the sting I felt every time I remembered she was still experiencing pain.

'That's great news. If you're ready for business, there are a couple of urgent messages for you. Dylan Lucas from Best Breaks Travel called. Something about All Class becoming a preferred supplier. Also, someone who said she was Maddison Parker's manager at Globe General Bank wants you to call her about finding a replacement for Maddison. And they have additional positions they need to recruit.'

Andrew beamed when he saw me. 'Chief! You're here. Ouch! Your face!'

'Send a group-wide email telling everyone to stop worrying about my face! It's nothing.'

Andrew laughed and looked like he was about to embrace me, then stepped back. 'Good news. I'll have the Financial Services Sector Tender finalised within the hour. Timing's down to the wire, but I love a challenge.'

'Andrew, you're the best.' I pulled him into a hug.

When I let him go, colour rushed into his cheeks. He patted down the Batman image on his tie. 'I better go and ...' He hurried away.

There was one more thing to do to make my day perfect.

I psyched myself up in the bathroom room where I checked my reflection. Today my makeup was perfect. I'd left my hair loose. For once, I'd embraced the bouncing waves with a direction of their own. A woman can achieve anything on a good hair day.

I'd also replaced my engagement and wedding rings with a pearl and marcasite one my mother had left me. Amid all the sad memories of her illness, I clung to one bright image – Mum's smile whenever she saw me. She was a strong and brave woman, and I was getting a glimpse of that in myself.

I marched into Sandi's office.

She was at her desk, focussed on her computer screen.

I slammed the door behind me.

Sandi jumped and half-stood. 'Jac, what are you ... You look awful.'

'You're not so flash yourself.'

Sandi's polished glow had dulled and wisps of messy hair framed her drawn features. Her mascara was smeared and her lipstick had faded, leaving patchy colour on her mouth.

She sat and reached to click off her monitor.

'Computer trouble, Sandi?'

'No, I'm trying to log in and it won't ... forget it, I'll work it out later.'

I sat in her visitor's chair and sighed. 'It's a pity to lose all this, Sandi.'

She glowered. 'What do you mean?'

'A nice office and a good job working with people who trusted you.'

'I don't have a clue what you're on about.' Her glare sharpened with the lie.

'Yes, you do. I'm guilty of being too trusting. But you, you're guilty of being a thief.'

Red-faced, Sandi rose, arms by her side with her fists clenched. 'What exactly are you accusing me of? I've done nothing wrong.'

'Nothing wrong? You stole clients and tried to wreck All Class's database.'

She tilted her chin. 'You can't prove anything.'

'I can, but unfortunately, approaching clients isn't a criminal activity.'

I frowned.

Sandi's fists unclenched. 'So, even if I had done something, you can't do a thing about it.'

'Let's see. I could take action along the lines of a breach of your employment contract. It would mean hours in court and enormous legal expense. It's all too time-consuming.' I waved the idea away.

Sandi smirked. 'As I said, you have nothing on me.'

'Not so fast,' I said.

Her nostrils flared.

'I do have all the evidence of your scheme with Jason Keene. I have copies of all your client correspondence and those between you and Jason. I have evidence you – shall we say – 'shared' assignments with him. Globe General Bank, for example. They had six vacancies: you logged four and gave him two. I have emails and text message records on the company mobile phone. You were a bit slack there on a few occasions. You should have stuck to your personal phone.' I blinked a few times for effect.

Sandi's colour ebbed. 'Clients can deal with whoever they choose,'
she said.

'True. Technically, I can't restrict you or Mr Keene from earning your livings.'

Sandi smirked then tipped her nose up in triumph, oozing self-satisfaction.

Fortunately, Angel had instructed me in Fraud Law 101.

'Except there's a crime called ... let me see ... oh, yes. Something about making and using a false document. I can't remember the exact wording. You and Jason Keene created emails to lie to clients about candidates' availability and assignments being cancelled. I have evidence you sabotaged the database, which is a criminal activity. All those little nails of proof demonstrate you planned and stood to gain from the deception. Those little nails will hold down your career's coffin lid tightly. I'll leave it to the police to sort out.' I gave her a double thumbs-up.

Sandi flopped into her chair and hung her head.

I stood and stretched out my palm. 'Hand over your access card. Pick up your handbag and get the hell out of here.'

Sandi took the lanyard with the card from around her neck and threw it on the desk. At the door, she paused and faced me. She opened her mouth.

'Don't bother, Sandi. You're the only "no class" part of All Class and I'm glad to be rid of you. You won't get a job in this industry again. Meantime, you might want to seek legal advice.' I smiled.

Sandi's chin quivered before she turned and strode out.

'Give my best to Jason,' I called after her. I bounced around in celebration. I was mid-prance when Andrew appeared in the doorway.

'Tender's ready to be lodged, Chief,' he said.

Paulette scurried up behind him, her face flushed, her tone as if reporting a global disaster.

'Sandi's lost it,' she said. 'She stormed into reception and knocked over my flowers. Then she threw the magazines everywhere and tipped up the waiting room chairs. What's all that about?'

'That,' I said, 'is her official resignation.'

CHAPTER TWENTY-FOUR

On the drive home from the rehabilitation centre, Draga stared out of the window as the houses flashed past. The wound was healing and in the shaved patch, silvery strands of hair had started to sprout back.

I wanted to tell her how sorry I was for all the worry and trouble I'd caused her, especially for her being on the receiving end of Thug's gun. But in the three weeks since the shooting, I'd failed to find the right words. Whatever I came up with was never enough to express what I needed to say. Even if I grovelled for the rest of my life, I wouldn't be able to make up for any of what had happened.

We travelled in silence until Draga asked, 'How you be do everything in house without me?'

'We managed.' We had, with a great deal of humility on my part. On the plus side, Ant had mastered the washing machine and the dishwasher. I'd mastered the vacuum cleaner and the hotplates. We were verging on being domesticated.

'And Mr Ruin?'

'Rohan's staying with Judy. She seems to have forgiven him.' I winced, thinking how I needed the same from Draga. 'The investigation into his business isn't over yet. I don't know what will happen, but I can't help him. He has to face up to the fraud.'

I reflected on Rohan's predicament. Depending on Geoff Campbell's still-to-be-made decision, he was facing charges and a prison term. He wouldn't look any better in a prison jumpsuit than I would've.

'Maybe I go one day see Missus Judy. See if I sell her the

Avon, make her bit happy.'

I stifled a smile and Draga waggled her finger. 'I tell you, Missus Jac, I can make her buy. Believe me.'

'Let it go, Draga.' I laughed, relieved she'd retained her dogged optimism.

The next thirty minutes passed with scant conversation. 'I'm sorry' kept coming to my lips, but each time I pursed them against the inadequacy of my words.

We pulled up at the house. A gardening crew had worked for days and now, in the morning sunshine, the place was perfect. The real estate agent had erected the 'For Sale' billboard two days ago. The photographs on it showed an elegant house interior, like the 'after' photographs straight out of a home renovation show. The images promised a life of luxury and fine things. But, over the past weeks, I'd learned image isn't everything.

Draga stared at the billboard, not blinking.

I helped her from the car.

Her face was even paler than when we'd left the rehabilitation unit.

'Where you will live, Missus Jac?' she asked, a tremor in her voice.

'I've found a place close by. I'll rent until everything is sorted out. I didn't want you to worry while you were in the hospital and then rehab.
The new place isn't as flash, but it's the right thing to do.'

Draga sighed and her expression clouded. 'Da, be better for you and boy.'

'It's been good for Ant already. He's been a big help.'

Her eyes widened. 'Boy help? How?'

'To pack, mainly. All the sorting out is part of a fresh start, away from the old life.'

'Is for best, Missus Jac. When marry people unhappy for long time, come other trouble. For everybody.'

She was right as usual. If I'd faced up to my disintegrating marriage earlier, I could have extricated myself with less pain on all levels.

'Smile, Draga. You should be excited. I know it's disorienting to move from the rehab unit to home, but you'll settle.'

She gave a small shrug and said nothing.

Inside, the furniture had been arranged for styling the property, but most of the cupboard contents were packed up. Draga's usual pristine kitchen was in disarray. The doors gaped open on half-empty cupboards and the benches were covered in appliances and utensils, ready to be boxed.

Draga's hands went to her cheeks. 'What happen in kitchen? Look like house be rob.'

Ant burst in. 'Hey, you're home. Awesome.' He launched himself at Draga and flung his arms around her neck, and then relaxed into a tentative hug. 'I don't want to squeeze too hard in case I hurt you.' He looked her up and down and laughed 'You look pretty good for someone who got shot.'

'Thank you, little Ant.' Draga wiped the back of her hand across her eyes. 'You look nice, too. I can see you dupe much bigger. You must be eat much.'

Ant checked his backside. 'It's not that big. Blame it on Jac. She's the cook.'

Draga fanned herself. 'You cook? In kitchen?'

'You think I wasn't paying attention all these years?' I put the kettle on and retrieved a mud cake out of the fridge. It was store-bought. My nascent culinary skills didn't extend to baking yet.

'Did Jac tell you she gave me a job?' Ant asked. 'It's a traineeship. I'm helping Andrew with computers and stuff.'

'You not go back with mother?'

'Nah. Mum doesn't care where I am, as long as I'm out of her way.'

Draga smiled. 'Ah, Missus Jac. You find place to put the love.'

I still didn't know if children were in my future, but no matter what, I had Ant for as long as he wanted to stay. This was my new normal and I liked it.

'And I'm not in trouble with the cops either,' Ant said.

'What happen Mr Detective Angel?' Draga asked.

'Case closed,' I said. 'He's checked on Ant a couple of times.'

'Tell her the truth, Jac,' Ant said. He turned to Draga. 'She's had dinner with him about five times and they talk on the phone all the time.'

'Not all the ...'

'Missus Jac! You make arrangement with Mr Detective?'

'You make it sound as if I'm a registered informant.'

'I must sit,' Draga said.

I pulled out a chair for her. 'I'm not rushing, and I don't know where it's going, but Angel's fun.'

'He's a cool guy,' Ant said. 'I'm thinkin' of joining the police force when I'm qualified. They must need infotech staff.'

'What?' I asked, before catching his wink. 'Don't freak me out, Ant.'

He laughed. He did that a lot these days.

Draga rubbed her forehead. 'I zbunjen – confuse.' Everything change much fast. You have much work to do. Be better you take me in my house. I be out of you way. I ask my cousin help me when I go home.' She licked her lips. 'But I not know how much she can help because she must go work every day.'

What an idiot I was. 'No, Draga. I thought you understood. The new house is big enough for all of us – you, Ant and me. Did you think we'd leave you on your own? You're part of our family. You can stay with us whenever you want, for as long as you want. I'm your business, remember?'

Draga's face crumpled and she lowered her head, her chin

quivering.

'Please don't cry,' I said. 'We have another surprise for you. Go get it, Ant.'

Ant returned and with a wide grin, held out a broom with an enormous red bow tied around the head.

Draga stood and placed both hands over her mouth. Her eyes misted. She gazed at the broom as if it was an objet d'art.

'Go on, take it,' I said.

Draga examined the broom head. 'Oh! Is nice, this shape can sweep corner much clean.' She gripped the handle tenderly and then positioned herself in a sweeping stance. She pushed the head along the floor with practised rhythm. Her cheeks glowed pink. 'Is light. Is beautiful broom. Thank you, Missus Jac and little Ant.'

'You're welcome.' I hugged her, nuzzling my face into the warmth of her neck and the familiar scent of 4711 Cologne. Relief and love bubbled to the surface in a rush.

I pulled back to look directly at her, realising the words I needed to use weren't my words. I needed to use hers.

'Draga, oprostimi.'

'There is nothing to forgive, Missus Jac,' she said, a wide smile lighting her face.

She picked up the broom and waltzed around the kitchen with it.

I watched her dance, my heart light.

ACKNOWLEDGEMENTS

A few lines of acknowledgement cannot fully express my gratitude for the encouragement and support the following people have given me during the long journey of bringing this book to life.

My husband, Martino, and my family, who make me believe in myself.
Your love is the air I breathe.

Chris Nardo, for the cover and text design.

Sherryl Clark and Demet Divaroren. Without you, I might still be staring at a blank page. A special thanks to Sherryl for her additional editorial work.

Raffaele Lucisani, whose assistance with this work took me back to our childhood. It felt as if we were kids at play again.

ABOUT THE AUTHOR

Lucia Nardo began her career as a social worker and community development manager, later moving into a corporate career as a company executive and business writer for some of Australia's largest corporations. Since leaving the private sector, she has published nonfiction titles, articles, and short stories. Lucia has taught creative writing in the TAFE sector,
and conducts writing workshops in the community. She lives in Melbourne, Australia.

www.lucianardo.com